Alice's Masque

Having worked for many years in education, Lindsay Clarke is now a full-time writer living in Somerset. His previous novels are *Sunday Whiteman* and *The Chymical Wedding*.

By the same author

SUNDAY WHITEMAN

THE CHYMICAL WEDDING

LINDSAY CLARKE

Alice's Masque

PICADOR
in association with Jonathan Cape

PICADOR

First published 1994 by Jonathan Cape Limited

This edition published 1995 by Picador
an imprint of Macmillan General Books
Cavaye Place London SW10 9PG
and Basingstoke
in association with Jonathan Cape Limited

Associated companies throughout the world

ISBN 0 330 32459 4

1 3 5 7 9 8 6 4 2

A CIP catalogue record for this book is available from
the British Library.

Printed and bound in Great Britain by
Cox & Wyman Ltd, Reading, Berkshire

ACKNOWLEDGMENTS

For their searching criticism and patient encouragement I want to thank my editors at Jonathan Cape, Tom Maschler and Pascal Cariss. The careful readings given to an earlier draft by Jeremy Reed and Rosie Jackson helped me to strengthen the final version, as did the stirring example of Chloe Goodchild's singing voice, and a timely insight offered by Ann Douglas. I owe a special debt of thanks to Charles Harvey and Suzanne Lilley Harvey who showed me far more of what was happening in the Cornish sky at sunset on 23 September 1991 than I was finally able to include; and I want to record with gratitude and affection the degree to which I was confirmed in the work by those members of the small international community of Schumacher College who took part in Theodore Roszak's course on 'Earth, Soul and Imagination' in the summer of 1991.

Once again what is of value here is largely attributable to the care and faith of my wife, Phoebe Clare.

For
my mother, my wife, her daughters, and mine

And ther seyde oones a clerk in two vers,
'What is bettre than gold? Jaspre. What is
bettre than jaspre? Wisedoom. And what is
better than wisedoom? Womman. And what
is bettre than a good womman? Nothyng.'

Chaucer, *The Tale of Melibee*

CONTENTS

Part One
OUTWARD

Love is a thyng as any spirit free.
Wommen, of kynde, desiren libertee,
And not to be constreyned as a thral;
And so doon men, if I sooth seyen shal.

Chaucer, *The Franklin's Tale*

I
SWAN

For most of that September afternoon the three women had been working quietly together in a sheltered cove on one of the more rigorous stretches of the Cornish coast.

Two of them had sketchbooks at their laps. They lifted and dipped their heads, like drinking birds, between the white dazzle of cartridge paper and the patient, naked form of a much younger woman who reclined below them on a greenish slab of rock. She lay on her back in the fifth pose of the session, one hand loosely cupped in the spread of hair beside her face, the other resting in the plump curve of her hip. Though her eyes were open she had evidently entered that passive state of grace in which a relaxed model appears so little aware of her observers that she might be quite alone.

None of the women had spoken for some time.

Their shadows were lengthening now, blacker across black Cornish stone, and the surf too was extending its reach among the inshore rocks. Further out, a warm late-summer sunlight altered constantly over the dense bottle-green blue-black of the incoming swell.

The woman nearest the sea moved a graphite pencil swiftly across the pad with a flowing motion of her body that lent strength to the lithe strokes of the sketch, though her wrists were thin. A cropped quiff of auburn hair and the baggy, petrol-blue dungarees made it difficult to age her, but Leah was perhaps thirty years old. There were shadows in the soft places round her eyes which gave her frown an unintended severity as she glanced up and saw a tremor pass across the model's freckled skin.

She said, 'Are you getting cold, Amy?'

The model shook her head. For an instant her fair hair seemed to flake off into light, then she released a sigh that was heard by the elder and nearer of the two artists, a large-boned woman in corduroy trousers and collarless shirt, who looked up, tanned and wrinkled under her bonnet's floppy brim. 'We can stop if you like,' Alice offered, and consulted her watch. It hung by a ribbon from the fob of a silk-backed waistcoat which must once have completed a three-piece suit. The tawny buttons could never have fastened across her bust.

'No, really, I'm all right for a bit longer.' The naked young woman wriggled her haunches against the rock. At seventeen her body was mature but the candour of her smile remained untarnished. 'I was just remembering a dream I had last night.'

'Ah,' said Alice, but it was Leah who broke the ensuing silence: 'So are you going to tell?'

'I don't think so.' In other company Amy's blush might have been more deeply suffused. Here it offered complicity.

'I see. Anyone we know?' Leah clicked her tongue over the drawing, regretting a too emphatic line. She reached for the eraser on the rock beside her.

Keeping her eyes closed, Amy said, 'That would be telling!'

From rosy pink the water in the jamjar where Alice rinsed her paintbrush swirled into a cloudy mauve.

'Amy, you're incorrigible,' she remarked mildly.

'Does that mean I can't get enough?'

Looking up, Leah saw that this ignorance was assumed.

4

'It means,' she muttered, 'that you'll probably come to a bad end. Like me.'

'You? You're not doing so badly. Is she, Alice?' When no agreement came, Amy added, 'Stephen's a lovely man. I hope you're not going to be beastly to him tonight.' But Leah only pursed her lips askew, and said that if they were going to carry on then Amy should shut up and keep still. The younger woman widened her eyes at Alice, who smiled, shook her head, then assessed the skein of washes on her pad.

Perhaps some of these colour-relations might one day be threaded across the warp of the large tapestry loom in her workshop. As for the pencilled figure beneath — it had promise and might sit well in the foreground of a new piece she had in mind, a last big composition, one that would tax all her skills. Alice was well into her seventies now, and the fringe under her bonnet was whiter than a stoat as she looked up against the glare off the sea. 'My bottom's seized up,' she declared, sensing how the mood had changed, 'I think I'll call it a day.'

Leah fetched a long sigh and closed her pad. 'Hopeless anyway,' she said to the waxy lumps of limpeted rubble that seemed to ooze from a fissure in the rock like frozen foam.

'Well he is,' Amy insisted airily. She drew up her knees and clasped her hands at her shins, then rocked on her buttocks two or three times before sprawling out on the warm slab again. 'Nice, I mean. Stephen.'

Leah slipped the graphite pencil into the bib-pocket of her dungarees and stared irritably down at the complacent nakedness. 'The man you were just dreaming about — was he nice?'

Momentarily Amy considered the advantages of a lie, but 'No,' she admitted, avoiding the significant tilt of Leah's brow, 'not exactly.'

'Oh dear, you're not still walking out with that awful Robboe?' Alice was not unconscious that her antique turn of phrase might exasperate. And it did, a little.

'That was ages ago.'

'Another villain then.' Leah got to her feet and gazed into the tangy light above the sea. 'We want our heads testing, that's what we want.'

Miffed, yet finding no immediate means to exclude herself from this verdict, Amy cast about for a large pair of red-framed sunglasses and put them on. Alice clicked the lid of her paintbox shut.

'What about you, Alice?' the girl asked, for though she would have denied it under accusation, a provocative demon was tempting her further down what she had already recognized as a risky path. 'You like Stephen, don't you?'

Alice considered the young nurseryman in his absence. He was, she thought, too easily ruled by Venus, too much the supplicant, but she said, 'He's very charming.'

'There you are then.'

'Though I sometimes wonder whether he isn't trying to make up for a want of character by an excess of principle.'

Immersed gratefully in the dark pool of her sunglasses, Amy wondered what character might be if not the willingness to stand up for one's ideals. 'Anyway,' she resumed eventually, as though all doubts had been aired and dismissed in the pronouncement, 'you couldn't ask for anyone more thoughtful.'

Whether or not the remark was intended as a reproach to Leah, it was so taken, though she saw the truth of it and felt badly. All day she'd been ruing the moment of weakness that had let Stephen press his invitation. In her present state the dinner he planned could be no more than a misery for both of them. She was, in fact, making up her mind to cancel as she stood, biting her lip, staring out to sea.

Alice sensed her distress. She guessed also how closely it verged on anger, and would have come to Leah's relief had not Amy spoken first. 'It wouldn't hurt you to be nicer to him, Leah.'

'Not that it's any of your business.'

'No, but . . .'

'And in my experience – which I think you'll agree leaves yours looking a bit thin – a lot of men are thoughtful till the going gets tough. Then they either turn nasty or collapse.' Leah released her pent breath on the ocean air. 'You can settle for that if you like. I shan't.'

Amy glanced at Alice, whose anxious gaze was fixed on Leah, who once more stared out to sea. It was as if all three women had been brought up anew against an unhappy fact.

Leah stepped down over the rocks to a glossy span of sand where the surf opened and closed with a soft hiss, like an ivory fan. She slipped off her espadrilles and flexed her toes in the foam. The chill touch brought a moment's remorse: precisely because Amy lacked experience she should have kept her own bitterness in check. But there it was, take it or leave it. One might as well tell the truth.

Meanwhile Amy's fingers lightly stroked the skin between her breasts. She felt badly for having pushed Leah this far, and – in the same complicated moment – aggrieved by her friend's bad-tempered reaction. Where men were concerned it seemed that nothing was straightforward, even when there were none around. Perhaps especially then.

So she turned her head away and watched Alice take a tobacco-tin from a khaki haversack and roll herself a thin liquorice-paper cigarette. The three women were no longer quite present to each other. They were screened in thought. There was a feeling of recklessness left in the air.

It recalled for Alice the day when she had first found the

house that stood a couple of miles inland from the cove, at the head of a wooded glen. That had been almost half a century ago, at the time of her disgrace.

She had been married for four of her twenty-six years, but she was out walking with her lover that day along one of the noblest stretches of cliff on the Cornish coast. They had taken flight from scandal for a while. London was at the far end of the world. The times were briefly free, and everything that happened seemed to resist all talk of chance.

A sudden squall blowing in off the sea had drenched them. Alice pulled off her glasses as they ran for whatever shelter might be found in the lee of an old sheep-fold. By now the rain made them useless anyway. Then she stood, panting, with the wall of the fold between her back and the veering wind as he leaned to lick the bright raindrops from her cheeks and nose. She kissed his chin, then his mouth. His hand loosened the belt of her coat, and she heard him murmur, as though in extenuation, 'We can't get much wetter anyway.' But she didn't care. She was still holding the glasses tightly when, moments later, she gasped at the touch of his hand on her skin.

Rain splashed about their heads. It made beads in his hair. She could feel the rough stone damp at her back. Then the air was cold about her thighs.

'You'll have me pregnant,' she whispered as he reached to free himself, and, uncertain whether the words were uttered as warning or as wish, she closed her eyes.

When they opened again the rain was shining.

Alice had gazed through its veil, across his shoulder, at a house standing on a low rise across the field. Had it been there before? She did not recall having seen it, she would have sworn there had been only open pasture. But the rain had blurred her vision, and everything was changing all the time in this passionate, drenched light. In any case, there the house now was, astonished to find itself newly arrived on the spot where it must have stood for centuries. It seemed to lean against the sky.

The stone walls were white-washed, the roof was of bluish slate, so the house nestled on its site with the sometimes bleak, sometimes gleaming coloration of a gull. Two or three slates had been dislodged by a gale. Water gushed from the throat of a blocked downpipe, and where the windows were not covered by fading blue shutters they were broken. All this was taken in by a single encompassing glance. She was immediately certain that the place had stood empty for some time.

With a moan her lover came. Sunlight glanced off white walls. Between the white swirl inside her now and the clouds brightening in the sky, Alice knew that this was where she must live. The thought came to her like a key placed in the hand: *this is your house, your place; here you belong.*

The rain sailed by, the day gathered brightness to itself. All things gleamed with the actuality of their existence. And somehow it was possible to sustain this cool, meditative distance on everything yet be, in the same undivided instant, ardently a part of it all. For everything was softly eliding now. It was all coming clear.

And so, as simply as that, in a moment beyond volition, the matter settled itself. She would live here in this gull-coloured house by the sea. She would become a professor of light and shade, of sea-squalls, and of brief, angelic visitations. Far from London, she would grow so hard to see that sooner or later she must vanish from the past entirely.

And her lover?

Well, he would vanish with her. There could be no demur.

How enthralled by life she had been that day, how unwise

not to observe more closely that moment in which his eyes were black and nervous as the flight of choughs above the cliff!

'Then I don't see what's to be done,' Amy said, increasing the effort in her adolescent frown. 'It looks like they're damned either way, doesn't it?' Then she sighed a little huffily. 'I mean, you warn me off villains like Robboe . . . Okay, I can understand that. Yet neither of you seem to have much time for a lovely man like Stephen either.'

Leah looked up from the shallows where the surf scurried about her ankles and sand yielded beneath her feet. The earth itself was growing unstable. 'Now you're getting the idea.'

'What idea?'

'That there's a design fault. That by and large they just won't do.'

Amy lifted herself on to her elbows and turned her head in protest towards Leah. 'But that's horrible. It means there's no hope.'

'Oh there's always hope,' she was answered. 'That's just the trouble. Even when you've realized they hate us you still go on hoping to turn up an exception.'

'Do you really think they do?' Amy saw how Leah's shrug disdainfully invited her to examine the evidence for herself. She did, and said, 'But Stephen doesn't – '

'Or if they don't hate us,' Leah interrupted, 'they're afraid of us, which amounts to much the same thing.'

Amy wrenched herself round on the rock and appealed to Alice. 'Is she right?' But if Alice was uneasy with talk so amply couched in generalities, there were more complicated reasons why she found herself pondering an answer at a length which exhausted Leah's patience.

Leah stooped to pick up a stone. It felt cool in her hand

10

with its rusty marbling. 'Anyway,' she said, angered by her own anger, 'I really don't want to talk about this.'

Agitated now, disappointed in Alice and disturbed by Leah's abrasive mood, Amy rolled over on to her stomach. 'I can't believe it,' she said, for she had read the accounts of amorous men offered by various congenial writers, and liked to imagine herself adored. 'It doesn't make any sense.'

'Nobody said it made sense,' – though Leah might have been speaking to the sea and to the hard line of the horizon.

'I mean,' Amy asked, perplexed, 'what's there to be afraid of?'

Leah snorted and threw the stone into the sea, which came and went undeterred. Again, apart from the iterations of the surf, silence closed round them.

And Alice was thinking: *there may be lands where light is of a hard, bright, constant quality, but ours is no such land; it's a fickle realm rather, of rain and shine, of trembling maritime uncertainty, where things blur and shift and reshape themselves with every trick of light; a place of hints and vanishings, of delicate advances and recessions where, instead of things inarguably existing, one is offered gleaming intimations of the possibility that they might exist.*

But she was not thinking just of England, no, nor of Cornwall in particular. It was simply a thought characteristic of this strange afternoon when such changes of mood had glanced about the cove with the fluency of light and shade. As now, for instance, when she vanished again in worries about Leah.

Sometimes Alice felt she knew Leah no better than on that damp day when the knock came at the front door and Alice (who had been about to take a bath) opened it irritably on a gawky trench-coated stranger with a suitcase at her feet. Her gaze was slightly askance; the dusky rain gusted at her back, pattering on the gaberdined shoulders; a taxi with dipped headlights idled beyond the gate. When Alice spotted the large portfolio knotted with black ribbon leaning against her thigh, her first thought was, *Oh hell, another pushy bloody student!* though for the moment Leah had said nothing. Hair blew damply about her brow. A mild astigmatism further attenuated her gaze. She seemed infirm of purpose. Yet even as Alice clutched the bathrobe to her bosom, demanding, 'Well?' her senses were making a swift descent through time.

'Alice?'

The question had been uncertainly put. It was answered with no larger conviction, for Alice was wondering how this cousin – was it Dilly or Jo? – could have remained so young while she herself had grown ancient as a turtle in the years between.

Then Leah had admitted her name. 'We *are* related,' she claimed, 'but you won't have heard of me.'

And how should she have done when, by mutual agreement, Alice and the rest of the family had seen nothing of one another for half a century? But even this quick, impatient inspection had shown how there was in this finely boned face an individual gloss to the family's idiosyncratic features which made it neither Dilly's nor Jo's; but close, unsettlingly close. Almost close enough to be some cruel imposture.

Imagine, she had thought, *imagine the shock of having a long-adopted child turn up on you. Imagine the heart brought up short like a stopped clock!*

'Do you remember', Leah asked, 'your cousin Roland?'

There was an access of wistful, bemused affection at Alice's lips. 'Rowly? Of course.'

'My grandfather.'

'I see.'

12

The monochrome day had shuddered in the wind. Rain dripped from the close-cropped chestnut hair.

'Oh dear,' said Alice. 'I suppose you'd better come in.'

'The thing is . . . the taxi . . .'

'You don't have the fare?'

'It's not that. But it's getting late. I haven't fixed up anywhere to stay. If you don't want me here for the night I'd better . . .'

Alice took the point distractedly. Did she want any of this? By one's late seventies, surely, one had earned the right to go unbothered. One might, rudely, insist on it. Oh bugger, bugger! After all this time! 'Why didn't you ring first? Or write even?'

'I know,' said Leah. By which she meant, evidently, that she did not know.

'It might have been wiser.'

'Yes.'

'Kinder even.'

'I'm sorry.' And Leah had looked down at her shoes, then back, appraisingly, into Alice's suddenly haggard face. The younger woman's eyes were a greenish, tarn-water grey, though splintered unusually with flecks of sharper colour: amber, cornelian, violet, a vivid cranesbill blue. There was no entreaty in them, no desire to charm; only an indurate submission to what might happen next.

This too Alice felt she recognized, though there was, she observed, no wedding ring on the hand vaguely pushing back a tress of damp hair. 'Pay the man,' she said, and reached down to pull the suitcase through into the hall.

Yet even when Leah was across the threshold they had looked at one another with no enthusiasm in Alice's gaze and no immediate gratitude in Leah's. Silently each was acknowledged as the other's problematic destiny. There was a possibility of mutual dislike. Then they were both

13

aware also of the sound of water drumming in the tub overhead.

Alice said, 'I was just about to take a bath. I've been couching some woad. I must stink of it.'

'Yes.'

'Not that badly I hope.'

'I'm sorry, I didn't mean . . .'

'Anyway, I'd better turn . . .'

'Don't let me stop you. Please. I can wait here while you take your bath.' Leah had indicated the oak settle in the hall, a piece of furniture on which nobody had actually sat for years, and the uncertain gesture recalled Alice to her better nature. How strange to be so rattled after all this time! How reprehensible!

Shamed by her halting hospitality, she smiled at last and said, 'I think we can do better than that.'

And gradually they did, though it was still a cause of some surprise how Alice's original concession of a meal, some wine, a chat, a bed for the night (and perhaps a glance at whatever the portfolio might hold) before gently ushering this unbidden relative out and on her way, had expanded into a stay of months. On the whole, happily so, though Leah was not an easy presence about the place. She was often moody and self-absorbed and secretive. But one thing at least had soon come clear: far from being an emissary sent by the family, she was as much a refugee as Alice had once been, though not in flight from the family itself, but from some equivalent catastrophe, the gender of which was presumably male. Virtually nothing had been said of this, however, for if their provisional alliance across the generations lacked that touch of ruthless intimacy which seasons friendship, it did so at Leah's insistence.

She had made no bones about this from the start. Pressed too closely on that first evening, she lowered her

14

glass and said, 'You're asking me to account for myself?'

'I wouldn't put it quite so fiercely.'

But the accompanying smile went unanswered. 'I don't have to, you see.'

'Of course not, if you don't wish to.'

'That's why I came away – so I wouldn't have to account for the past any more. Not to anyone but me.'

'Then why come to a member of the family?'

'Do you still think of yourself that way?'

'No, not really.'

'Because you cut free. Because you saw life didn't have to be the way it was. You stepped out of the net. There was nothing holding you.'

'It seems', said Alice, 'that you have the advantage of knowing rather more about me than I do about you.'

'Not really. Just enough to get the feeling that you might understand.'

'Without question?'

Leah gave a little shrug, but said nothing.

'So I must take you as I find you?'

'If you prefer lies,' Leah answered, 'I can give you lies.'

'Why not the truth? Are you running away from it?'

'Changing it,' came the quiet reply. 'Or trying to. Like you did once, I've left the claims of the past behind.'

'Yet you've brought what looks like a full portfolio?'

Alice had been pleased to see how the increased spin on her response elicited a smile. 'They're all self-portraits,' Leah answered. 'I'll show you, if you like.' She brought the portfolio to the table. The sheets of paper lying inside were all patiently blank.

Yet they had been lies, of course, reclusive lies.

Weeks later the shadows of an otherwise undelineated past still showed. They were active among them now, in the

15

cove, where Amy was staring down across her naked midriff at her feet. The toes were curling and uncurling as though with purposes of their own. Her ankles, she realized, would probably always be too thick for perfection now.

'But if you're right,' she murmured to Leah's turned back, 'there's no justice.' For a time, while Alice re-lit her cigarette, she was left alone with that cold thought.

'It's not quite that bad,' Alice exhaled. 'They don't have it all their own way. Though I'm still often shocked by their rudimentary grasp of what we are.'

Leah splashed a foot through the surf. 'They're three parts asleep. They want to be left that way.'

'And we keep poking them?' Amy grinned.

'We're the bloody nuisance.' There was more than a touch of malice in Leah's glance and voice. 'We remind them of everything they'd rather discount. We're the place where chaos might break through and upset their orderly schemes.'

'They do smell the danger in us', Alice agreed, ' – the fact that we'll behave ourselves only up to a certain point, and then we're quite likely to turn into ruthless, half-crazed creatures with a she-wolf's morality. Or so it seems to them.'

Across the generations the three women were drawn into sudden collusion, and less by conscious assent than by the outwardly invisible fact that for a brief duration each of them had been visited by the same pattern of images. The pictures came from a source deeper than personal fantasy, deeper even than racial memory, and they were travelling so quickly that none of the women had time to register the event as a shared experience before it was over and each of them withdrew into their separate and quite different emotions. Yet before those fleeting scenes dissolved, all three of them had been shown something of what it was like

16

on those frenzied occasions when the midwives and spinners used to go hunting in packs for any man stupid enough to fall into their clutches.

Only Alice recognized what she had seen. The dream had arrived through her words, she saw it most clearly. She already knew how such hunts had been raised in parishes across Europe less than a hundred years before she was born – sometimes in the night after the delivery of a child, or on certain feast-days, or whenever a wild moon took the women that way. Calmly she accepted the episode as a moment from her ancestry still charged with residual power. Leah, by contrast, experienced a savage pang of elation that faded quickly into disappointment, though its sensuality intensified her restiveness; while Amy was aware only of a frantic commotion that left her excited and ashamed. She stifled it at once.

As though it had never disappeared, the cove reassembled itself around them, and the three women returned to the day.

Alice was saying, 'In any case, they have a shrewd idea just how much we're holding back.'

Leah snorted at the sea. 'And what are we supposed to do with it?' she demanded.

'Yes,' Alice sympathized, 'all that wicked energy has nowhere much to go these days.'

'Except round and round inside us, till it comes out as a thin, malicious whinge of resentment when what we really need . . .'

'Is to howl out our despair?'

'Yes.'

Alarmed by the hiss of that final syllable, Amy had listened uncertainly to this exchange. Yet she was fascinated too by the thrill of adrenalin coursing round her system. She had never heard Alice in this vein before: small wonder her mother was dubious of the association.

17

'Well I don't feel that way,' she said eventually.

'Nor should you,' Alice answered, 'not as long as you can help it.'

Amy removed her sunglasses to gaze more intently into that nut-brown, patrician face. She found no condescension there, only the patient beauty of great age, which so often took her by surprise. There came a flickering recognition that the older she herself got, the less she seemed to understand; then her thoughts moved on. 'It's hard to think of you that way, Alice. I don't see you as despairing.'

The soft wattles at Alice's throat wobbled a little as she shook her head in a smile. 'Of course, I'm rather past it all, my dear. But not so far that I can't remember. It took me an awfully long time to honour the animal in me . . . to see that my most vital part could be messy and violent and full of fury. That it had a perfect right to those feelings, and needed to shriek and rampage far more than I'd ever dared to let it do.'

'And what happened when you did?'

'Trouble, of course. But I was already in trouble anyway. I just didn't know how to make it work for me. Then one day I decided to let rip.' Alice stubbed her cigarette on the rock. 'Very satisfactory! Apart from anything else, it's so much healthier when we mourn our sufferings out loud like the Irish keeners. Or turn them into noisy hymns of pain and protest like the women do in Africa. A good wail lubricates the system. And it's quite remarkable how it makes things happen.'

At that moment Leah, who had been standing in a trance-like state of attention with the surf swirling round her calves, threw back her head and bayed at the sun.

The sound began as a hollow, abdominal moaning from her upturned throat, then gathered force and volume as she released an indrawn gasp of sea-air back upon the elements in a protracted, baleful howl.

18

Gulls rose from the sea and flapped away. A sparrow-hawk that had been foraging along the cliff-face veered off for another cove. Amy shrank inside her skin and came out goose-flesh. For a moment or two even Alice was embarrassed by the ugly, raw fervour of the sound, which went on and on – a withering complaint against creation – until Leah exhausted the last of her breath and turned back to her companions with a spent, dazed wonder on her face. A wave splashed against her, leaving the hitched legs of her dungarees wet through. For a few seconds she was grinning with stupefied satisfaction. Then, in silence, the tears came rolling from her eyes.

For much of its duration the noise of the howl had reached above the tumbling sea-surge, high over the rocks, and was carried in gusts up to the cliff-top where a man walked his dog along an otherwise deserted stretch of coastal path.

Both man and dog were brought up short by the sound, though the dog soon lost interest and scouted off among the blackthorn thickets. The man, however, could not so easily ignore a noise which had shocked his heart, so he turned into the breeze off the sea, the better to hear and identify it. Far out on the swell, an orange figure in a lobster-boat calmly hauled in a flagged pot. There was no other visible presence. In any case, the sound had come from a place much closer, below him, on the cliff-face or among the hidden rocks. He took a few steps off the path, but the slope was too sheer, and the furze too thick, to obtain an angle of vision. If there was a beach down there he didn't know of it, and he could see no access.

Uncertainly he sought to persuade himself that it had been an animal's cry, but its quavering pathos had troubled him. Or was it conscience, or some unconscious flow of sympathy, which left him uncomfortably certain that its source was human? Certain too – though he would be reluctant to admit this the next day – that it was a woman's cry, the cry of one in some considerable distress. So what to do? If this cliff was as sheer as the others then no one could survive a fall for long. It would, in any case, be difficult to fall by accident, and there were more certain drops to choose for suicide. Also the sound had been vigorous enough, and not identifiably a call for help.

What to make of it then? Some incident in a boat under the cliff? Something with which, at this height and distance, it was neither possible nor desirable to become involved.

Impatient, uneasy, he stood for a space with his ears pressed against the breeze, listening for a resumption of the cry, or some consequence. He heard only the surge of the sea. The man looked at his watch. His right foot tapped the ground. He picked his way back to the path and stood uncertainly, looking in vain for witnesses or aid. Then he strode off, more hurriedly than before, out of this story and back into his own.

But elsewhere, much further afield, things had already begun to happen.

Some time around mid-afternoon there came a break in the rain, and Ronan's spirits lifted. He was speeding westwards where a dove-grey blur of sunlight hovered across the land as tranced and discontinuous as his own vague processes of thought. The old Rover was sweetly tuned; he was making good time. A couple more hours should see him at the coast, breathing sea-air and looking for a place to stay. Until then he was in an agreeable state of free fall between experiences, and everything felt subtly different. Air and space were extending freely round him, the breadth of England wheeling by – green paddocks and rough pasture, flanks of turned earth the colour of iron oxide, and a far blue prospect of misty hangered hills.

He had almost forgotten how good it was to leave the city, to breathe easily under the enlarging sky, to feel this blessed freedom from constraint. It was as if he'd prised himself free of his outworn life and it had come away clean. Ronan leaned his head out of the open window and took the rush of damp air at his mouth. He gasped at the force of it, feeling his mind turn suddenly nomadic. He saw the finally unownable land spread out before him, unfolding itself, all invitation. Old griefs expired. Decisions had been made and taken, everything put at risk. Again the gamble of it brought his heart to his mouth, but the road gleamed ahead of him like polished slate, and every approaching overpass began to take on disproportionate significance, as though it marked a frontier checkpoint or an entrance on another world.

Forty-seven now, balding behind the frontal sweep of his hair, Ronan smiled at this last extravagance, and thought, why not? To put one's foot down hard and go, just go, with no more thought for destination than for consequence. To flex the will so far beyond its ordinary range you simply vanished: no trap-doors, no magic cabinets, just instant transmission into elsewhere – gone! His smile widened with the realization that if things worked out, another world *was* waiting for him – out there on that marvellous reach of coast which had basked in the day's only sunshine while he'd fretted through the rainy frenzy of the motorways. So he wasn't just crossing the country after all – he was transiting between worlds; and this sudden absurd exhilaration was the closest he'd come to a sense of un-trammelled liberty since the adventures of his youth. It increased his appetite for speed.

In the lane ahead a grimy hire-van rattled along at a steady takeable seventy. Ronan checked his rear-view mirror where the Peugeot that had followed him for miles still coasted uncomfortably close. Time it was shaken off!

Already he was drifting out and reaching for the indicator when the picture in the mirror shifted. Some distance back the hunched figure of a motorcyclist in black leathers and a scarlet helmet had bobbed into the outer lane. An impatient click escaped from Ronan's lips. He pulled back, and glimpsed a white movement from the corner of his eye – not in the mirror-glass, but to its left, nearer the edge of his vision, up ahead, perhaps two hundred yards away: a swan was winging through the livid air, white against the grey unstable clouds, descending rapidly.

For a second or two the sight impressed itself on his mind with bright, heraldic clarity. His mood changed again, he felt a familiar yearning flex the muscles of his heart; and he was gone from the moment, returned to the bedroom of her flat where they lay between cool sheets and she was reading aloud, one rainy afternoon, some poem – a love poem – about a swan. He heard the dusky cadences of her voice, the scatter of rain against the window-glass. He saw the soft hollows made by her collar-bones, and the skin gleaming at her shoulders. He saw the sudden brake-lights of the white hire-van ahead – they were glowing red and he was closing in on them with reckless speed. He saw that, senselessly, the van was skidding to a halt. His eyes widened, the heart jumped; but even as he gasped in shock, Ronan understood.

Deceived perhaps by the sheen of damp asphalt, imagining a river there below, the swan was about to alight on the busy carriageway. The driver of the van had seen what was happening and, in an effort not to collide with the descending bird, had stood on his brakes.

Instantly Ronan's own foot shifted too, but by the time his shoe-sole reached the pedal certain things were clear. The Peugeot was too close on his tail and travelling too fast to stop. If Ronan braked, his car would be crushed between

22

the halted van and the oncoming saloon, or tossed like a beer-can into the traffic on the other side. He ran the sequence through his mind. He saw the pictures.

Yet there might still just be time and room enough to swerve out round the van before the more distant motor-cyclist entered the same space. It took the merest fraction of that time to calculate that if an accident was about to happen his own chances would be better swerving than braking; and so, with part of his mind already in court pleading blamelessness, Ronan pulled down on the wheel.

There came the long protest of a horn.

Ronan's drawn breath sought to make his car seem needle-thin. Then the van was slinking intimately past his left-hand wing-mirror as, in another dimension, through a different, blacker wedge of the spectrum, the astounded biker veered towards the rough grass round the central crash-barrier at his right.

The second-hand on the dashboard clock had advanced almost no distance at all since he'd seen the lights glow red, but there was leisure enough for him to admire in breathless gratitude the diligent, jinking slide with which machine and rider somehow finessed the perils of that inconstant gap before speeding furiously on. After that, there was no space left in Ronan's mind beyond the patch of road directly in front of his own wheels where, slowed by the curved resistance of its wings, the swan was touching down.

The great bird stumbled there. It might have been making a flustered curtsey to the traffic passing on the other side as, slowly, in a puzzled beseeching of patience with such untypical disarray, the swan craned its neck towards Ronan's advancing vehicle, and vanished beneath its hood.

There was a bump, a dull, lopsided jerk, no more. When he glanced, as he must, in the rear-view mirror, he saw a gaudy shambles on the road. The air was afloat with white down. Someone might have been shaking out an old mattress there.

Some time later the rain returned. Ronan was speeding along, seeing as little of the road ahead as if his windscreen had been blurred by the backwash from a lorry's wheels. When he switched on the wipers the focus of his vision barely reached the screen. He felt sick and shaky, dispossessed of all rights.

Impossible not to imagine the driver of each approaching vehicle staring in horror at his blood-spattered front bumper where he had run down so vivid a creature as a swan and had not stopped. But what good would stopping have done – to stand helplessly over torn webs and smashed wings? A terrible thing had seized its chance to happen. The rainy air was tainted by the news. Nothing could ever be the same again.

Less than forty minutes earlier he had been driving unexceptionably along the highway. Impulsive perhaps; yes, abstracted; but not overly rash. Now – by way of a transition in which time had distended and his grip on events had slipped beyond retrievable control – he was coasting blindly through an unchancy, half-aquatic world where he was experiencing a still graver discontinuity.

Now it was like this: he could see his hands *out there*, holding the wheel; his skin might have been a shadow cast by some distant source of light. He felt himself to be shut inside his body in much the same way that the body itself was shut inside the car; yet it was all a much looser fit than before. He could feel the difference as a sort of mismatch, like an inaccurate adjustment in a printer's colour register. It was as if he were instantly present to himself as his own ghost.

The sensation was of sudden decompression, all the

oxygen shocked from his air. There was sweat at his neck. He might have forgotten his own name. His head filled with the sound of distant screaming.

All the certainty with which he had set out that day diminished to a sense of panic. The lies he had told no longer wore the aspect of minor theatrical triumphs; they merely confirmed a giddy sense of irreality. False in its pretexts, as probably also in its premises, this entire westward enterprise began to feel unsafe. In this condition nothing could work out well for him.

Yet he did not turn back, for that, at this late stage of the game, seemed the one avoidable humiliation.

2

BLOW-HOLE

When he arrived in the harbour-town of Porthmallion, Ronan took a room in a small and, as it turned out, rather dispiriting hotel.

Brian Pollard, the proprietor of The Anchor, was the retired skipper of a merchant-vessel, a man whose features had been brutalized by drink and authority. Having foundered now on the lee-shore of a large mortgage, he lacked a talent for geniality, even common courtesy came hard. His wife had turned into a creature of apologies and explanation. Her eyes appealed everywhere for help.

It was she who showed Ronan up to his room. As they passed a rear window on the stair he noticed her husband down in the courtyard, admiring the Rover in its two-tone green livery; but there were, Ronan knew, no obvious traces on the bodywork – the rain had seen to that. Apart from a new dent on the bumper the old car was in almost mint condition. It was accustomed to envy.

'There's a lovely view of the harbour,' Stella Pollard encouraged. She stood in the open doorway of the room, alert to her guest's response. Fortunately Ronan's back was to the woman and his wince at what had been done to a once generous Jacobean chamber was invisible. This was mere interim space, untouched by the imagination. A single night here already felt too much.

'It'll be fine,' he said, and found something depressing in the wan gratitude of her smile.

'What brings you to Cornwall?' The enquiry felt more than a casual formality. The woman wanted to talk, to linger, but his mind was elsewhere. In the face of his distracted silence, she offered a suggestion: 'Just a holiday, is it?'

'Yes, something of the sort.'

In neither words nor glances did Stella Pollard express the anarchic impulse of thought welling up from a life devoid of gentle touch. She fingered the button at her throat and said, 'Well, I hope you'll be comfortable with us.'

As soon as she was gone Ronan threw open the sash-window and released the room's synthetically freshened air. He listened to the jeering of the gulls.

It was an hour or so before sunset. The tide stood nearly at full. He could hear the slap of water against the quay where a bronzed young man was writhing from his wetsuit, and a few older people stood about gazing at the mixed flotilla inside the harbour bar. The light was filled with salt and the iodine smell of seaweed. Ronan caught his breath but felt none of the excitement he might have anticipated earlier – only the unappeasable tedium of the sea, and the way the day was ending with an aimless air. He had a dead swan on his conscience still. His mind was numb with it.

He crossed to the bed, reached for the smaller of his two travelling-bags and took out a footpath-map of the area. The sheet's crisp folds opened on a wide expanse of blue, then revealed the irregular bulge of the local coastline to the right of the map. Close to its midpoint were the harbour and grey-shaded town of Porthmallion. A few inches lower, and a little way inland, lay Treligo village, just east of the spanner-shaped promontory of Pengerent Head and north

27

of the wide, gentler swathe of Gleave Bay. Between these small centres of population the ancient field-boundaries were marked in spidery reticulations like the hair-line crazing of a glaze.

Ronan looked down on Treligo with a raptorial eye. The letter had supplied no return address but the regional postmark was unblurred, *and she had to be in or near that village*. He was sure of it – he remembered the name of the place, what she'd said about it, that day at the exhibition. She had to be here, somewhere inside this narrow span of land. He took in the symbols for the church, the chapel, the public house. He imagined her walking the quiet village street or out on the cliffs, her long hair blowing about her back and shoulders, reddening in the evening light. He murmured the gaunt names of the outlying farms and homesteads: Tregareth, Treleaze, Menadu, Roseleye, Perangarth. She might be inside any one of them, almost near enough to hear the shouting of his heart, and so close he was famished by the need to have her with him right now, here in this shoddy room. Had he been a fool not to go directly to the village, to find accommodation there, and start in immediately asking questions?

Not in this state. In such a small place he might have bumped into her even as he was taking bags from the car, or their eyes could have collided in the bar-room of the pub, and he would have been left fumbling to explain himself. He was in no shape now for a chance encounter at a time when everything would depend on delicacy, on care. Better, after this awful day, to hole up for the night. He needed to be calmer, to recover the certainty with which he had first set out. He needed sleep and darkness to be kind.

Ronan lay back on the bed, the map still open beside him. When he closed his eyes the room filled with his longing and was soon too small a space to contain it. Out across the town it ranged, over the cliffs and the gloomy inshore fields, reaching for her, letting her know he was here, that he wanted her back, that he needed her now as he had never needed in his life; but finding no requital in that disconsolate landscape, his thoughts turned inward again, towards sleep, consuming time, until he was back where the two of them had last been at one together.

Against the creamy light that filtered through calico drapes she was throwing back her hair. Then her face was close over him. He found the longing reflected there, the wondering surmise: how could there be so little time left when they were so deeply ventured on one another? Impossible! Yet even as he reached out for her she was displaced by a curtseying swan. It went down before him in a wreck of plumage, then was gone.

In the hall at Roseleye, Leah had just replaced the telephone in its cradle for the third time in half an hour, and had done so with such unnecessary force that Alice came out of the kitchen to contemplate the slender, provisional figure standing at the foot of the stairs in a dolphined T-shirt and knickers.

'I've been trying to get hold of Stephen,' Leah explained. Remotely the fingers of her left hand scratched a place on her thigh. 'He's not answering.'

'He's not the only one.'

Leah sighed at the dry reproach. A shaft of evening sunlight made the down on her arm glow a little. She felt molested by it, she was aggrieved at her own visibility. She wanted to return immediately upstairs, away from Alice, who was drying her hands on a chequered tea-towel, but her will was in pieces. An air of helplessness prevailed between these two women. It might also have been exasperation, and not for the first time Leah thought of packing her bags and leaving with no more explanation than had preceded her arrival. Surely, as far as Alice was concerned, it could only be relief?

This had been a stupefying day. Even before the unsatisfactory conversation in the cove Leah had been aware of her growing nerviness: hence the sour, sharp tone with Amy, hence the cramped flow of her line. Yet she could find no sufficient cause for her tension, and so, as she stood in the surf, the howling seemed to come from nowhere. It took possession, shook her in its grip, and dropped her, leaving her so depleted that she could conceive of no further use for the remaining day than to lie on her bed and cry till she slept, and sleep, God help her, until some quirk of cosmic invention found means to make her miserable self tolerable once more.

She had hurried back from the cove ahead of the others, but when she reached her bed she could neither weep nor sleep. When Alice came to see her she lay in silence like a woman coated with pain.

Two hours later she had remembered that, for reasons far beyond memory and belief, she had agreed to go out with Stephen that night. Nothing felt further from desire or possibility. And now Alice was saying, 'I wish you'd talk to me, Leah,' and that too was barely possible. Yet there was such concern in Alice's gaze. Even their exasperation was an active ingredient of the care these women had for one another – almost at times despite themselves. It brought its obligations too.

Barefoot in the hall, holding the banister for support, Leah found a degree of distance on what she had to say. 'I thought', she conceded, ' – before I came here, I mean – I thought that I could change things just by making it happen. I thought that if you could *imagine* things differently they would have to change.' She took in Alice's nod. 'Like the time I fell off my bicycle, in traffic – not long before I left,' Leah explained with no obvious logic. 'I hit the kerb and came off, banging my head and biting my tongue, but I wasn't really hurt. And when I got up everything seemed to have shifted key around me – the bell on my handlebars, the fruit in boxes outside a shop, the cracks in the pavement. I stood there with the taste of blood in my mouth and I'd never known ordinary things seem so actual and vivid. But in the same instant it felt as if the whole street was on the point of changing into something else . . . was eager for it even.' She looked up with an air of defiance. 'I suppose you think I only saw things that way because I'd banged my head.'

'On the contrary,' Alice responded quietly, 'I think we need to knock ourselves on the head every now and then in order to see through things.'

'That's right. That's what I mean. It was after that accident I began to see the world differently. I saw it as fiction – and as bad fiction mostly, the work of aggressive, mediocre minds. And I thought that once you'd seen through it – once you'd seen it not as something fixed in stone, but as stories – stories that could be differently told – then everything would become malleable somehow. It could all be changed.' Again Leah looked up, but without eagerness. 'And it turns out to be true,' she added with a thin, countermanding smile. 'But there's a problem. Replacing yourself. That's the hardest thing of all.'

'Except,' Alice agreed, 'that we don't have to keep on telling ourselves the same story either.'

'No, but . . .' Then all further promise of intimacy suddenly expired as Leah lost faith in this chary venture of confession. She looked down at her watch. 'Look, it's getting late. I can't get through to Stephen. When he turns up will you tell him I'm not well?' Her glance of appeal

31

found no favour in Alice's eyes. 'Or you could just say I can't handle seeing him tonight. Would you do that for me?'

'I could, but I won't.'

Leah stared in disbelief. The tone of the refusal had been neither short nor without sympathy, but it was refusal none the less.

'I mean,' Alice added after a significant moment, 'you're not actually ill, are you?'

There were impartial lights in which no one could dispute that Alice was an ugly old woman.

'I feel dead,' Leah said. 'I feel dead inside.'

'Then resurrect for goodness' sake.' Alice withstood the outraged glare. 'Obviously the present story isn't working. Try another. Go out with Stephen. Nothing's going to change if you stay here.'

'I'm barely human,' Leah protested. 'I'd probably savage him.'

'Well that might be lively! You should definitely go.'

'Alice . . .'

But Alice shook her head. 'If you choose not to talk about anything that matters, or to end a conversation the moment it gets difficult, then don't count on my complicity when you're feeling sorry for yourself. Don't count on it anyway. And certainly don't ask me to comfort your admirers.' She folded the tea-towel, smiling agreeably. 'I think you should come down out of the moon palace and keep your promises.' But as she turned away into the kitchen Alice was wondering – not without anxiety – whether challenge might serve where sympathy had failed.

Ronan woke to a calamitous sense of loss. For months now that feeling had imbued his dreams, though the circumstances and object of the loss seemed to alter with such frequency from dream to dream that the links were far from obvious to a man poorly educated in the idiom of the night. There had been times too when his nerves were so eroded by depression, or by the drugs he'd taken to contain its ravages, that nothing but this seemingly random debility of feeling survived those dim regions of sleep from which no light of memory escaped on waking. Not this time though. Too vividly he recalled the vanishing swan.

The map crackled beneath his hand. He lay on the bed as at a long drop's edge. When he pushed himself upright he let go of the dream. It fell backwards into the dark.

He checked his watch and found that he had slept for less than quarter of an hour. Then he was out of his clothes and standing under the hot gush of a shower as though consciousness itself might be washed away and nothing left but raw sensation.

Minutes later he was down in the bar of the hotel radiating a desire to be left alone over his drink.

He was joined there by a burly young American with a moustache who had come, he said, to Cornwall in search of ancestors. Evidently he did not observe Ronan's lack of interest, or could not credit it, for he was soon furnishing names of places and people, of a ship even, a late seventeenth-century barque that had crossed the Atlantic to some New England haven, bringing this man's forebears to where Ronan wished, in silence, the crass young pilgrim had remained. But then he remembered how he too had once been a traveller in foreign parts, and young; and having admitted the American so far into its sympathy, his imagination ventured further, seeing the delicate ship breast the Atlantic's swell, thinking of the souls it had carried, and recalling that he too was a seeker again, and insecure. His nods became friendlier. He put a question or two, attended to the replies. A responsive question was asked and answered. It was established that Ronan too was a stranger in these parts, though his interest in the area was left unspecified. The American – his name was Prewett – bought more drinks. There was a silence in which, eventually, Ronan heard himself say, 'I killed a swan today.'

Prewett rubbed the back of his hand across his moustache. 'Come again.'

Ronan had observed the shift of focus in his eyes. 'A swan. I ran it down. In the road.' Why was he doing this? What fantasy of absolution had crossed his mind? He felt, and – from the uneasy expression on the younger man's face – might have looked like the Ancient Mariner. It was, perhaps, the same obsessive glitter in his eyes that caused the American, again, to glance away. Ronan perceived misunderstanding. 'I didn't mean to,' he added quickly. 'It landed right in front of my car. Couldn't stop, you see. No chance. I ran right over it.'

'Jesus!'

Ronan stared at his drink, unshriven.

Prewett said, 'What do you do with a thing like that?'

Regretful of this impulse of confession, Ronan shrugged. 'That's just awful. I mean, a *swan!* That's a big bird.'

'Royal.' Ronan took in the American's puzzled frown. 'Over here swans are considered royal. They're the property of the queen.'

'I see.' Prewett tried for lightness. 'I guess she can't keep track of all of them.' But Ronan was already elsewhere. He did not smile. A moment or two later he heard the soft drawl add, 'Though my old man would say God does. He's a preacher, back home. Not a sparrow falls, you know?'

Ronan was seized by the appalling thought of what it must be like to live inside a universe which was everywhere the manifestation of omniscient consciousness. No secrecy, not even in the silence of the mind.

'Do you believe that?' he demanded.

34

Narrowing his honest eyes, the American soothed his cheek with a fingernail as he thought. 'Hell, I don't know. I guess there's a sense in which everything connects . . . like touching a web, you know?'

'I think it's meaningless. Pure hazard. That it should have been my car. Not the next, not the one before. Mine. In the same space, that moment . . .'

'Sure.' But the assent came more as consolation than conviction, and there was a further protracted silence, from which the younger man looked up, concerned, into his companion's whitened face. 'Hey, are you feeling okay? You're looking kinda peaky there.'

'I'm all right.' Ronan ran a hand through his hair. 'I think I need some air. Excuse me.' Relinquishing his drink, he stepped through into the lobby of the hotel where Brian Pollard sat behind the desk with its telephone and register, its brash vase of carnations. He looked up from an examination of his cheque-book stubs.

'You'll eat with us tonight?'

'I suppose so, I don't know.' But the thought of food made him nauseous. He blanched, saying, 'I have to step outside.'

Dusk was closing over the quay where young men with lank hair and fringed leather jackets smoked together, one of them straddling a Japanese machine of conspicuous power. When Ronan looked up he saw the ramparts of black cliff above the harbour and the unsteady sky beyond. Needing to walk, to clear his head, he found the sign for the coastal path and mounted the steps that had been let into the steep cliff-side. Then he struck southwards, feeling the breeze cold against his face, hearing the sea toil in the darkness below. He was walking quickly, like a man with purpose, panting from the climb.

Soon the sky was almost completely dark. He trudged

through rough tussocks of grass where the land sheered away to a bulky overhang of cliff. A wind had risen from the gloom, dampening the air against his cheek though no rain came. Ronan lacked direction in the unreliable light, but he couldn't face the thought of the hotel – that bullock of a landlord, the dismayed creature his wife, the dire room. There must be other, livelier bars along this coast.

Beneath him the sea detonated like a quarry. He had walked for more than two miles when something came floating towards him out of the night. It touched his face, there, and again, softly, there. A gentle winnowing contact, kinder, less thin than driven rain, blurring across his lashes and brows.

Seeds, he thought at first, some form of wind-blown pollen, whitish in the milky light. But not at that season surely? Then moths perhaps, or some smaller night-flying insect? Puzzled he watched them waft past, sailing and dipping on the runnels of the wind, ever more thickly, until at a further inquisitive touch he put a finger to his face and felt a brief, sudsy dampness there.

Foam then. But wasn't he too high above the breaking swell for spray to reach him? Even as the question shaped itself the swarm had passed. There was only black wind at his face.

Ronan advanced. Some distance ahead came the thump and smack of sea on rock, followed by a demolishing roar of falling masonry. Huge slabs of marble might have reared and toppled there. Instants later their collapse was swallowed in a deep, receding gush. Again the air thickened into a flurry of white foam. He was caught in a shoal of small damp stars.

The cloud-cover broke and the night tilted, a little tipsily. His stomach was empty. In his bloodstream whiskey colluded with ionized air. Lightheaded, he saw himself at the helm of a listing windjammer, spindrift in his face as he doubled some risky cape. He was leaning on the wind.

A louder, almost stunning din of impact and collapse convulsed the air. Then he came upon the blow-hole's edge.

The tide had passed full. It was mainly the force of wind that drove the big seas through an arched gulley into the narrow throat of rock, but the power of those congested energies was terrible. They blazed whitely under the gleam of a fat moon. Ronan stared down. He might have been watching the turmoil of a trapped whale.

Yet nothing there was animate. The violence spent and restored itself without malice or ambition. At each collision the waters leapt and sucked and churned as they had done for millions of years before the first glimmering of mind. They remained impervious to its existence.

The wind shuddered at Ronan's ears. At bay against the fact of matter, he gazed dizzily down. These were the enduring things – blind wind, blind sea, blind rock. Devoid of everything except existence, they would go on and on. The whole shoot was reducible to the exhaust from combusted stars. Again the night gusted. Briefly the moon staggered in its tracks. And what nonsense this made of belief in divine intelligence, or any other consoling fiction!

Oddly these bleak reflections brought a kind of liberty. They pushed his troubles into steep perspective. Even the horror on the road seemed small, for every crash of swell against these rocks might be the smashing of a swan. Staring into the tumult, he seemed to see it so. Swan after swan was dashed to pieces there. Yet that was not the end of it, for from their ruin rose apocalyptic wings. Even as he watched, a voracious winged creature, neither fish nor beast nor bird, soared out of the depths to taste the sky. He gasped at the prodigious beauty of the thing. The night was left scoured and shining: a man might cleanse himself in its abrasive light. He saw himself standing on the brink of things with dark-adapted eyes. There were no final sanctions, no meaning outside the human mind. He'd been right, therefore, to put everything at risk rather than eking out a safe but spurious existence.

The blow-hole offered up its hollow-throated roar. For a few moments longer Ronan stared into the turbulent shaft at his feet, then walked on until its clamour was submerged in the general grievance of the sea.

On a rise near the edge of the cliff, the path turned inland for a hundred yards or so. He saw the lights of a small hotel in the black wedge of cove below. The personal world had resumed itself: it was coming to meet him. But the same wind that had driven off the cloud was gathering more, and his mood veered with it. His path dipped towards the cove. The moon withdrew. There was only the cold smell of night and the cover of the sky, inkily coalescent with the fathomless black sea. Everything was leaking into everything else. He was uncertain even of his own boundaries.

After a time he perceived that his breath was a kind of sipping on the darkness. He was filling himself with it, sip by sip, and the cold was more than the touch of the night at his face: it was maturing to an inward predilection.

Conscious of his unstable condition, in awe of it, Ronan made for the lights of the cove.

In a difficult moment towards the end of the meal Leah realized that she had not once looked fully into Stephen's face. There had been a number of parrying glances, plenty of temporizing stares and frowns, the occasional tolerant smile. He had been treated to the full sidelong repertoire of her habitual refractory way with men – indeed with almost everyone these days. Yet not until now had she looked evenly across at him and encountered the difficult and resolute man inside – a man who, only a moment before, had said something so unexpected and acute that for an instant she was uncertain whether to be furious or disarmed.

But she had brought this confusion on herself. She should not have listened to Alice. She should never have let the young nurseryman bring her to this expensive table where a candle made dancer's bows, and where, when she looked out of the wide picture-window into the Atlantic night, she saw only the lights of other tables reflected there. *The Intimate Isles*, she thought: this was where men and women were supposed to go together, this was what they were supposed to do. They went out by night, in finery, to small enchanted hotels, and ate the milky flesh of monkfish and sipped good wine, and talked to the murmur of other couples afloat on the same crystallized ballroom dance of conversation. This was courtship ritual. She knew every move, countercheck and turn. The whole order of service was familiar to her; from swooning palate to turned coverlet. She knew exactly how to ease or frustrate each little ceremony of experience.

The problem here was that this was an earnest, kindly man, and she was in poor shape, and she could see, for the moment, no other exit from the ring he was drawing round her than his imminent hurt.

Only a few awkward moments earlier she had tried to fend him off by saying, weakly enough, 'Stephen, I think we should just concentrate on trying to be friends.'

But he'd half smiled, half frowned his refusal to be deterred. 'No, we can't do that. At least not yet. We might end up as friends, but I'd have to count that a major defeat. We'd be friends who might have been lovers – in my version at least. And that's a sad thing to be.'

She said, 'I would make you sad in any case.'

'But not only that.'

'In the end.'

'Already she's talking endings and we've barely begun. How can you be so sure?'

'Because I know me.'

'As you were.'

'As I am.'

'And how is that?'

Though she was less than two years older than Stephen, it suddenly felt like twenty. 'I'm chock-full of sadness,' she said, but defiantly, without self-pity. 'Sadness and bitterness and anger and hurt. They're all communicable. You don't need any of them.'

'And you do? You need to hold on to them?'

'I told you – they're what I am. I'm full of them. Up to here.' She tapped her head and looked impatiently away, and it was then that he said the extraordinary thing. 'For a moment you almost had me convinced. But now I don't think so. I don't think you're *full* of anything. On the contrary, you feel empty to me. It feels as though . . . as though you've been excavated.'

Evidently it was not a word he had intended to use. It had presented itself and he seemed astonished by its appearance. Both of them were shocked by it, and seeing that she might be about to stand and walk away he put a hand over hers in restraint. She would not allow it, but neither did she rise.

'I don't mean it cruelly,' he said, hearing too late that it could not have sounded otherwise, 'but there are times when you make me think of the blow-hole up on the cliff – all those big elemental noises, full of sound and fury, like you, your moods, that air of suppressed violence you give off. But it can only shout like that because it's hollowed out and empty, because it's become the shape of what isn't there any more, of what's been taken away.'

There were, dangerously, tears at the back of her eyes. The air was constricted in her throat. She lifted the napkin from her lap and patted the place where she was biting her lip. Then she held it there, in purdah.

A wiser, or a more callous, man would have persevered. Lacking the sure instinct of one, and the insensitivity of the other, Stephen allowed her eyes to arrest him. For an instant he could have taken back every word, but he would not apologize for truth; though there had been, if truth were told, an edge of reprisal in his tone.

'Oh shit!' He pushed his plate away and slid the legs of his chair noisily to one side so that he was sitting with his fist pushed against his nostrils, staring into the night. Leah, meanwhile, desired nothing more ardently than her own extinction, but settled for one of the ways she had learned in recent months to disappear. She made for the moon palace stairs.

'This monkfish is excellent.' Her voice was ice on a marble slab. 'Perhaps it will go some way towards making up the deficiency.'

He did not respond.

'I wonder why they're called monkfish?' she went on. 'I mean, presumably they're not celibate. They must breed, mustn't they? Or perhaps all female monkfish are nuns? Do you think they do it by immaculate conception?'

'Leah.'

'Can we leave it?'

'I really didn't mean to hurt you.'

'I believe you,' she said, but her tone denied it.

'At least . . . not very much.'

Again she encountered his eyes, though she was prepared this time, control was resumed. 'You're an honest man. Sometimes it's engaging.'

'I suppose I've completely blown it now?'

'Like the blow-hole,' she said, 'there's nothing to blow.' She spoke from the sparse rocky places, yet she was amazed to find a lively rivalry growing there, like thrift.

'What I was trying to say is that I think I could love you if you'd give me half a chance.'

And how, she wondered, would he cope if she unleashed all the black raging inside her – if, along with what he thought he wanted, he also had to take the full force of all that (out of consideration, out of stupid affection even) she kept kennelled up in here?

'Why should I do that?' she asked, and pushed away her plate.

'Because . . .' But he seemed to think better of it. 'No reason,' he smiled ruefully. 'No reason at all. I'll just have to make my chances, won't I?' He gazed across at the withdrawn face, aware of difficult thoughts happening in places to which he had no access. She made him think of a black iris unfurling its flag into dusky purple, for there was a mystery to her life that beguiled him, and with a yearning close to pain. 'Can I ask you something?' he said. 'What happened to you? Before you turned up here, I mean.' But in that moment the waiter appeared asking if he might clear the abandoned plates. Exasperated, still polite, Stephen nodded and leaned back. The job was swiftly done. They agreed to skip pudding but take coffee. The waiter withdrew, and when it became clear from her silence that she had found cover behind the diversion, he said, 'I think someone must have messed you about pretty badly. Am I right?'

'Yes,' she answered. 'Me.'

'Single-handed?'

'No. It was a collaboration. It took at least four generations of my family.'

'And a man?'

42

'Several.'

'But one in particular?'

'Yes,' she conceded, 'a particular man.'

Having forced the admission, he now found himself touched by jealousy. 'Tell me about him.'

'There's no need. It's quite over.'

'Then why do I get the feeling he's here with us right now?'

Her face drew shadow from the candle flame. Her unease took a further turn. 'I don't remember you being this pushy before.'

He smiled, not altogether easily. 'Something Alice said – after last time. It got me thinking. I'd been doing my best to impress and succeeding with no one but Amy . . .'

'Who adores you, of course.'

'It's you I want. And Alice knows it. Anyway, having watched my noble ape approach fall flat, she suggested that too much abnegation makes a man go blind. I took the point.'

'Alice', said Leah feelingly, 'is a manipulator.'

Which might, he recognized, be true of the speaker too, for she had slipped his hook, and now here was the further interruption of coffee with bitter mints.

They were left a little at a loss with one another. He was frustrated by her elusiveness, and fascinated by it. Yet it was exhausting too; and so, sensing that he was a match for her only if he kept things simple and direct, he said, 'Doesn't it get lonely, keeping everything to yourself like that?'

Leah looked up sharply at this common gambit – the knight's move, a familiar preliminary to the taking of the queen. Every unattached woman was lonely by definition. Most attached ones too. Wherefore knights considered themselves serviceable. But, for Leah, her loneliness was proud estate. She was not so lightly laid, not now, not any more.

He was, apparently, sincere, which made the question difficult to bear.

Excavated, angry, sad, bitter, lonely – yes, dammit, all of these, and there was nothing to be done about it, nothing at all – she looked her watch. After ten-thirty. Even in silence the pressures built.

Her need to leave this place was urgent now.

He said, 'Have I upset you again?'

With stiff fingers Leah lightly tapped the table's edge. 'It's been a weird day, Stephen. I'm really tired. If it's all right with you, I'd like to go home.'

He held her gaze for a long moment, then nodded his assent. He caught the waiter's eye.

Leah got up to go to the loo where she stood for a space, staring at her treacherous reflection.

There were times when she could not bear what had become of her. She loathed the fractious, unappeasable creature staring back from the mirror. When all credible self-esteem was gone, what point continuing?

Then she blew her nose and found her face in mourning for the loving woman who had lived there once, who must – please God – survive there still, though walled-up alive some time ago, and ever more deeply immured by each involuntary act of self-protection. Leah was scared to think how little air could now be left in there.

By the time she returned the bill had been settled. The waiter came with her coat. He was tipped and thanked, then they stepped through into the public bar of the hotel. She was leading the way. Stephen said something behind her, and she was about to turn when she saw a face she recognized at the bar.

For an instant she thought it a malevolent trick of imagination, but the profile turned three-quarter face, and there was no mistaking the high-boned darksome glare.

44

All colour blanched from her. She was stunned out of coherent thought, yet elsewhere a cold, executive function of her mind calculated possibilities: if he was here, in Cornwall, near Treligo, then it must be because he knew where she was, where she lived. Someone had broken trust; she was quarry again; her nerves had known it. She needed time to think, she had to get away.

In the same frozen instant she saw that recognition was not yet mutual. She remembered how severely her hair had been cut since they were last together – it might take him a second or two to work out what was troubling in this couple leaving the restaurant.

Too late she reached a hand to her face in concealment.

Now the shock was his. In the half-gloom of the bar his eyes were white with it.

Then Stephen was beside her where she had stopped in her tracks. He was looking down at her, puzzled, concerned, 'Leah? Are you all right?'

She shrugged off his arm, hissing, 'I have to get out of here,' and made for the door where darkness came at her, big and clear.

Flight aggravated panic. She had never been to this hotel before, she did not recognize the cove or the cliff, her bearings were lost. Unable even to find Stephen's car, and exposed to a night in which the ways were no longer safe, she sought to wrap herself invisibly inside its windy hollows.

3
MISSING

The next morning, shortly before nine, an oldish man with blowing hair stood talking to two police officers, neither of them uniformed, on the north-facing edge of Pengerent Head. His face was still haggard with shock. For the same reason perhaps, or simply because such unaccustomed attention made him garrulous, his answers tended to be longer than the questions required. Something about him almost seemed eager to please. Yet what he had to tell could not be less than dreadful.

His name was Sessions. He was a retired librarian who had moved from a dormitory town in Essex on his retirement barely a year before. His wife must have been dying even before they came, he explained, though neither of them had known it, and he was widowed within a few months of their arrival. He had no family hereabouts and no close friends. Grief had left him desolate and remote. His need for sleep had become as frugal as his need for food, so most mornings it was his practice to rise before dawn and walk out to the headland where he would stand in silence and outstare the night.

So far the young detective-constable with the notebook had written down only the witness's name together with his present and previous address. Now he lowered the pencil from his lips to jot down: *Widowed. Alone. Insomniac.*

Then he considered whether to add some comment to the effect that the old man, who was wiry enough and strong, might also be just a bit dotty with loneliness. Undecided, he glanced across the cliffs where a helicopter scouted the coastline between the headland and Porthmallion, hovering every now and then like a hawk at stoop. Even at this distance the sky was loud with its commotion.

It was the Inspector who had put the questions, and if he too was impatient with the straggling answers it did not show. George Nankevill was approaching retirement himself. He had listened to this sort of complaint before and wondered what they expected, these pensioners who came down from Up-along bringing their nest-eggs with them? That the angel of death might overlook the quiet nooks in which they secluded themselves, or pick them off in handfuls, two at a time? There was hardly a village on his patch without its complement of dazed strangers whose spouses had died on them. Like unemployment and the derelict winter villages, it was one of the modern blights on the Duchy. What did they expect?

But let this one ramble, he thought. It might save trouble later if he could establish from the start that this shocked dismay was the genuine item. 'Any particular reason why you come to the same spot every day?' he asked.

'I like its remoteness. You can be fairly sure of having the whole dawn spectacle to yourself out here. It's a good place to think.'

'What sort of thing do you think about?'

The old man offered a diffident smile. 'Time. Change. The big things and the small memories they bring.' He glanced up again and saw encouragement in the Inspector's eyes. 'I like to catch the first crack of light among the stars. I like to think about how all this was formed, millions of years ago.'

'On that sort of time-scale human life can seem pretty insignificant.'

'Or even more precious . . . depending how you feel.' Reginald Sessions uttered a sigh, then looked back at his mild interrogator. 'Who could do such a thing, Inspector? What kind of man could do a thing like that?'

The response was no more than a noncommittal shrug, an almost gallic raising of the brows behind thick-rimmed glasses. 'We don't even know that it's not suicide,' he lied. 'What makes you think it's not?'

'I just assumed . . .' The man was perplexed by the question. 'The times we live in, I suppose. The things one reads about and hears on TV. All these people . . . the helicopter . . .'

The Inspector too glanced down at the activity in the cove. As though it were a matter of no more than casual interest he said, 'So tell me again. About this morning, I mean. Tell me just what happened.'

That morning Reginald Sessions had woken later than usual. By the time he reached the coastal path dawn was already hardening inland. He had taken his normal route out on to the headland past the mounds and ditches of its Iron Age fort. He noticed that the grass was damp from the night's rain.

'I'm surprised not to have heard it,' he said. 'But then I took paracetamol for a headache last night. It must have deepened my sleep.'

'Do you often get headaches?' the detective-constable asked quietly. This was the first case on which he'd caught the distinctive smell of an evil larger than mere villainy loose in the world. What he had seen in the cove left him agitated and queasy. He was keen for a quick kill.

'No, not often. Only if I watch too much television.'

'Which is what you were doing last night?'

48

'That's right.'

'On your own?'

'As usual, I'm afraid.'

'And you didn't go out at all?'

'Just to the door, for a breath of fresh air, about ten-thirty. After the news. There was no sign of rain then, which is why it surprised me . . . the damp grass, I mean. I went to bed soon after, tossed and turned a bit, then dropped off.'

'Go on,' said the Inspector.

The elderly man thought himself back to that time no more than a few hours ago, which now seemed an age away: just after dawn, the sky marbled, the breakers flaking softly in white streamers from the rock. Valerian and sea-pinks in the pale light. The air, he remembered, was damp and sweet.

'There's not a lot to tell. It was a clear morning. Fine. No one about yet. The boats hadn't put out from Porthmallion. I spent some time watching the cormorants out on the islands.'

The Inspector followed his gaze out to the two large, offshore outcrops of rock which were known locally, for no obvious reason except perhaps their blackness, as the Pot and Kettle. 'You must have sharp eyesight.'

'I had my binoculars. I always take them. I took them off when I got back home to ring the police.'

'You rang from home then? Why not the box in the village? Wouldn't it have been quicker?'

'Yes, but I needed to sit down . . . to collect myself. I'm sorry if . . .'

At that moment a call sign crackled from the radio in the police car parked on the cliff-top. The DC closed his notebook and went to answer.

'No matter,' the Inspector said. 'Go on.'

After a time Sessions had swung the binoculars inland,

tracking a flight of choughs along the cliff. Then he spotted a kestrel hovering above the cliff-face. He lowered the lenses in search of its quarry, and it was then that he glimpsed the woman on the beach.

'The first shock was the realization she was naked. I thought she was sprawled out on the beach after a dawn swim. Skinny-dipping – isn't that what they call it? Of course, I lowered the binoculars immediately. I didn't want her thinking I was . . .'

'But you must have looked back?' The Inspector smiled at the man's confusion. 'Don't worry. It's only natural. Anybody would.'

'After a while. But not with the binoculars. Not at first. She was in plain sight, and once you knew where to look . . . It was then I sensed that something was wrong. It must have been cold down there but she wasn't moving at all. And there was something not right about the angle of her arm . . .'

'So you put the binoculars back on her?'

'And adjusted the focus, yes.'

'Could you tell she was dead?'

'Not then. Not till I got down there.'

The man's voice was a little shaky now. He sensed a change in the quality of attention. 'I had to see if there was anything I could do,' he explained. 'I'd shouted out to her before that, just to make sure. But there was no answer, no movement. I knew she was unconscious at least. It took me some time to find a safe way down, but I don't think it made any difference. Her head . . . You saw. And she was so cold . . .'

'So you came away?'

'I was feeling a bit faint . . . and worried about the climb back up. I'm not as young as I was. And I was trembling, you see.'

50

In fact, the old man had sat among the rocks for some time, out of sight of the torn, bluish flesh and the hair matted with blood and kelp. He was panicky and fearful, wondering where the angels of mercy had been when the young woman cried out for their protection. At the same time he was contending with his anxious desire to walk away as if he had found nothing. He remembered those feelings but could say nothing about them now, and for a few moments both men seemed preoccupied with the bleak pictures fixed on their separate memories. Then, like one losing interest, the Inspector sighed.

Somewhere at large in the country was a man about whom there might be nothing special at all except that he had been on these cliffs the previous night and was now a sex-criminal and murderer, if he had not been so before. It was beginning to seem unlikely that this aging ex-librarian in a beige anorak was anything other than he claimed to be – the unfortunate finder of the body. The only touch of evil on him was on the Inspector too, and on everyone who had been down to the cove. It was always the same in Nankevill's infrequent experience of murder: for a time, in the presence of the victim's remains, its odium seemed to stain the very light.

'And you didn't recognize her?' he said. 'You've no idea who she is?'

The haggard man shook his head. 'I'm not sure even her own father would know her. Not now. Not like that.'

From the open door of the parked car the DC called. 'Excuse me, sir, the Super wants a word.'

George Nankevill rasped a hand across his chin and muttered, 'Somebody will miss her somewhere. We'll find out who she is soon enough.' He turned away and crossed to the car. There was a brief murmured conference at the car door before he climbed in to use the radio.

Left alone with his thoughts, the witness wondered whether some significant detail had escaped him. He was retracing the line of questions when, belatedly, and with a sickly pang of alarm, he realized what had been in the Inspector's mind throughout.

'But surely . . . ?' he gasped aloud, then worked the zip of his anorak nervously up and down before turning for reassurance to the uniformed constable who stood some distance away, where the path down to the cove had been ribboned off. 'You don't think they think I . . . ?'

'I shouldn't think so, sir.' The policeman's eyes shifted back along the headland towards the small gathering of onlookers brought there by rumour; then down to the beach below, where a tent flapped in the stiff breeze among the rocks. A photographer replacing lenses in a leather bag glanced up as the helicopter banked overhead and the sound of its rotor shuddered on the air.

Now the old man was trembling again. There had been no reassurance in the constable's response. The knowledge of his isolation shut round him. There was no one to turn to. On this bare cliff-top there were no mercy angels.

Mr Sessions stared out to sea, then skywards where clouds the colour of the local slate were moving swiftly in off the Atlantic. There was a feeling of acceleration in the air. His hands were clenching and unclenching as he waited to see what would happen next.

As usual at that hour of the mid-morning Alice was alone in her workshop. She sat at her wheel, spinning the last of the wool she had carded earlier. Three more rolags lay on the bench beside her like little sleeves of smoke. Soon Dora Pascoe would come down from the house, her chores half done, and a smell of coffee would overlay the smell of fleece in this lofty space which had been a mill-building once. Together they would savour the first cigarette of the day.

There had been rain in the night. Alice could hear its aftermath in the swollen volume of the stream. It sounded beyond the creak and whirr of the wheel. Somewhere on the glen's green air, a blackbird sang, and all would have been well except that a baleful noise throbbing across the sky had set her slightly on edge. She presumed an exercise by the air-sea rescue people, for on this tranquil day disaster seemed unlikely; but on this coast one never knew, and she was glad when the helicopter's din abated and the morning returned to scale.

In a dusty beam of sunlight slanting down from a high window where a gantry had once hung, Alice's body swayed to the rhythms of the wheel. The treadle rose and fell under her foot, the spindle hummed to itself, slowly the bobbin fattened with yarn.

Alice re-entered a trance of industrious repose.

Since Barney had died five years before, she had grown used to solitude. During her time of grief she began to prefer it even, for her work brought demands enough to keep her occupied without the moral adjustments and delicate accommodations of feeling that came from having another person about the place. And there was much else: a store of reading to be done, and the garden to tend; she took an astrologer's interest in the motions of the heavens, and an aging outsider's view of the changes on earth. There were memories and dreams to assimilate; and, more rarely, her waking excursions into the visionary realm, of which she spoke to no one, yet which had furnished the most striking imagery of her work in later years.

Then Leah had arrived, and things had changed, and not all the changes were agreeable; so she had been glad of the chance to spend a little time alone again, the previous night, in the house which had harboured and nourished her imagination for more than half a century.

When she first became mistress of Roseleye, Alice was just twenty-six years old. She had relinquished the scholarly promise of her career as a medievalist, together with a prosperous married life and the respect of her family and friends. In their place she had her disreputable lover, an artist's unquenchable ambition, and this doddery old house in Cornwall: unquestionably the better of the bargain, though the family solicitor who had profited from both divorce and conveyance (and was now – God bless his venal soul – long dead) could never have seen it so.

'I'm advised the price is too high,' he'd declared when he looked up, sighing, from the file of documents that had already accumulated around the purchase.

But Alice had arrived in his dowdy Gray's Inn chambers resolved no longer to be discountenanced by the narrow-eyed man who sat across from her, wobbly-jowled, with small divots of hair at his cheeks. Nothing must halt the magical process by which, after that first stirring day at the coast, she was coming at last into her own.

'I do not wish to haggle,' she answered, flushed and smart in her heather two-piece.

'But, my dear young woman, have you studied the surveyor's report on this find of yours . . . this Roseleye?'

'It's pronounced *Rozelly*,' Alice corrected, placing the stress firmly on the second syllable.

'I see. Well, whatever. Listen to this, pray.'

Rising-damp, beetle, woodworm, a worrying crack in the stonework of the gable-end – the solicitor read the gloomier passages of the report aloud, then wondered drily what particular virtues the property might have to set against this impressive tally of dilapidation.

Over the previous weeks Alice's feelings had been

sufficiently excoriated. It seemed that the single blessing from her previous life was childlessness, for the divorce would have been intolerable otherwise. Her former husband, who was a fashionable gynaecological consultant, had not been about to endanger a rich private practice by playing the gentleman, nor did Alice expect it. So she was prepared, publicly, to accept the guilt of this sensational affair as entirely hers; but she had long since wearied of the legal profession with its expedient fictions and pinchbeck rhetoric. She saw no reason now to justify herself before this condescending specimen.

'I understand', she said, 'that my parents have given me a free hand in this matter.'

'That is the case, although . . .'

'Then it does not need your consent?'

His was now the cold voice of a senior partner unused to challenge or correction. 'Nevertheless it is my duty to point out the evident unwisdom of this purchase.'

Sighing, Alice wondered in silence how fat a man might wax from pointing out the evident. Hugely, it seemed. She perceived also that he had concerned himself with the dull business of this conveyance for no larger purpose than to add the weight of his judgment to the sum of her indignities.

'You know the extent of your settlement,' he persisted. 'Have you considered what proportion of it will be swallowed up by essential repairs?'

'We intend to do much of the work ourselves.'

'Do you, by George?'

He was thinking (and she could see him thinking): who would have thought so plain a woman could perpetrate such scandal?

And the plain woman's thoughts were no more charitable. She was imagining suit, waistcoat, shirt, tie and underwear removed, and the fat man left, dimpled, gartered and ridiculous in his leather chair.

Eventually the solicitor sniffed. He lifted the watch unnecessarily from his fob and spoke to it. 'Well, that is your own affair, of course.'

'Yes.'

'Though I'm damned if I know how I'll answer your father when he asks what possessed me to approve a contract on a property in this condition.'

Alice imagined them in the club together, lords of the parcelled earth, shaking their heads over port and cigars. How good, by contrast, to find herself in these badlands, affiliated with the reprobate and wild.

She favoured the man with a patient smile. 'I suppose you might tell him that there was one compelling reason why I wanted this house, whatever its condition.'

'Which is?'

'The situation.'

Apparently this dull answer had disappointed. 'Two miles inland? No sea-views there, I imagine.'

'None. But something better.' Alice paused to relish the sudden ambiguous precision of her thought. Then quietly she uttered it: 'You see, Roseleye stands on the threshold of the otherworld.'

If a glint of scorn had brightened her eyes, there had been nothing overtly captious or fanciful in her voice.

The solicitor further narrowed his gaze. A dismissive puff of his lips intimated much. In particular, that Alice might have made fools of her husband and her family, but she must not think that she could do the same with him.

'It's quite true,' she insisted, on the wing of her inspiration now. (She was remembering the wicket-gate at the foot of the derelict garden, the stepping-stones and the stream that wound through the glen before cascading into a small gorge that opened on the sea. She was remembering the waterfall with its cauldron-pool, and the scraps of rag tied to the brambles there, and the posy of wildflowers that someone had daintily laid in a jar among the stones.)

'In fact,' she insisted airily, 'you can't walk far from its door in any direction without recalling that all the islands of Britain were once co-extensive with the otherworld, and may be so still. That's why I love it, that's why I want it, and that's why I most certainly shall have it. Now may we please proceed with the purchase?'

Aghast at this sublime irreality, the solicitor searched among his papers for the deed of conveyance. Any doubts that the family were doing the sensible thing in paying off this impossible daughter had disappeared. The otherworld indeed! He wished the silly vixen well of it. Evidently she had become too crazy by half to prosper in this one.

A few moments later he was witnessing her signature and ringing for a clerk.

So in the end enough money had been settled on her to put the buildings back into repair and to survive modestly for a time; and as her side of an agreement that the resolute woman had never come to regret in the following years, the family had seen nothing of her since.

On one score, however, her detractors had been largely right. She would not hold her lover long, they warned: he was younger than Alice, of deplorable provenance, unreliable, and with too racy an eye on the main chance to content himself with the tedium of life on that rainy peninsula. They gave her six months of deluded happiness at most before he upped and scarpered; and she must not think that she could come running back.

Alice had her own magnificent reasons for hearing none of this. She was a prudent, dutiful wife no more. She was no longer the judicious scholar, tying her imagination down with weights as she lectured earnestly on courtly love and the romances of the grail. The doctoral thesis, of which her fussy supervisor entertained such hopes, would never be completed now. She had transcended the need. She had been propelled by this scandalous affair into her proper destiny.

Or perhaps she had simply been returned to it. For Alice had loved the old romances of the Middle Ages ever since she first marvelled over them in her childhood books. Their landscapes were the landscapes of her soul – the misty woods and lakes, the savage heaths, the blue and gold enamelled sky in which an intelligible starry firmament made music – these were her imagination's native land. As an undergraduate she became more deeply intrigued by those tales in which the amorous latin temperament fused with celtic glamour to refine the legends of the grail. Here, she later thought, was a congenial theme for many years' research. A stimulating, harmless life might be passed that way; but, unsurprisingly, the patient scrutiny of textual variants and philological cruxes had failed to requite the longings of an unhappily married woman with a taste for marvels.

Then passion ignited her life. For a time there were secrecies, concealments, lies, all of them hateful to one whose every impulse was to proclaim herself found out by joy. So the truth was told and all hell broke loose. By then, however, Alice had seen clearly what she had only glimpsed before: *fin amor* – the adulterous love exalted by the troubadors – was more than a poetic fancy; it had been a sacramental experience, an erotic heresy celebrating the deep knowledge of the heart. Through the ritual of its devotions ardent spirits had once been conducted into the secret gardens of the soul – and it could happen still.

Now Alice was not, of course, the first to make these claims, nor even to believe that the key to such rites was hidden in the romances of the grail. In her lectures and seminars she had referred often to the work of Jessie Weston, though always with the arch rider that Miss Weston's acquaintance with the occult orders of her own day might have stimulated an overheated imagination to outrun her critical intellect. But Alice could have eaten those words gladly now, for through the illuminating rapture of her own adulterous love she had grasped what all but a few initiates had long since forgotten – that the romances were the tantric scriptures of the west.

Her supervisor was profoundly dismayed by this conviction. Like the princes of the church before them, the learned doctors of the academy had orthodoxies to defend. Alice's only evidence for her findings was that questionable stuff experience, and no one knew what to do with a scholar who *became* her thesis.

This was the least of Alice's concerns, for her life was irretrievably altered. If colleagues, family and friends believed her deluded, this came as no surprise: she had never expected understanding from those with no share in the experience. But she was initiate now in the heresy of love, and for her it was all true – vividly, deliriously, self-evidently true.

As for her partner in the mysteries – well, he lasted longer than her critics hazarded. Having survived their ordeal at the hands of the press, they retreated to Roseleye where he remained for almost two years – though the second was often wretched when they were together, and worse during his intermittent absences. Then he left on one of his unexplained trips to London and this time he did not come back. Alice had been amazed to discover how few of the things left in Cornwall were actually his.

It was the summer of 1939. Shortly afterwards the world declared war on itself.

Diminished to insignificance by this universal tragedy, his defection gradually became endurable. And, by then, Roseleye had disclosed consoling mysteries of its own.

While converting this building from ruined mill to weaving-studio Alice had removed the rotten boards and joists of the upper floor, leaving only a narrow gallery to be achieved by the worn stone stairs. The door beneath the gallery opened now and Dora Pascoe came in, carrying an electric kettle.

Alice braked the wheel with a hand greasy with lanolin. She got up to stretch her long bones and returned, content, to the present. It was a spinner's privilege to busy herself in more than one world at a time, and the wool gathered on the bobbin gave palpable value to the hour she had just spent elsewhere. But turning to greet Mrs Pascoe now she sensed something very wrong.

Under hair as fay and wispy as the seed-head of a dandelion, the cleaning-lady's face was more than usually dour. She stood in the doorway with the free hand cupped at her cheek saying, 'You won't have heard then?'

With a reflex of alarm Alice remembered the throb of the helicopter across the morning sky. 'Has there been an accident?'

'Worse,' said Mrs Pascoe. 'Dear God, the times we live in!'

The postman had rehearsed his version of the morning's events only moments before. By the time the story had reached him it was already embellished by rumour. Nor was the cleaner beyond adding a touch or two of her own, for how else to come to terms with what was both terrible and unseen? Its shadow fell on Alice's imagination now, and to Dora Pascoe it seemed that horror had been intensified in the sharing rather than diminished. For a time the two women teetered together while, unheard by either, the room was loud with their breathing.

'And they've no idea who she is?' said Alice.

'They say she was bashed about something terrible.'

Unconsciously Alice reached a hand to her mouth. She was thinking how frail the threads were that bound us to life, but she said only, 'So they don't even know if she's local?'

Mrs Pascoe shook her head, muttering, 'Terrible, terrible.' And the breeze through the open door further disarrayed her hair. Since the loss of husband, son and brother in the same foundered smack, the cleaning-lady had been a little crazed. Disaster had unravelled her life. For years now she had lived alone in a squalid caravan from which neither friends nor social-workers had been able to budge her. One could discern in those eroded cheeks a lifetime of accomplished suffering.

She bared her large teeth. 'My first thought was for young Amy. You know the way she carries on. But the postman says he saw her out riding beyond Perangarth, so it can't be her.'

'Thank God!'

'But it's still some mother's child.' A stalk of a woman in her floral pinny, Mrs Pascoe crossed to the Belfast sink where it stood on breeze-blocks under a pair of old brass taps. 'Who could do such a thing?' she murmured over the noise of the filling kettle. 'What sort of monster would do a thing like that?'

An urgent part of Alice's mind was trying to recall the noises of Leah's return to the house the previous night; another, less voluntary part presented its spontaneous answer to Mrs Pascoe's question. It escaped her lips as on the breath of thought. She said, and was astonished to hear herself saying, 'The Nameless Knight.'

The whisper could not be heard above the water's splash. Mrs Pascoe half-turned her head. 'What's that?'

61

'The Nameless Knight,' Alice repeated, wondering at this trick of light inside her head. Then she looked up, scattered, agitated. 'It's nothing. Just something that came into my mind. From an old story.'

'It's an old story, all right, God help us all.'

Dora Pascoe plugged in the kettle, then took a packet of untipped cigarettes from the pocket of her apron. 'Will you have one of these?'

A hand still at her mouth, Alice declined. Her thoughts were swinging on a binnacle. She said, 'When you were in the house just now . . .' and swallowed. 'Did you see anything of Leah? I don't remember hearing her come in last night.'

The flame on Mrs Pascoe's plastic lighter stopped short of her cigarette. For several seconds, while Alice read the cleaning-lady's eyes, the room was conspicuously still. She remembered the premonitory howling in the cove. The sound of the helicopter's rotor throbbed about her head. Alice uttered a little panting sigh.

'Just a minute, my dear.' Mrs Pascoe lit her cigarette. 'Don't you go jumping to confusion now.'

But variants on the same vile picture were in both their minds, the same unfocused thought that not since the gods first ranged the planet with their murderous, randy appetites had it been a safe and homely place for woman-kind. Images of laurel entered Alice's head, and of a nightingale that cried 'jug jug' to dirty ears.

'Where did she go then?' demanded Mrs Pascoe from the quivering present. 'Who was she with?'

'She was going out with Stephen. He was taking her to dinner. Somewhere in Porthmallion, I think.'

'Then she's probably been cuddled up with him all night.'

Alice took in the sly, gratified smile. She had already considered this impulsive possibility, and failed to square it with the knowledge that Leah had gone out with Stephen only because of the pressure she herself had applied. She shared the doubts with Dora now.

'Yes, but you never know,' the cleaning-lady answered. 'Not nowadays. And anyway he wouldn't have let her come back on her own. He'd have seen her safely home.'

'Unless they quarrelled. Leah can be so difficult.'

'Even so, he'd have . . .' Mrs Pascoe drew down her mouth. 'Unless . . . Unless you think he . . .'

'No, not Stephen. Surely?'

Experienced in malevolent turns of fate, Mrs Pascoe swiftly lost confidence in her own effort at reassurance. Rarely constant on a single theme, her mind now yawed on a bleak wind. 'That's just the worry of it,' she said, as though concluding a systematic argument, 'it could be any of the devils. It could be any one of them. They don't seem to know when no means no. Not when they're hot down there.' Mrs Pascoe's arms were crossed at her narrow chest. She was swaying a little.

Alice steadied herself against the bench. 'I can't imagine that Stephen would hurt her. Not like that.'

'Course he wouldn't. I'm sure you're right. He's a gentleman is Stephen. She's probably just sleeping it off in her room this minute.'

'I think,' said Alice, 'I'd better make sure she's all right.'

When she stepped outside the workshop a solitary magpie flapped across the stream. Alice faltered a moment, torn between her desire to hurry up to the house and a powerful urge to follow the green, lichened smell of the dells downstream to the fall. There she might collect herself. She might find that absconded place inside herself where all things could be borne with patient equanimity. But there was a need, instantly, to know.

Sighing, driven by her agitation, she turned right, taking the muddy track uphill to the house.

The air was sweet and mild. Gnats danced against wood-shadows. Sunlight glittered from the puddles. The sky was mirrored there.

Alice felt the knock of her heart. She had forgotten the old ashplant that usually helped her up this slope. Here and there she had to catch at branches for support. Lines from the old story chattered round her head. She muttered the couplets aloud, amazed to find the precise scholarly accent of her Middle English still intact and fluent after all these years.

Panting and murmuring, Alice climbed the path to her house. Anxiety that had mingled with anger was mounting to outrage now. Yes, *outrage*, that, precisely, was the word. She was refining it in cool-headed, philological reflections.

And how odd that such thoughts should return after decades of neglect, and that she should have these lines still stored by heart, memorials of a once true passion. How delicate an instrument the human organism turns out to be! How far more rarefied and subtle than the partial stuff of mental explanations! These men, these men!

Alice passed through the wicket-gate (if it is not to rot she must repaint it soon) and on past her vegetable garden. A pair of wood-pigeons clapped their wings near the crown of the silver birch. Cloud was building from the west, and with it, maybe, rain.

Recognizing for the first time how empty her life had in fact become before Leah's arrival at Roseleye, she opened the back door into the kitchen and stood there calling, 'Leah.'

There was no answer, so she walked through into the hall and shouted again up the stairs. On the upper floor there was no sound of movement even. Alice was nearly at the stair-head when she heard Dora Pascoe come into the kitchen calling, 'Is she there? Is she all right?'

Not stopping to answer, Alice crossed the landing to knock on Leah's bedroom door. (At ten past eleven, however late her return last night, she had slept long enough.) When, again, there was no reply she tried the latch.

The door opened on the half-gloom of a curtained room. A dress which Leah must have considered and rejected still lay draped across the bed. Its colours were reflected in the long mirror of the open wardrobe door. Leah would have checked her appearance there before coming down to meet Stephen. Despite her mood she had looked well, Alice recalled, in the viridian silk shirt and short black skirt, with the moonstones glowing at her ears and throat. Then she was gone, and Alice had not heard her come back because she had not come back.

Down in the parlour the always slow tall-case clock chimed the hour. Alice crossed the room to draw the curtains. Under a clatter of wooden rings the drapes sighed along the pole. A cloudy morning light came in.

In a trance of dismay she pressed her forehead against the window-glass. For a moment or two her eyes were closed, then she was gazing down, beyond the mist of her breath, across the front garden, to where a car drove past the house, very slowly, on the other side of the lane. The driver's side window was open and a man was looking out at Roseleye.

The face seemed eager and nervous, perhaps lost, perhaps seeking a particular address. His eyes scouted the house-front and as they shifted upwards to the window where Alice watched, their stares met for an instant. Then the head was pulled back inside the car, which accelerated, changed gear, and moved off quickly down the lane.

In other circumstances Alice would not have given the incident a moment's thought – Roseleye was a pretty house, passing tourists often slowed to admire the mature trellised roses along its white façade – but this morning it filled her heart with dread. The man's furtive glance had caught her attention, then ducked away. It had been like having the phone ring and picking it up to hear nothing but a tense, fraught breathing down the line.

For the first time in as long as she could remember Alice was afraid.

4
VISION

Beyond a closed door, in the still-room of the Anchor Hotel, a dish-washer completed its cycle and relapsed into immobility. Brian Pollard shifted restlessly in the new silence.

It could only have been minutes after the local radio-station's morning newsflash that he'd phoned the police, yet his call had received no serious attention until now, and he was out of all patience. Already he had demanded what point there was in appealing to the public for information if you then sat on it for hours. He'd received no satisfactory answer; and, having repeated his evidence, he was further aggrieved by the Inspector's phlegmatic refusal to be impressed. What more did they want? Blood-stained laundry? The weapon itself? A signed confession?

George Nankevill knew how many calls had been prompted by the appeal over the air-waves. He knew that each of them was being followed up, mostly by men without his seniority. And he knew that Pollard's frequent complaints about the failure of the police to deal with 'the louts and rowdy elements' that hung around Porthmallion Quay had made him no friends at the station. Of course the duty-sergeant there had logged the call, but Nankevill understood the sergeant's dry sigh when he said, 'It seems we have a swan-killer on the loose as well.' Neither officer cared for the vigilante mentality.

On his arrival at the hotel Nankevill had been ushered through into the private back-parlour where he began to realize that the person with the most interesting tale to tell was being allowed no room to speak. She sat with tautly laced fingers on an armless chair, her calves crossed and thin beneath her skirt. She swallowed frequently, and looked away when she became conscious of his gaze.

A little hungry now, a little bored, Nankevill reviewed the facts.

A male guest in his mid-forties had booked in for a single night, drunk a couple of taciturn whiskeys in the bar, then walked out for a breath of air at about 7.30 the previous evening. He had not returned by 2.20 a.m., at which time Brian Pollard woke in discomfort where he had nodded off at the reception desk. Seeing no reason further to inconvenience himself for a man who could run down a swan in the road then brag about it among strangers, the hotelier had locked the doors and gone to bed.

'Deliberately?' Nankevill had pressed. 'He deliberately ran over a swan?'

Pollard's eyebrows insisted that nothing abominable in human nature could surprise him. Yet he had not, the Inspector noted, confirmed deliberate intent. Regrettably the American, Prewett, who had passed on this story, had also checked out of the hotel, making for St Mauger. Nor was the Inspector's faith in this hearsay evidence increased by Pollard's low-grade impression of an American accent.

The point was, the hotelier insisted, that his wife had bumped into the man around 6.30 that morning, early, soon after she'd unlocked the outside doors. He was trying to sneak back to his room, still fully dressed, unshaven, rumpled. His clothes were damp. There was mud round his trouser turn-ups and caked on his shoes. He'd obviously been out all night, didn't apologize, gave no satisfactory account of himself. Frankly, they'd been glad to see the back of him when he left without taking breakfast. He'd paid up, the full tariff, cash in hand without quibbling. They'd have thought no more about it if it hadn't been for the newsflash. Then it was obvious.

'If you'd been quicker off the mark,' the hotelier concluded, 'you could have caught up with him hours ago. I'd got his registration number, and a two-tone green Rover P4 110 shouldn't be hard to spot. But he could be anywhere by now.'

'If we need him,' Nankevill said quietly, 'we'll find him.'

'What do you mean "if"? Isn't it obvious?'

'I mean, he doesn't seem to have been too worried about covering his tracks, does he?' Then he turned away. 'What were your feelings, Mrs Pollard . . . when you saw him this morning?'

Stella Pollard adjusted the skirt at her knees. 'Well . . .' – she cleared her throat – 'I didn't know about the murder at the time.'

'That's why I'm interested. Tell me about him. Did he frighten you at all?'

'It was a bit of a shock, seeing him like that. He looked more embarrassed than anything. I wouldn't like to say.'

'Did you speak to him?'

The woman gazed askance into the past. For several hours her husband had been convinced it was a murderer who had met her unexpectedly at the turn of the stair. Because she could not quite bring herself to believe it she had been dizzy with the thought all day. 'I said good morning. I said we'd been worried when he didn't come back.' But what she did not say, either then or now, was that she had lain in crisp sheets the previous night, lubricating her way to sleep with developed memories of the few moments when she'd shown him up to his room and they stood alone together: she, breathless for approval, as in the presence of fame; he, lean and warily intense against the window's gauzy glare.

'Did *he* say anything at all?'

There was, she thought (for the meeting on the stair had become an illustration from a magazine), no need for words. Yet how, she wondered, if the man was in truth a murderer? Suppose she had acted on the barely suppressed impulse to confess her loneliness, her longing? Again, that metabolic thrill of terror. She gasped a little at the teasing, secret thought. And wondered whether the impassive policeman had discerned it.

Stella Pollard glanced out of the window where, momentarily indifferent to death and lust, a gull preened its wing on a post. The fitful light was blue again. Drying linen took the shape of wind.

'He said he'd met a friend . . . that he'd lost all track of time.'

And only after he'd brushed past her did she observe the mud left on the carpet by his shoes.

Her curls, Nankevill decided, were too sootily black to be quite natural. 'Did you believe him?' he asked.

'There was no reason not to. At the time.'

'You didn't wonder where they'd been all night?'

'No not till later when . . .'

'Yes?'

Stella Pollard hesitated.

'She means when I heard the radio,' her husband said.

'No, there's something else.'

Aware she would have to answer for this, and that there would be other consequences too, the woman was looking at neither man. Pollard turned towards her, the twill of his trousers stretching across bulky thighs. 'Well?'

She twisted a button on her chiffon blouse. The sad

70

breasts rose and fell, as her hand moved to the pocket of her skirt and took out a folded sheet of paper.

'I found this in his room.'

'Why wasn't I told about it?' her husband wanted to know.

'I forgot about it,' she lied, ''till just now.'

George Nankevill reached out an open palm into the tension between them.

Sighing again, the woman relinquished the creased document into his custody. Evidently it had been torn from a spiral-bound notebook, screwed up and thrown away. The Inspector put on his reading glasses. A crabbed black script came into focus, barbed like fence-wire across the page:

After whiskey on the cliff last night: underground, climbing downwards, stone warm to the hand. Not much headroom, conscious of the weight of rock over me, panicky because it will be hard to turn round in there. Then the passage opens on a cave. A smell of earthquake in the air. A woman sits with her back to me, doing something with her hands. I know it is L. I call out her name. She turns, and is hideous, old. I see she is stitching a shirt from the feathers of a swan. She says, Not here.

Then where?

Are you so sure you still want to find her?

When I say yes she laughs. Two bangles of light come spinning out of the gloom, one gold, one silver. They stop with their circles partly overlapping. Now the hag is speaking through the space where the lights mingle, but she speaks with L's voice. She is telling me to look for a place where there's nothing to choose between light and dark, where neither sun nor moon rules the sky, and it's not night, not day, not winter or summer either, the water there neither fresh nor salt, the tide doesn't ebb, doesn't flow.

I say, Impossible place, unmeetable conditions.

She says, If you want me you'll find me there. Infuriated I lash out.

God knows I didn't know what I was doing then, I didn't know what would happen, almost I had stopped caring. At earlier and later times I wanted it ended, but not then, not at that moment. I just thought that people have to do the things I see them doing, it cannot be stopped, best not to worry over consequences. But the vital thing was struck down cold inside. And so, again, seeing her so, the shock of it. Now only darkness here, the old loathing for myself, the hatefulness and fear.

George Nankevill picked his way through the scrawl twice in silence. When he looked up he was conscious of the tension between husband and wife, which was not his problem. 'And you're quite sure he wrote this?' he asked. 'It couldn't have been left by another guest?'

'All our rooms are cleared every day,' Stella Pollard answered defensively. 'It wasn't there before he came, and no one else has been in there since.'

'Then you'll have no objection if I keep it?'

'Not at all,' Brian Pollard intervened, 'not if it helps you nail the bastard.'

Shrugging bleakly, the Inspector pocketed the paper. 'It might have no bearing on our enquiries, of course.'

'But you're pretty sure it does.

'In cases like this,' Nankevill said, 'nobody's innocent till someone's found guilty.'

*

'Hasn't he come yet?' Amy doffed her riding-hat and shook out her curls, then the surprise in her face faded to disappointment. 'Or has he gone already?'

Mrs Pascoe had known too much loss in her life to bear even a stranger's grief with equanimity, so she failed to understand how Amy could appear so nonchalant and breezy on this dreadful day. Nor did she approve of the fat-haunched grey tethered to the gate-post, or of the way its rider had taken to entering Roseleye with barely a knock, thereby giving a further turn to her nerves.

'Who would that be?' she asked, plugging the vacuum-cleaner into the dining-room socket. Irritable with tension, her voice was pitched to daunt this chatterbox from dawdling here, near lunchtime, when she would soon be picking at the food.

'The man who was asking for Leah.'

Mrs Pascoe glanced out of the mullioned window, as if in search of such a person. 'Alice won't be happy,' she said, 'if that horse eats her Nelly Moser.'

Amy had small patience with needless obstacles. 'Where is she? In her studio?'

'If she is, she won't want you down there. Not now.' Mrs Pascoe's foot had already advanced to the switch on the machine when a fearful thought occurred. 'What man?'

'A man in a car. He stopped me outside the village to ask if I knew where Leah lived.'

'And you told him?'

'Why not?'

'Because he might be a mass-murderer, that's why not. And you should have more sense than to be caught riding round on your own at a time like this, let alone talking to strangers.'

If Amy found this response bewilderingly pessimistic it was because she had slept late, skipped breakfast, gone straight to the stables to saddle the grey, and knew nothing of the morning's atrocious news. She listened, horrified now, to Mrs Pascoe's account of what neither had seen. For a few cold seconds she was one flesh with the dead woman. Then her heart quailed, for the dead woman might, it seemed, be Leah.

'It turns me over to think about it,' Mrs Pascoe wound up her anxious narrative. 'And Alice is worrying herself sick.'

As though the world consisted only of forbiddable possibilities Amy declared, 'It can't be Leah.'

Yet somewhere also she readied herself for a larger grief than she had ever known. Silently, shamefully, almost in the same breath, she thanked whatever stars that it was not her own young body in the cove, that her heart could still kick about in its stall like this, alive to the criminal black fact that now there was nowhere safe. And look how her imagination teetered. Not since she'd thought she was pregnant had she drifted this close to the world's edge. Again, from those starless depths, flashed bolts of remorse for her many derelictions. There must be no more rows, no sulks, no risks. She would take vows of diligence. She would be a better person.

Then she dared to ask, 'Has Alice phoned the police?'

'She's thinking about it.'

At least this first nail had not been hammered home. Amy summoned her native optimism. 'I think she's with Stephen,' she said. 'I could tell she fancied him really. That's why she was so hostile. You can always tell. She was just a bit scared, I think. I'm the same way myself . . . With people I really care about.'

Too nervous for patience, Mrs Pascoe grunted.

Again she applied her foot to the switch, but Amy's thoughts were faster. 'That's why she was in that funny mood all day. You have tried ringing him?'

'He's got one of them answering machines.'

'What about at work?'

'He rang to say he'd be in late.'

'There you are then.'

'It's not him we're worried about.'

'They're in bed. Don't you see?'

Relieving as this thought was, Amy was not altogether sure she liked it. But further speculation was irresistible. 'He's skiving off in bed with Leah and they're telling each other their life-stories. *Après sex*. I bet you a fiver.' Her frown gathered. 'And now there's another man looking for her. God, she's amazing!'

But Mrs Pascoe's thoughts were darker. 'When was it that you spoke to this man?'

'About half an hour ago.'

'And he didn't say what he wanted?'

'Just Leah's address.'

'So where is he then?'

'How should I know?'

The young woman and the old woman glowered at one another. Finally the switch was pressed, and the room filled with the din of suction.

'Do you think I should warn Alice?' Amy shouted.

'I think,' Mrs Pascoe shouted back, 'you should take that horse home.'

But Alice was not in her studio. Filled with rage and terror and dread at the death in the night, she had crossed the stepping-stones downstream and climbed the path under the canopy of the glen before taking the half-hidden stairway down into the fall's wild cell.

She had been standing for some time by the edge of the pool at the foot of a sheltered defile so steep that the waters were in constant churning shadow. When she lifted her gaze she was surprised how bright the light on the high rocks and the grass, how blue that cloistered crack of sky. Between them, flexing like a limb against the sleek, greenish-black ledges of the crag, was the waterfall.

The night's rain had swollen the volume of the stream. It surged from a high cleft in the outcrop rock as from a gash in darkness. Then, with so radiant a gleam you might think a black sleeve had been turned inside-out to reveal a shimmering white lining, the slender torrent plummeted for sixty feet.

Three times, over thousands of years, at ever lower levels, the force of falling water had scooped a deep cauldron-shaped trough out of solid stone. Each trough had broken under pressure, leaving smooth ruins like damaged sockets in the face of the crag. Now the fall had hollowed out another basin at its foot, and for the past few centuries the overflow had splashed through an arch in the surrounding rock before stilling its turbulence in a shallow pool. Soft rainbow colours glided down the spray.

With her fingers trembling at the ashplant's handle, Alice gazed up where the fall poured itself as a rush of sound and light among the shadows of the gorge.

She was remembering the first time she had come here – how she had rounded the natural buttress of rock and, for a few blazoned seconds, stood alone by the pool with the damp light spraying about her face, and it was as if she had been nudged into astonished recognition by the genius of the place. Then her lover had stepped round the rock. He did not immediately speak, but the moment had passed. Alice felt torn back into time. Yet in those instants of silence, in the presence of the man to whom she had given herself unreservedly less than an hour before, she had seen how her life would always be subject now to more than human loyalties.

And he had been puzzled by the sudden distance between them.

'If we'd known,' he said, 'we should have waited to make love here.' There was a lucid instant in which she saw how finally vulnerable they might be to one another. Then she said, 'I'm glad we didn't,' but the tone of her answer might have injured him, so she added, 'I wanted you *then*. And this place . . .' Her gaze wandered around the leafy cell, almost shyly now. 'It's sacred,' she dared. 'We have to learn its rites. Look, have you seen?' She pointed out the rags tied to the thorns, and the almost hidden jar of votive flowers. Then she reached out to close his arm around her waist, and as they gazed up into the shining fall she whispered, 'It's like *la fossiure a la gent amant.*'

But he had been a janitor at the university not a student, and her images were strange to him, and he knew no French – neither modern nor this antique idiom. So she told him the story of how Cornish King Mark had come upon his wife, Iseult, sleeping chastely with Tristram in such a secret place as this – 'the cave of lovers' – and how he had believed them innocent because of the naked sword that lay between them.

'Then more fool he,' he'd smiled, teasing her solemnity. But she held her chin high to take the fine spray on her face, and he thought his rough humour might have chafed her spirit, so he spoke in reparation through a blur of kisses at her cheek. 'I know you're right. It feels inhabited. It feels as though we would have been watched.'

'Yes,' she whispered back, 'oh yes,' and it seemed that everything consisted of the streaming rainbow light, endlessly inheriting itself, as transient as it was timeless; and just as nothing in those moments could ever be the same again, so not a scruple of their radiance could ever truly vanish.

*

Or so Alice had always believed, yet an extinguishing shadow had been cast across this day. The walk up the glen had failed to calm her. She'd jumped at the flap of pigeon's wings. Ferns and the oily green gloom of ivy leaves oppressed her. She saw where knotweed tangled the banks so thickly that the stream was reduced to a dim ribbon under its dense growth. After her grip almost slipped from the chain that had recently been fixed in the rock to ease the steep descent to the fall, she had tried to deepen her breathing but her lungs were lumps of grief, for when she imagined the face of the murdered woman it was Leah's face that she saw, dirty and bloodied; and nothing could displace the picture from her mind. It seemed to shut the sky.

Alice stared up into the glittering tresses of the fall. She remembered the conversation in the cove the previous day, and what had been said about men's fear of women. The words were ashes in the mouth. She heard Leah's howl, it echoed inside her. A lifetime's injured bewilderment turned her briefly into a pillar of hatred then.

But that went nowhere. It became, in its way, another crime against the light.

Unblinking, Alice stared into the plunging water till it felt as though her mind must drown under its velocity and weight. There was no release in that torrent of light, only the sense of a world collapsing round her; and so, in search of the solid, the substantial, her gaze shifted away to the gleaming rock-face beside the fall. And then it seemed that the world around her was indeed dissolving, for the entire wall of the crag was floating swiftly upwards, in a greenish-black shimmer of energy, towards the unstable sky. Alice felt a prickling inside her skin, a dizziness. She remembered the feeling of being sea-sick as a child. Somewhere also she understood what was happening: that her eyes, having adapted to the water's downward plunge could not, in the same moment, accept the rock as stationary. A simple optical illusion had reduced it to a veil-like flow of particles travelling as rapidly as the misty fabric of the fall itself, though in the opposite direction. Yet it was as if, by a quick switch of attention, she had caught matter out in its pretence of solidity. For an instant she might have been watching a delicately painted stage-set tremble.

Then the nausea passed, her pulse-rate slowed, and there was a stillness which seemed a quality of the light, while the noise of the fall diminished to a susurration in the chambers of the ear. And everything was sentient: the trees, the ferns and fungus, the stones, the water itself, all were tuned to the same prophetic frequency. The whole glen was a mind, and Alice was deeply immersed in its thoughts, which were the events now unfolding against the screen of the fall, where quietly, as little more than a shapely condensation of the spray, the figure of a woman stepped through the veil of matter in that rocky cell, and the masque began.

Neither acknowledging Alice's presence, nor disregarding it, the lady advanced to the edge of the pool where she stood in marbling light, holding a large bronze hand-mirror at her side. The mirror was circular, wider than the span of a man's hand, and its reverse was chased with an abstract design of trumpet-scrolls, from which, startlingly, the head of a fantastical beast emerged. But the lady's features were mild, and her form matronly under a white linen gown that draped in ankle-length folds from the girdle at her hips. Though she appeared perhaps forty years younger than Alice, the penetration of her gaze might have been older than the slab of amber rock near which she stood. Not vigilant, not unwary either, she was simply *there* in silent announcement that one mode of time had been suspended

79

and another resumed. She glanced up at the fall which ceased its movement and hung, glistening in its dark cleft, like a white mare's tail. In the same lucid instant the turmoil of the cauldron-pool was stilled.

Sunlight flashed off the mirror as the lady lifted it. From Alice's angle of vision, the lens reflected the surface of the pool and she was dazzled at first by the surface-glitter there. Then her eyes were drawn to movement among the deeper shadows. A moment later, in much the same way that the mirror's abstract pattern had resolved itself into an animal's head, new images appeared. She was peering through the glassy surface into a torch-lit chamber where two men were arguing.

One of them sat hunched at a long table. The cowl of his robe had been thrown back, and his grizzled hair was tonsured in the Roman style. The skin of his face was swarthy and much-lined, the eyes close-set, severe, the lips as frugal as a crack in rock. A plain wooden cross dangled from the rope with which his robe was belted. The other man was burlier, of a more princely bearing except for the limp that marked his restless pacing back and forth before an open fire. Thick red hair crested over his brow, he was densely bearded. Under a brooched mantle his tunic glinted with gold thread, and he wore massive armlets clasped above both wrists. Evidently he was the more powerful figure of the two, and certainly commanded the devotion of the pink-eared mastiff that lay by the hearth watching his every move. But his demeanour was agitated, anxious even, and for the moment authority seemed to lie with the other, the monk, who sat with fingers steepled at his chin.

Though Alice could hear nothing she sensed that the lame man was under pressure to commit some action, the prospect of which terrified him as much as he desired it. A fierce exchange between the two men came to an end when the monk rose from the table, holding up his cross as if to say, 'In this sign conquer,' and, breathing heavily, the crippled prince turned away from the other's fanatical stare to gaze into the fire. He stood in its heat for a long time before looking back at the proffered cross and nodding his submission.

Daylight opened again – blue morning lifting out of early mist. Alice heard the sound of the fall and of a man singing. The strains of a harp tingled on the air. Her angle of vision escalated with the music, widening, becoming steeper, until she had a sharp, buzzard's eye view of the whole length of the gorge through which a procession was winding in spring-time ceremonial from the direction of the sea.

Garlanded with primroses, violets and golden saxifrage, people were shouting and singing as they followed a man who rode a white mare bareback through the glen. He held a branch that glinted silver. The horse's mane and tail were braided with wildflowers, its flanks painted with blue dye.

In the rocky cell of the fall, nine women awaited his arrival. They stood arranged in a chevron, four on each side of the little gorge, with the ninth at the apex, white against the rainbow spray. All were dressed in white gowns, and each held a ritual object: Alice saw a drinking-horn, a basket, a platter, a pan, a knife, a chess-board, and a gorgeous tunic with a matching mantle. The woman at the fall held a silver bowl which was chased and embossed with elaborate designs; a sword lay on the amber stone at her feet; a chariot with shining harness rested on its shafts at the foot of the crag.

As the procession halted in the clearing the music died. Lithely the young man dismounted and stepped forward to shout something that Alice could not understand. The horse stamped a rear hoof, a shiver passed across its flank. The shout was repeated twice more, and after a long, uneasy moment another figure emerged from a leafy place among the rocks. He was limping as he advanced into clear space.

Under the eyes of the women and the urgent crowd, the bearded cripple and the beardless youth measured one another silently until the younger man began a brisk, ritual exchange of challenge and reply. When it was completed he turned to address the women, holding the silver branch aloft with an oiled arm, and shaking it so that a tinkle of small bells shivered on the air. Then he demanded something of the crowd, which roared its assent. Smiling, he turned to confront the lame man once more, lifted the branch and struck a token blow across his shoulder. The bells jingled. The mare swished its tail. Then the challenger put the branch aside and leaned forward, flexing his arms, readying himself to fight.

In the same moment the cripple glanced up to the high bastions of the crag and shouted. Immediately an armoured man stepped from behind an outcrop rock. For an instant he seemed merely to point at the challenger with an outstretched arm; then Alice saw the javelin speeding down into the gorge.

It pierced the young man's lower belly, driving him by the force of its flight some yards backwards to the ground, where he lay with his feet kicking, gripping the lance in both hands, too shocked to cry out. Suddenly his tunic flushed with blood.

For a long instant, until the mare gave a fretful neigh, it seemed that time too had been transfixed. One of the women dropped the platter she was holding and began to scream, and there was a clatter of armour as men with drawn swords scrambled down the defile to stand guard beside their lame leader. Above them, both ridges of the crag were lined with archers. The crowd uttered a stunned, beseeching moan, and there was confusion then as people

82

tried to back away, the air of festivity gone, dispersed in a welter of fear and panic, and a numbing sense of desecration.

The lame man turned, swept up the sword from the stone and brandished it, shouting over the noise of the crowd, which was brought to silence, though nothing could stop the howling of a baby, nor the sobs of the fallen man as blood bucketed inside him and brimmed from his mouth.

Sweating, wild-eyed, the cripple harangued the throng for a time before turning to face the woman at the fall. She stared at him unflinching, saying nothing. He snapped out a command. Still she did not move or speak. There was a moment's stand-off until, finding he could neither break her stare nor sustain it, he signalled to one of his men who snatched the bowl from her grasp and lofted it like a trophy. A few soldiers cheered. One took a jewelled bridle from the chariot and harnessed the mare to stop it careering through the crowd; another put his foot to the chest of the wounded man and withdrew the javelin. Suddenly the air smelled of blood and flowers.

Sick at heart, Alice watched the cripple limp towards the woman at the fall, where he loomed over her with the sword trembling at his side. He grabbed her by the hair, wrenching her head down sideways towards the ground. Some of her women cried out and moved to protect her, but soldiers forced them back as she fell. Blood broke from her temple where it grazed the rock. She was dazed and speechless when the cripple yanked her legs apart. Again the soldiers cheered at her first gagging cry. Then they turned in gangs on the other women.

Alice shut her eyes in refusal, but the dark was filled with images, and the screams were amplified there until her refusal to see became an intimate, personal betrayal of every struggling woman in the glen. Assailed by waves of pain,

83

unable to withdraw or intervene, she watched through a glaze of tears as the thing was done. The sun was high now, the sky blazing. Over the screams of women and the passion of the fall, Alice made out the sound of the harp and of a voice chanting, a male voice remembering and recording this, turning atrocity to song, gathering up every cry that rose from the glen and arranging them in a lay to haunt the generations, until at last it was finished, and the scene gave a little shiver as though it were painted on silk and a breeze had rustled it. Then it vanished in the shimmer of the fall.

In the same instant all the particular anxiety that had brought Alice into the glen expired. It was gone from her like a pain that had run its course. In the ensuing clarity of mind she felt herself to be on the brink of a single tremendous insight. It had to do with the crime against nature and the crime against love; it accounted for the tragic split between the worlds, and lent graver meaning to the old stories that she had always loved. She felt certain that she was about to be given a further, revelatory glimpse into the source-book of this island's heart, and though her eyes were still blurred with grief, the prospect of that impending disclosure filled her with a terrible elation.

Then the neon-blue bolt of a kingfisher flashing across the pool startled her back to normal consciousness. She was standing in freckled sunlight, blinking. The figures had gone. The fall was clamouring at her ears.

Not half a mile away Amy was piling her curls under the riding-hat in the hall at Roseleye when the telephone rang. She decided to wait, curious to know whether it was the stranger calling, but when the ringing went unheard over the vacuum-cleaner's din, she picked up the receiver herself and said, 'Hello.'

'Amy? What are you doing there?'

'Thank God! Where *are* you? Everyone's worried sick here. They think . . .'

'I know. I've just heard. That's why I rang. I knew Alice would be worrying. I should have rung last night but . . .'

'Don't tell me.' Even in relief it was hard to keep the twinge of malice from her voice. 'You're at Stephen's, right?'

'Yes, but . . .'

'At' – Amy checked her watch – 'eleven fifty-two a.m. on the morning after the night before. Hmmm!'

'Amy, let me speak to Alice.'

'She's not here. She's down at the studio trying to make up her mind to ring the police. You were a missing person, you know, until a minute ago.' Then Amy remembered the picture of Leah that had sickened her mind at Mrs Pascoe's account. 'Anyway, at least you're all right.' Her voice declined to a whisper. 'It's scary, isn't it? – what happened last night.'

'It's horrible.'

'Like a hole in things. Something torn, like the sky, and only black showing through. I don't understand why they want us dead. I think I'm really frightened, Leah.'

'You should be. It's bloody terrifying.'

'I wonder who she was. You haven't heard anything?'

'I don't think they know yet.'

'And the man. It must have been a man. He could still be around here. We might even know him.'

'Yes. There are police everywhere.'

Amy recalled that Stephen's cottage overlooked most of the little harbour-town. She visualized a sparely furnished, masculine space smelling of aftershave and magazines. It felt enviably secure. She said, 'I suppose they'll catch him?'

'He might be across the other side of the country by now.'

'Or abroad even.' But neither notion consoled. Amy

caught up with her own swift thoughts. 'Listen, I want to know who this other . . .'

'Look would you get Alice for me?' Leah interrupted. 'I've really got to talk to her.'

Then, invisibly to her, the dining-room door opened and Mrs Pascoe looked out, brandishing the nozzle of her machine at a conversation that should not be there.

'It's Leah,' Amy hissed. 'She's all right. She's with Stephen. What did I tell you?' She watched the cleaning-lady lift a hand to her flat, pinnied chest, then spoke into the receiver again. 'It's Mrs P. She's hoovering. Very relieved.' When her brisk smile glanced off Mrs Pascoe's glower she turned her face to the wall. 'So who's this other man then?'

'Oh God, has he been there?'

That tensely gasped demand was not exactly an answer but it told Amy two things: that Leah knew the stranger was in the area, and that the knowledge worried her.

'I thought he'd be here when I arrived,' she said. 'That's why I came actually, but he hasn't turned up yet.' Amy remembered the harassed eyes frowning up at her from the car. 'Interesting face,' she conceded, 'but he's a bit worn-looking, isn't he?'

'You've met him?'

'Of course. He asked me where you lived.'

'He didn't know?'

'Didn't seem to.'

'You didn't tell him?'

'Shouldn't I have done?'

'Oh God!'

Contrite, doubly guilty now, Amy said, 'I'm sorry Leah. It never crossed my mind . . .'

There was silence down the line.

Thinking quickly, seeing no way of mending things, Amy held Mrs Pascoe at bay with a flapping hand. 'Who is he anyway? It's not your father, is it? Are you in trouble, Leah?'

When neither confirmation nor denial came she said, 'It's someone from your past, isn't it?' Then, aghast with possibilities: 'You're not married, are you?'

Leah, who had taken in nothing but noise, spoke over this latest speculation. 'Look, I've got to get back there. Tell Alice I'm . . .'

'I think Mrs P. wants a word.'

'Tell her I'll be back as fast as I can. Tell them both I'm really sorry. Oh God, this is too much.'

Amy heard the line go dead. She paused a moment before hanging up the phone. Like a cherub in an old map, she blew through puffed cheeks and lifted her eyes to meet Mrs Pascoe's exasperated frown.

At that moment both women heard the sound of a car pulling up in the lane outside the house. Their eyes widened, and Mrs Pascoe's chance to rebuke the visitor for taking liberties expired.

Amy was first to the little leaded window by the door. Her drawn breath took in the jaded fragrance from the vase of cut flowers on the sill. 'It's him,' she whispered. 'He's here.' The cleaning-lady was quickly at her shoulder, peering out at the vehicle, from which no one immediately emerged. The two women exchanged uncertain glances, for Leah was not here and neither was Alice, and it was not their business; yet a marauder was at the gates and something must be done.

Amy said, 'I don't think she wants to see him.'

'Why not?'

'In fact, I'm sure she doesn't.'

'Then we shan't let him in.' Which, on this horrible day, was Mrs Pascoe's preference anyway.

'He might just sit there.'

'Let him sit.'

'But she's on her way back.'

Dora Pascoe's mouth sagged in thought. Large resources of silence and obstinacy were available when she found herself pestered, down at the van, by social workers and health-visitors and that kidney, but this was not her situation. And it certainly wasn't Amy's. Evidently one of them should fetch Alice, but these were risky times and she neither liked to leave the girl on her own here, nor to man the door alone. She stared into difficulties beyond her competence.

A door clunked shut.

'He's coming,' Amy hissed.

In fact the man was standing by the mare, breathing into her nostrils, stroking the tender muzzle where the grey nose dappled into a pinkish dove-white. To her own surprise, Mrs Pascoe muttered, 'The horse seems to like him.'

'She likes everybody.'

When the man turned, grimly, towards the house Mrs Pascoe decided it was only the presence of the girl that flustered her so. She assumed the dignity of her years. 'I'll do the talking.'

'But . . .'

'You heard.' She opened the door at the knocker's first rap and took even herself aback by the absolute declaration, 'She's not here.'

The man was buffeted by this contrary wind. He lifted a hand to his jaw, and nodded eventually as if he had expected no more. There was a silence, which Amy soon found fruitless. 'I told them you were coming. I thought you'd have been here before me.'

'Yes. I saw . . . the horse.' The man conspicuously swallowed. His gaze shifted away, down to the boot-scraper by the door-stone. 'Did she leave when you . . . ?'

The appeal in the drawn, returning face was so pained that Amy allowed herself an instant's pity.

'Oh no, it wasn't that. She wasn't here as it happens.'

Evidently this answer caused some commotion of thought. Then, conscious that his luck was pushed, the stranger said, 'Will she be back later?'

'I think that's quite enough.' Having accomplished all that was needful Mrs Pascoe was ready to shut the door on excess, but Amy was in the way.

'You didn't say what you wanted.'

For a moment, foraging for help, he studied the almost-innocent, glittering inquisition of her eyes. 'I'm a friend. She wasn't expecting me.' He fetched a hot sigh, and put a hand to the pocket of his leather jacket. Mrs Pascoe flinched, but only an envelope appeared. 'Look, I've written her a note. I wonder if you'd . . .' He held it up for the taking, making a final bid. The name that no one had spoken was written there in spiky capitals. 'Would you give this to her?'

Mrs Pascoe intercepted Amy's reaching hand. 'Yes, well . . .' She examined the envelope dubiously, then tucked it into her bib-pocket. 'I think you should go now.'

The man nodded again. He was about to say more when his glanced shifted, nervous and gaunt, between the fay, white head and the blonde curls, into the hall where a rear door was opening. Involuntarily both women turned.

Alice said, 'Who is it, Dora?'

'It's a man,' Mrs Pascoe answered, 'looking for Leah. Says he's a friend of hers.'

And Amy remembered there was an outstanding need for reassurance. 'She's all right, Alice. She was just – '

'I know.'

' – on the phone.' But her breathless news had been deflated by the quiet interruption, and in the second it took to wonder how Alice could possibly have known, the old woman was asking, 'Why are you all standing at the door?' She smiled up at the stranger. 'Can I help?'

Having pulled himself together to drive back to the house, Ronan had found the truculent glare of the pinnied cleaner and the frank, jodhpured figure of the young rider troubling enough. Now this other unsought female presence emerged from the hall with a gaze that held him like a book.

'I don't think so. I think it's . . . ' There was sweat at Ronan's neck. Even his simplest sentences were firing at half-cock. He felt doomed to a series of weird failures here.

Alice said, 'I think you'd better come inside.'

The invitation carried a damely air of command. It pointed to where he wanted to be. Yet if he crossed that step he must fall into imperious hands, and nowhere in sight was the one face that could put an end, good or bad, to this anxious endeavour. Ronan cleared his throat, then looked round as if a quick glance might catch Leah listening from concealment.

'It's perfectly all right,' Alice insisted. 'In fact, I've rather been expecting you. Or someone like you.' She frowned as she looked past the uneasy stranger, out across her garden. 'Is that a horse over there? Amy dear, you really are impossible. Do take it away.'

When she beckoned Ronan inside he hesitated a moment, still bleary from a night in which he had barely slept; but under the traction of the old woman's sympathetic gaze, he crossed the threshold. Names were exchanged. The house opened to receive him. He took at once to the smell of it, to the feel of the place with its nooks and corners and low oak lintels that had him ducking here and there. These rooms were homely in their mullioned light. They had settled inside staunch stone over centuries. The lax piles of books and papers and magazines gave them a lived-in air that quietly recommended peace.

For the first time since he had crossed into Cornwall, Ronan felt arrived; yet he was bemused by this sudden elevation from intruder to welcome guest, and uncertain how to play things now. Sighing with a queer mix of apprehension and relief, and glad that Alice's offer of coffee left him alone in the parlour for a time to collect his thoughts, he sank into the plump upholstery of an old velvet chesterfield.

A book lay on a low table in front of the hearth. Stamped in gold on the maroon binding over a simple coat of arms he read the words *Le Livre du Cueur d'Amours Espris*. Curious, Ronan opened its pages at random and found himself looking at a picture from a modern reproduction of an old illuminated manuscript. Inside a gilded margin, an open boat with five passengers aboard was putting ashore by night on a rocky island. Two women watched the landfall – they were angling from the moonlit cliff under a sky full of golden stars. One of them reeled in a gleaming mackerel as she gazed down where the little pinnace lay hove to, stern first, with its sail furled. There was a hushed, spellbound sense of arrival to the moment. You could almost hear the surf.

It was how this moody Cornish coast might have appeared to a visionary painter more than five hundred years before, but so finely, so strangely, was the nocturnal beauty of the scene achieved that Ronan felt himself privileged with a glimpse into a medieval dream.

From the commentary on the opposing page he learned that the island was a way-station on the voyage to the Isle of Love, and the two women – their names were *Compaignie* and *Amittié* – were waiting to welcome the voyagers after a stormy crossing.

Ronan's hands trembled as they held the book.

He could remember little of the previous night except for

a windy cleft above the sea where he had raged for a time, then dozed, and woken as the rain began, with a whiskey bottle half-empty on the rock beside him. He had no idea how long he had walked after that, or where, or how the scratches on his hand had come, or when the skin had broken at his shin. He knew that his waking mind had been a foundry of hot rage which sleep had done no more than darken.

Then, back at the hotel, he had found the doors bolted, and could have wept because he was dirty and wet and lacked the face to wake the manager with explanations. Abject, for an hour or two he'd endured brief spasms of sleep in the back seat of his car, and dreamed the kind of dreams that made his heart lurch these days, dreams he would rather have left in those deep trenches of sleep from which no light escapes.

He was dismayed by the wreck that met him in the morning's mirror when he entered the hotel. Still more so by the nervous woman's scrutiny on the stair. And again, later – perhaps worst of all – when he'd driven past this house intending to stop but not stopping because the sight of the old woman watching from an upstairs window had precipitated a further humiliating crisis of the will.

All morning Ronan had felt as wary with himself as with a suddenly distempered dog. He could not remember when he had ever been so vulnerable. Yet here he was, inside this homely room at last, and little though he believed in signs and portents, this illustration from an ancient allegorical romance seemed to offer omens that here was a place where he might catch his breath in the time before Leah arrived.

And after that? He didn't know any more.

Ronan closed his eyes. In the otherwise silent morning he heard birdsong and the clop of a horse's hooves in the lane, then he caught the smell of autumn on the breeze through the partially open window. He sat on the sofa with the book open at his lap, feeling the velvet's pile under his hand, and yielded to Roseleye's benign, archaic grace.

5
COVE

When Mrs Pascoe glanced through the parlour door in passing she thought that Ronan was asleep. This she reported, in some disgust, to Alice who remarked without surprise that the man had looked tired. Alice carried the tray through from the kitchen a few moments later and found him lightly dozing. The book she had been studying the night before lay open at his lap. He was frowning a little as he slept.

Ronan had drifted out of consciousness through the muted night-scene of the picture in Alice's book, but it was not those images of dark landfall that informed his dream. He was in a whiter place, under the lights of an operating theatre, one among a number of medical specialists conferring over an unconscious patient. He listened as a psychiatrist worried in abstract nouns about the patient's pathological detachment from all sense of fellow-feeling with the human race. There was a judicious nodding of heads among the rest of the team, swiftly followed by agreement on the need for surgery. Discussion had already shifted to the most profitable angle of cranial attack when Ronan burst out with a muddled expression of dissent: the problem wasn't with the man's brain, it wasn't physical at all; the trouble was he'd lost his soul!

A brief, cold silence was broken by murmurings of

consternation. Witheringly the consultant surgeon asked him to explain precisely what he meant by this. Ronan opened his mouth to answer; he had certainly meant something by it, something that seemed urgently important at the time, and very clear, but now that he was asked he couldn't for the life of him remember. So the rest of the team was left waiting as, in a hot fluster of embarrassment, consciousness returned.

His eyes opened on shady daylight. He was looking at an old woman who sat beside the opposing corner of the ingle-nook fire-place, smiling at his sudden discomfiture. A delicious smell of coffee singed the air.

'I see you were admiring René's book,' Alice remarked, reaching for the coffee-pot. 'It's rather fine, isn't it?'

'I think I must have nodded off.'

'But it is a dream book, so perhaps that's understandable. White or black?'

'Black please.' As if to signify that he was now fully awake, Ronan closed the book at his lap and frowned down at the gilded blazon of its title, but for the moment Alice was glad enough to keep the conversation on this familiar ground. '*The Book of the Heart as Love's Prisoner,*' she translated. 'You may have seen: it tells how René went to bed one night and dreamed that his heart was plucked from his chest by the god of love.'

'René?'

'Of Anjou. King of Sicily. Known in his time as Good King René.'

'I see. The book was made for him?' Carefully Ronan placed the volume aside before he took the brimming cup.

'No, he wrote it himself. He may have done the paintings too. There's a tradition that he was a pupil of Jan van Eyck. I don't see why not.'

'It's amazingly beautiful,' Ronan murmured, and covered

95

his further thoughts by assuming the lightly flirtatious air that usually endeared him to older women. 'If it's a love story I hope it has a happy ending.'

'It's rather more interesting than that,' Alice replied, adding milk to her coffee; and when he asked her to say more, she appraised the request wryly, wondering whether she was merely patronized. Deciding not, she said, 'The story follows the adventures of the captive heart which is portrayed as the Knight Cueur endeavouring to rescue his lady from the various enemies of love. After many trials he frees her from the stronghold of Resistance, but then they are attacked by Shame, Fear and Denial. His page, Desire, is killed, Cueur is grievously injured, and the lady seized by Denial. There's no hope of recovering her this time, so Cueur is taken by Compassion to a hospital on the Island of Love, where he passes the rest of his life in prayer and meditation. Would you care for a biscuit? I can only offer you digestives, I'm afraid.'

Ronan helped himself, saying, 'So he joins the ranks of the walking wounded?' He smiled ruefully. 'I know a number of them. Though I can't say that allegories have ever had much appeal for me.'

'It's not a fashionable form, of course.'

'Because there's always the feel of a fix about it, don't you think?' Only part of Ronan's mind had been engaged but he saw that Alice was considering his remark with more seriousness than he'd intended. She said, 'If you mean it's at pains to relate the moral structure of the imagination to a larger order of meaning, then yes,' and paused to brush biscuit-crumbs from her trousers. 'But perhaps you meant something different?'

'I meant that the form looks a little naive over against our contemporary understanding of what complicated creatures we are.' But Ronan wasn't looking for debate about medieval literature, of which he was largely ignorant, so he withdrew into levity. 'Actually I was thinking that this must be the first heart-transplant operation on record. Pity it wasn't a success!'

'Are you so sure about that?' Alice smiled. 'At the end of the book René wakes up clutching his chest, and finds his heart exactly where it should be. I sometimes wonder whether contemporary psychology achieves as much.'

Ronan heard the mischief in her afterthought, but he also felt the presence of a peculiar, countervailing vision with certainties of its own. It deepened his curiosity about the woman, and troubled him a little too. After a pensive moment he said, 'Our dreams are surely darker.'

'Perhaps because we honour them less?' Alice took in his dubious frown. 'We certainly keep a tighter grip on our hearts!'

They looked at one another searchingly then, the poised, reflective woman and the uncertain man. He was thinking that she felt as quirky and hospitable as this ancient house she lived in; that there were decades of experience mapped across her face and, behind it, deeper repositories still, where who knew what crone's store of wisdom had been laid up? Wondering vaguely whether there was any stranger creature on earth than a doughty old woman, he recalled the hag in the cave from the previous night's dream; but this was a much more approachable figure. He was thinking – or was it a mere freak of his loneliness to imagine it? – that she might be enlisted to his cause.

But his sudden abstraction seemed to have left her at a loss. He wondered what must she be seeing as she looked across at him? An agitated, questionable figure, already middle-aged. Too old surely for Leah? – and long compromised by decisions taken too early, out of ignorance or ambition or scarcely understood desires. And far from content – even though the well-cut clothes and expensive watch proclaimed him among the beneficiaries of a spend-thrift, unjust age. But that wasn't all. There were other, lighter qualities: the exuberant Irishman in him with a talent for generosity, and an appetite for beauty, for risk. And his laconic sense of humour – dear God, what had happened to that in recent months, where had that got lost? Ronan sensed in this stately old woman a nimble spirit that would have risen to his wit in better days. It made him want more than her approval now: he wanted to excite her delight. He saw that what he really wanted was for Leah to come back and find them laughing together there.

'Tell me,' said Alice, disappointing him a little by the conventional approach, 'have you known Leah long?' But when he glanced up, the hooded, hazel eyes regarded him across the rim of her cup with larger candour. 'What are you doing here?' they demanded agreeably enough. 'What do you want with her?'

Ronan took back the initiative. 'Long enough', he replied, 'to love her very much.' But he was shocked to recognize this as the first public avowal of his feelings. The words had come hot to his lips. They felt dangerous on the air.

'Ah!' said Alice. 'Then perhaps it's not so peculiar that she has never mentioned you.'

He puzzled over this unembarrassed response, wondering what might be learnt from it. He saw she would be freer with information only when eased further into his confidence.

'I'm afraid we parted unhappily,' he admitted.

'And not entirely by your choice?'

'That's right. Though the fault was mine.'

'So you've come here hoping to remedy it?'

'Exactly.'

Alice considered the turbulent figure across from her. 'I think you may find that difficult,' she said and, when he answered that he was prepared for that, 'I wonder.' Invisibly he winced under the edge of her smile, though Alice was already recollecting that this stranger must know Leah more intimately than she did herself. His face betrayed a lover's knowledge. Pain was obvious in the dark search of his gaze where a vertical line creased his forehead from the place where his eyebrows almost met to the peaked hairline. It might have marked the tense frontier between the hemispheres of his brain. Alice found stories in the lean, sensitive features, which were complex and vain, and she was glad of that, for she could take only charitable interest in men who lacked occasion for vanity. Yet she had also seen nobler possibilities there, of which his unhappy condition might be either the ruin or the precursor. It was hard to say, for those inconstant eyes might promise more than they intended to deliver, and it needed no unusual insight to divine a powerful, egotistical will beneath the surface of his present disarray. She said, 'At least I understand now why you were eager for a happy ending to Cueur's quest!'

For a moment, thinking himself mocked, he hardened his gaze; but if Alice had secret thoughts they simply regretted the way so many men chose to confine themselves within the limits of the will as though trust must expire beyond that safe perimeter. 'Did you let Leah know you were coming?' she asked.

When Ronan shook his head she said, 'Then you *are* in for a hard time!'

'Harder than you know.'

'Why so?'

'She wrote telling me not to look for her.'

'Then why have you come?'

99

'Because I had to.' The assertion was quiet but absolute. Alice acknowledged its honest force, and looked away, exempting him from further explanation. Perhaps for that reason he chose to explain. 'Her letter rang with loneliness,' he claimed. 'There was no life in the words, no real conviction. It felt as though she was concealing a life as arid as mine.'

There might, Alice knew, be a measure of truth in what this man had read between the lines; but how easy to discover in those vague spaces what was eagerly sought, and not found, in a letter's deliberate words. By the same token he seemed to be reading her own silence now. 'Can you honestly tell me she's been happy since she's been here?' he demanded.

'It may', Alice admitted, 'be too strong a word.' And when Ronan opened a significant hand – point proven – she asked, 'Do you take satisfaction in that?'

'On the contrary – I hate myself for it. I hate it that it makes me glad. But I don't see how it could be otherwise.'

'Are you so sure you understand her?'

'I understand what she's been going through. I know how much she hurts, how much we've hurt each other. But without each other ... we're empty, we're deficient. Deficient of life. There's no real meaning.' He took a moment to measure the impact of his statement, then added, 'The point is, it doesn't have to stay this way. Things can be changed between us.'

Alice felt caution grow in proportion to his intensity, yet she found herself warming to his insistent spirit even as she reflected that it would take an intense, difficult, arrogant man such as this to derail a nature as stubborn and passionate as Leah's. Also she was beginning to make educated guesses about the larger context of the damage that had been done between them.

Meanwhile, under her thoughtful scrutiny, Ronan felt anxious to justify his claims. He was wondering how to convince Alice that things had not always been like this. How to tell her, for instance, that from the moment they'd met he felt transparent in Leah's company, he felt made of light? He'd delighted in the way she'd exposed his cautious moves towards seduction as devices to avoid rejection first and commitment later. Wittily, alluringly, with alarming honesty, she'd held him at bay for weeks, and during that time his pleasure in her ways became intoxication. When they were lovers at last it matured into obsession. Over two tempestuous years Ronan came to believe that his passion for Leah was the final value of his existence – though how true that was he discovered only after he got back from a trip abroad to find her gone.

'And you believe Leah feels this too?' Alice asked.

'I'm sure of it.' But already Ronan had been swept away by his thoughts, back across the afflicted time in which he'd suffered his lover's disappearance like a bereavement. There was no denying that towards the end they had been able neither to comfort one another nor to let each other go. A number of corrosive encounters left both in agony, but the decision to end them had been Leah's alone. It was achieved by amputation. His therefore had been the greater shock.

'If she's honest with herself,' he added, 'she must.' Then he lowered his eyes from Alice's gaze to the book in his lap: *The Book of the Heart as Love's Prisoner*. Ah yes, he too could have written such a book, though with darker illustrations.

Alice had always been porous to the vagrant emotions of those around her – in her youth disablingly so, though she had gradually learned ways of avoiding inundation. On this day, however, she had already been in a heightened state of receptivity when Ronan arrived, and she sensed the full gravity of his condition now. 'I'm sorry,' she offered, sincerely enough but in an effort also to achieve a degree of distance, 'these months must have been difficult for you too.'

His heart welled with sudden gratitude, though the woman could have no knowledge how far her considerate remark failed to comprehend the depths he'd endured. Those months had been infernal. For a while he'd tried to reconcile himself to loss, even to congratulate himself on a timely escape from gathering complexities; but irretrievably it seemed, after Leah had left, every aspect of his life went bad. The work he'd once loved filled him with loathing now. He became negligent and forgetful, made stupid errors of fact and judgment; he was irascible with colleagues, bored by clients, sickened by the accrued habits of his days. He found himself eavesdropping on his own conversations: they were mere white noise. A gauze-like screen interposed itself between thought and action, and what was filtered out was meaning. He drank too much, yet to no more than distempering effect. As the weeks wasted by, the signs of distress became more serious until his state deteriorated out of all proportion. Suddenly, from no clear cause, he'd find himself drenched in sweat, or sitting in the lavatory, shaking, unable to catch his breath. Fear, a formless engulfing fear, fear more terrible than anything he'd known since he was a child, shook his heart. It passed through him like a freakish storm. At times his teeth chattered with it. Images of atrocity seized his mind. He would wake weeping with unnameable grief.

On his doctor's advice he took medication. The dark storm passed, but there was a sense of falsity inside the ensuing calm. False words, false deeds, false stories told inside the silence of his mind: these became his listless portion now. How to trust any part of such corruption to tell where truth might lie? Once the links between feeling and meaning were cut, what point in quests for value and significance? One settled for inanity. For a time his life had shifted into neutral then, which proved worse in its vacant way than the fear had been. Had he believed in the soul he would have thought it moribund inside him. In any case, shortly after his bleak forty-seventh birthday, Ronan caught himself staring down the hill to death.

If he was able to share none of this directly now, the atmosphere of the room was nevertheless loaded with it.

Seeking to ease the man's jammed desire to speak, Alice said, 'Leah's been here some time. Why didn't you come sooner?'

'I didn't know where she was until she wrote. But even if I had . . .' He glanced up like a man distracted. 'I don't know . . . I'd been in poor shape – out of my head really – then I ran into a friend of Leah's – her former flat-mate, Cathy. I was coming out of the library when I saw her at the cycle-rack unlocking the Silver Dream Machine.' He took in Alice's quizzical glance. 'It's the nickname I gave to Leah's bike. She must have passed it on to Cathy when she left. Anyway, that ordinary event – watching somebody else swing into the saddle and ride off into traffic . . . It hit me like a fist thumping down on my chest. It kick-started the heart.' Instantly he was returned to that swiftly crystallizing moment when he had run into the street to call the rider back – as though it had been Leah herself who would brake and turn and smile in sudden astonishment. But the cyclist neither stopped nor turned, and he had stepped unwarily into the path of a car that hooted and swerved as it carried a white-faced passenger shouting by. Ronan remembered how he'd stood in the hot street, amazed that the death he'd contemplated in the attractive middle-distance only the day before should have brushed so closely past him. His senses had been quickened by it. He could taste its exhaust acrid at his mouth. He saw how mortal his condition had become. He saw that he wanted to live, that he wanted to be alive again inside his skin. He wanted feeling back – be it pain or joy, or whatever intermingled refinement of the two had magnetized his time with Leah. 'I saw it then,' he said. 'I knew I'd been fooling myself to think I could live without her. I knew I couldn't carry on like that – not for much longer. I had to find her again, we had to reclaim each other. It was more than desire – you have to understand that – it was necessity.'

Ronan took in Alice's pensive gaze and smiled, a little embarrassed by his own vehemence; but it was true – every word of it. Now he was here in this ancient house by the sea; and Leah was on her way. She was coming closer by the second, and at that thought his heart was in his mouth with imminence. His eyes were closed: he was in the little pinnace at moon-rise, putting ashore after his stormy crossing; the cliffs loomed over him where the women fished, he saw their shiny catch. Then his eyes opened again, the room resumed its airy calm.

But Alice too was possessed by troubling certainties. She remembered Leah's howling in the cove. She knew how far beyond unrequited love that bitter sound had ranged, and she was beginning to wonder whether the Leah she knew was the real reason for Ronan's Cornish quest. With every moment that passed it felt likelier that he had been drawn to Roseleye by some more biddable figure of his own imagining. And, if that was the case, it alarmed Alice to think what might happen when the urgency of his unconscious need collided with Leah's own vulnerable yet refractory spirit.

In the next instant, as though caught on a swift breeze, her thoughts were entirely elsewhere. They were transported back to the glen, and her gaze travelled with them, so she was no longer looking outwards at the parlour of Roseleye but inwards into the shimmer of the waterfall. The Lady stood beside her still. Both watched as more figures emerged through the spray. Alice saw eight women carrying a ninth between them, whose naked body they laid down beside the pool. The hair was matted with blood, the face pitifully damaged; a gash in the dead woman's side continued to bleed as Alice became aware of another presence in the glen – the stern, distracted figure of a man whose robe and hair were the colour of stone, and who seemed less an emanation of the spray than of the unstable rock beside it. She watched him reach into the leather scrip at his belt and take out a crudely fashioned drinking-cup. The whorled grain of its wood was blackened with use, the lip cracked; but when the man handed the vessel over, it was received as a precious object by the lady of the fall.

She knelt beside the corpse and held the bowl at the gushing wound. When it brimmed with blood she held the cup to the dead body's lips. The dead mouth was made to drink. Alice was filled with primitive revulsion at the sight until she saw how the bluish tinge of the flesh was changing. A pearly suffusion of light was returning there. It was like watching dawn.

Then the image was gone. She was back in the parlour, blinking, confused. The wound had been healing itself. Alice put a hand to her eyes, the tips of her fingers pinched the bridge of her nose. 'I'm sorry,' she heard Ronan saying, 'I didn't mean to burden you.'

'Not at all,' she answered reflexively, surfacing again. 'I think it's good you've come. I think it was time.' She was smiling across at the stranger in her room – not the man in the glen after all, but not unlike him either; a figure with something of the same distracted gravity, who seemed to be relaxing back into the couch, with an arm loosely stretched

105

along its back as the parlour door rattled open and, with a white, raging face, Leah was suddenly across the room demanding, 'What the hell are you doing here?'

Of course she had planned stronger openings but his proximity confounded her. As she burst into the room and saw Ronan there, chatting with Alice, one arm loosely stretched along the back of the chesterfield, evidently relaxed, Leah's heart was stamping. Momentarily though, the question pushed him back.

'I thought we needed to talk.' His voice was hoarse, his cheeks flushed with the knowledge that he was overheard; and Leah's anger flashed in the parlour's tranquil light. How dare he seek to shut her back inside that plural pronoun? 'As far as I'm concerned,' she snapped, '*we* ceased to exist a long time ago.'

'I know, but . . .'

'I don't know how you can do this, tracking me down here, bothering my friends . . .'

'He wasn't bothering me,' Alice intervened from her chair, where she was still a little dazed by the power of what she had just seen. 'In fact, we were having a rather illuminating talk.'

Appalled by this defection, Leah briefly contemplated her friend with assassin's eyes. 'If you're going to listen to him you won't hear the half of it.' Then she redirected her fire where it belonged. 'There's nothing to say. You shouldn't have come. I want you out of here. I want you out of my space.'

They stared at one another, he in appeal, she with implacable menace. 'At the risk of pedantry,' Alice broke the silence, 'I might point out that this space is mine. I do so prefer it if *all* my guests feel welcome.'

Ronan collected himself. 'No, Leah's right. I shouldn't be

106

here.' Observing with a quick constriction of his heart that she had not changed her clothes from the previous night, he said, 'Did you read my note?'

Leah shook her head. She had flung the letter down unread when Mrs Pascoe informed her that its writer was still in the house, talking with Alice. But she had read his gaze.

'I asked if we could meet somewhere else. I said I'd wait for you at the pub till closing time this afternoon. I could still do that, if you want a chance to . . .'

'There's no point.'

Only in fury could she meet his eyes, and fury was hard to sustain under their entreaty. So she looked away, trusting her voice to close all doors behind her.

'I've come a long way, Leah.'

She heard that more than geographical distances were meant, but, 'It's over,' she snapped. 'I don't want you here, interfering with my life. I don't want you charming my friends and damaging my mind. Everything's changed, I've worked for these changes, and it's been bloody hard, and I don't want . . .'

By now there were tears of rage and grief in Leah's eyes. He said, 'You can't allow that I might have changed too?'

'God, I hope so.'

'It's true.'

'So how does your wife feel about that?'

A silence strummed between them, in which presently Alice cleared her throat. 'It appears you have a lot to say to one another after all. If you'll excuse me, I'll leave you alone.'

Leah watched in disbelief as Alice gathered the coffee cups on to the chased silver tray, and nodded amiably at the speechless pair before making for the door. A bumble-bee, which had entered through the slightly open window and failed to find its way out again, fretted against the pane. As Alice paused to worry over its struggle, Ronan got to his feet and hastened the other way round the sofa, reaching to open the door. The old woman studied this act of awkward gallantry through narrowed eyes. 'There's a magazine over there,' she said. 'You might use it to help that bee on its way.' Then she left the room.

Leah put a hand to her head and made a little moan. Though her moonstone accessories had been forgotten on the shelf in Stephen's bathroom, she was stuck in high heels and black cotton tights which had begun to irritate her as the day grew warmer. She was furious and miserable and trapped, and for the first time in months she would have killed for a cigarette.

For the moment Ronan was cooler. He picked up the magazine and faffled about for a while in a vain effort to persuade the errant insect out of an open window. Finally Leah could bear it no longer. 'Oh bugger the bee,' she exploded.

'There,' he said, 'it's gone,' and offered a smile.

But by now Leah had both hands at her face. She was saying, 'I can't breathe in here.'

'Would you rather go outside?'

'Don't be so bloody considerate.'

He stood for a time with his arms heavy at his sides before replacing the magazine where he had found it.

'Why are you doing this to me?' Leah said.

'I think you know.'

But if she did, she made no acknowledgment.

'These past months . . . not knowing where you were, not being able to see you, to speak to you . . .'

'How did you find me? Did Cathy tell you?'

'The letter you sent. It was postmarked. I remembered that day when we saw Alice's exhibition. I was sure you'd be here.'

She stared at him in disbelief. 'That letter was telling you to stop bothering Cathy, to stop trying to find me.'

His eyes brightened with conviction. 'If you'd really wanted me out of your life you wouldn't have written at all.'

'Oh God!' Her head craned back on the taut neck, but the white, slightly bulging ceiling was no sky to roll open and pluck her from this pass. 'But that was weeks ago,' she realized, irrelevantly, aghast.

'I came as soon as I could.'

'I see.' Scorn glimmered at her lips. 'This was the first convenient moment to terrorize me.'

'Leah.'

But she disdained his appeal. 'Last night . . .'

'I didn't mean to shock you. I'd no idea you'd be there. I didn't know where I was myself. Yesterday was a god-awful day. The weather, the drive, I hardly slept at all last night. You have to believe . . .'

'I don't have to believe anything.' But she felt the pull of those familiar, insistent eyes. 'I've got to get out of here.' She made for the hall where Dora Pascoe was asking Alice if she could come back for the night because she wouldn't feel safe in her caravan. Unable to bear the silent, anxious gossip of their stare, Leah turned away towards the back door, kicked off her heels and slipped into a well-worn pair of flat shoes. As Ronan entered the hall she hurried out into the garden. He looked to Alice who shrugged dubiously, while Mrs Pascoe avoided his eyes. So he followed his quarry through the door, and when he caught up with her she was picking at the paint of the wicket-gate that opened into the glen.

In those few moments alone Leah had been thinking that they might never be free of each other, and the thought seemed to diminish all options to fatality. It made her spirit quail. But she had needed air, and space, a chance to collect herself, for her feelings were different now, more complicated and troubling than the reflex of panic the previous night when, from a dark corner of the car-park, she'd seen Ronan standing at the door of the hotel. Leah had almost frozen then, but under the pressure of her hissed demands, Stephen had swung his car from its slot and out on to the road. Once more she'd caught Ronan's white stare squinting against the headlights as they turned, but he made no motion. Then, with Stephen gunning the engine round the cove and up towards the coastal road, the immediate menace was gone. Two or three times she'd checked the wing-mirror but no lights followed. There had even been a brief instant of sickly relief before she realized: he had no need to follow, he must know where to find her, he would pick his time.

Later, on the first straight stretch of road above the cliff, Stephen had braked and pulled into a bumpy lay-by, demanding, 'What was all that about?' Strapped in her seat-belt, with her eyes closed against the great sweep of night and sea, Leah had clutched the little sequinned purse at her lap. 'It felt like some kind of panic-attack,' Stephen pressed. 'Was it me? Something I said?' And, when she shook her head, 'Leah, I'm your friend. Why won't you trust me?'

After a time she had glanced across and seen nothing harmful there, nothing she could not control. And she had a need, however brief, for sanctuary. A moment later he was amazed to hear her saying, 'I've been thinking. Would you take me home with you after all?'

And so, to her immediate chagrin and dismay, she had woken that morning in Stephen's bed, ruing the weakness that had brought her there. She could hear him on the phone downstairs, telling someone he would come into work late.

110

Blearily she'd looked at her watch: eight twenty-five. She had slept for less than three hours. She turned over and buried her head against the day, and when Stephen tip-toed into the room she pretended to be sleeping still. Within minutes she was.

Nearly three hours later he had gently woken her. His worried frown left her instantly distraught. She wanted to explain herself, to apologize, to die. She should never have let this happen; she should never have made it happen. She was sure he must be blaming himself over the failure of their misprised effort to make love, for that tender débâcle had ended, soon after it began, in tears and a barely coherent confession of what was actually happening; and now – the morning after – she had looked into his troubled eyes and wished, impossibly, to erase it all.

But there had been more terrible things on Stephen's mind, for he had gone out shopping for breakfast only to return shaken by news which had left the entire neighbourhood queasy with terror and suspicion. Aghast at his words, feeling the light snuffed round her, Leah had begun to hate this strange, contaminated day. A woman was dead, the murderer unfound. Ronan was waiting. She would not cope well. Nothing was reliable now; especially, most perfidious of all, her own feelings. They were instruments of error, good for nothing but grief. The gentle talk that she and Stephen had salvaged from the night withered in this suddenly bleaker air. Leah was armed and hostile again. What else made sense in a world where women were objects of violent desire to be used, defiled, tormented, killed?

Left bristling with fear, she had tried to ring Alice only to find herself speaking to Amy. A few minutes later Stephen had driven her back to Roseleye, his equable nature sickened by shock and thoroughly confused. He

111

would have come with her into the house but Leah forbad him even to wait outside.

And why, she wondered now, had she done that? Because she was wary of Ronan's jealous temper, yes; but that wasn't the whole of it. On the silent drive back to Roseleye, Leah had felt her own emotions shifting like the light in rain. She was amazed by the changes working there. But Ronan had come for her; against all odds and obstacles he had sought her out; and if, after the grave damage that had been done between them, she could still rise to his renewed advances with an agitation of the heart that reached far deeper than her surface rage, then there was no help for it, and no telling what the consequences of her growing temerity might be.

Her breathing was unsteady as she heard him tread the damp lawn towards her. He said, 'You can't just turn your back on me, Leah.' And though the words were commonplace enough she was pierced by the dreadful truth they told.

'You should have let things be,' she murmured unmoving.

'I couldn't.' Unable to compel the attention of her eyes, he made his voice more urgent. 'I've lived without you for months now. I know what happened to me in that time and it wasn't life. It wasn't even a good imitation. My life stopped the day you left. You took it with you. I had to come for it.'

'But it's not like that,' she protested, helpless in the face of such error. 'It can't be like that.' She shrugged away as he reached for her arms, trying to turn her round. Avoiding his touch and gaze, she pushed open the gate and passed through. 'I don't know what to do with you,' she said. 'I've nothing to give. There's nothing left, don't you see? There's nothing here that's yours. You should never have come.'

Unable to hold still, and with the way back to the house now blocked, she turned aside, down the slope to where the path divided. The stream flashed and glinted in the glen below.

'Give me an hour to talk to you,' he urged. 'Just an hour, that's all I ask.' His tone insisted that only a craven or a frigid heart could refuse this concession. 'Then I'll leave. If that's what you still want, I'll leave.'

Under the damp green canopy of the trees his words came at her like a dare. They drew her gaze upwards to where he stood at the top of the bank with his hands open. His eyes sought to reel her in, rekindling the good memories, the occasions of joy and tenderness, of secrecy and risk, the old annealing heat of a passion absolute in its exile from the world.

Possessed by his longing, Ronan was suddenly back in the flat on that afternoon of summer lightning when, in response to some simple thing he said, Leah had astonished him by her deliverance into a love-making so complete it swept them through to a region where the entire flashing sky seemed resumed inside their skins. They'd lain in each other's arms for a long time afterwards, tranquil and reverential, speaking in whispers, listening to the rain through the pale light of the calico drapes; and when, later, he got up to bring her coffee, there was thunder in the milk. Thunder had touched their skins. A torrent of starlings thrilled across the evening air. They could hear the sky carrying the storm away.

As he gazed down on her now, the memory returned with such power that, for a crucial instant, she was drawn into its field; and she knew the smell of him, the taste of his skin, she knew the gripped frown of those deep-set eyes. Everything about him was familiar as a once-forgotten, now-returning pain. She wanted to shout up at him, 'I loved you, God damn you, I loved you so much. How could you do those things to me? How could you hurt me like that?' Only her fierce, vestigial pride prevented it; but it held her there too, even though she knew herself at risk. Always their love had thrived on risk, and those risks had ruined her.

They might, were she not very careful, ruin her again. But she saw also that the glint of confident ownership was gone from his gaze. And what if something new was trying to happen? It was possible, it was just possible, and in all conscience, in all charity, she could not refuse to listen. The ties between them were too strong for that, and it was not that she felt passive before them, rather that, in this different place, away from the old shadows, she felt her spirit quickening to his voice again. She felt the dangerous possibilities of renewal. So when, after a time, she nodded silently, her eyes were closed, but the delicate lids did not withhold complicity. She too, it seemed, was conjuring chaos here.

Ronan sensed the change in her. He smiled, reaching out a hand, but before he could approach she turned away, taking the left-hand path towards the stream. Sunlight glittered among the leaves of beech and sycamore. The path was muddy on this steep stretch, and difficult, and having won her assent it was somehow terrible for him to watch her slithering away down the wild bank in the shirt of viridian silk. He called after her, 'You'll spoil your clothes like that. Hang on, let me help.' But she pressed on, not waiting for him when she reached the stream and took the stepping-stones out across white water to where the path followed an easier route on the other side. He saw at once that it was not wide enough for two people to walk side by side, which was as Leah had intended, for she still needed time to feel her way into this encounter. She too had her terms. She would make him meet them. He would find that nothing came easily here.

They reached a place where the trees ended and the stream accelerated glassily over sleek stones; then the water swerved through a narrow throat of rock and plunged into a steep gorge. The path forked there, and she took the track that veered to the left of an upright, brightly lichened dividing-stone where it climbed through bracken towards the high cliff. Overhead the sky was an unsullied blue above the still hidden sea.

Head down, panting a little, Ronan concentrated on the climb until, at the highest point, the sea declared itself. He paused to contemplate its expansive sweep, then looked back the way they had come, and saw the stream far below him, taking its first dive into the gorge. The canopy of beech and sycamore crowded the glen beyond, receding inland much further than they had travelled. He had expected to see the house back there, but it was invisible on the far side of a rise where cattle grazed in sunlight. There was a warm hush across the land.

Things stood fair for a lovely afternoon; and they should have been together there, in love, devising futures, not striding out in this fanatical bid to end an hour. Ronan gazed out across the quiet littoral and felt the return of a yearning familiar from previous, more youthful excursions to the sea. It was the desire somehow to *possess* the landscape; and not by dealing for its freehold, but more intimately, more completely than that, as though there might be a way to make this place a property of the self, a quality that could be carried off, like a bride, to enrich one's life elsewhere.

For the first time he recognized the sensuality of the longing. It was less consuming than his desire for Leah, but not unrelated, and in that infatuated moment it felt as though the earth itself might have erotic claims on him, as though the yearning that had gripped his soul and brought him here would remain insatiable till it was answered by the earth itself.

Yet both the intensity of the desire and its impossibility filled him with a sense of further imminent loss. The thought, *I have to get out of the city*, flashed across his mind. Then, *We should settle down here, together*. But he was made more restless than ever by the thoughts, more intensely driven to change the way things were between himself and Leah right now. And every instinct told him only touch could do it; yet that, above all, she was determined to forbid.

She had stopped some yards ahead of him, gazing across to the next headland, tense and remote. He followed her gaze and saw the activity on that distant bluff where a number of cars were parked, their roofs shimmering in the heat. A small crowd was confined behind a cordoned barrier, watching a group of figures in conference on the cliff-top, but they were too far away for him to make out what was happening. As he turned to begin their conversation at last he caught the sleek gleam of her shirt from the corner of his eye, vivid against the gun-metal sea. She had walked on and appeared to be heading straight for the edge of their own deserted cliff.

Only after he'd shortened the gap between them could he see that she followed what was now little more than a rabbit-track between waist-high banks of hog-weed and coarse grass. Beyond her lay nothing but blue sky. She was approaching the sheerest of drops. Then the path debouched sharply to the right, and at so steep an incline that she disappeared.

Ronan hurried to catch up, but the path twisted as it descended, becoming a damp gulley between bushes of gorse and blackthorn. It was stepped here and there with outcrop stone, though at the next turn it dipped more steeply still, plunging under tangles of thorn dense enough to form a tunnel.

There was no sign of Leah. Smaller than himself, she must have slipped under the branches of the thorn-trees easily, but he had to crouch and slither, unpicking caught sleeves and shoulders. When he emerged, standing, high over the sea still, she was already far below him, out along a promontory of rock, following the path's hair-pin kink near the seaward limit of the narrow ridge. On either side, a jagged rock-face sliced sheerly away to where great slabs of stone were piled like scatter-cushions on the strand beneath.

Though the tide had begun to flow again it was still some distance out, and on the far side of the next headland two small islands had appeared. Ronan narrowed his gaze against the brilliant wind-glimmer off the sea. Gulls nestled in the swell. Under the edge of the horizon, a freighter coasted slowly westwards. He could feel the sleepless hours silting the back of his eyes. Suddenly he was detached from his own motives. Their moorings had slipped. But there was Leah, clambering down the last rocks above the small triangular span of sand, and as far as he knew she had not once looked back. Her indifference strengthened his compulsion, for it could only be assumed. He found it unthinkable that anything in her subsequent experience could have approached the intensity she'd known with him; but she was half-wild from this separation, unused to his approach. He could presume nothing now. Nothing except the scary, mutual knowledge of a life at stake between them. Yet when eventually he reached that stretch of sand it seemed devoid of life.

His first wretched thought was that she could be hiding anywhere among these rocks. They lay around him utterly still, quite silent, so fixed in their bed of sand and shell that it was hard to conceive the calamitous grinding of stack

117

against stack that had strewn them randomly along the shore. Two caves yawned under the cliff, their damp mouths sleeked with weed. Or she could be stealing between the rocks, eluding him at will. Anger grew at the thought of such perversity. He cursed aloud, agitated by the notion that she had already taken some secret route out of here, leaving him stupid as a stone while she back-tracked, clearing off, out of his reach. So had he crossed the country, killing a swan, and come through one of the worst nights of his life for nothing more gratifying than this travesty of his existing torment? He was beginning to think so when she stepped quietly from a dark crevice in the promontory of rock down which he'd climbed only moments before.

Something had changed. He couldn't place it at once, for he was still distracted by the damage to her hair. Only when she sat down a few yards away, on a rock angled towards the sea, did he observe that she was now bare-legged beneath the skirt. She took care to cover both knees with her hands as she dipped her feet into a fringed pool, wincing a little at the cold, yet the nakedness of her shins seemed to offer a first startling sign of returning intimacy. His hostility expired, instantly displaced by wistful tenderness.

She had consciously chosen a spot where there was no space for him to sit down beside her. Their eyes met. Hers glanced away, significantly, to her watch.

'Leah, this is so hard for me,' he sighed. 'I can't even begin if you keep checking the time like that.'

'You asked for an hour.'

She glanced up at the anguish in his face. Remorse stabbed her, followed instantly by anger. Why must she always render herself vulnerable to him? As long as he could reach this compassionate place, he held all the weapons. He could suborn her mind, exploit every feeling. There was no remedy. Again she looked away so that he should not see her confusion.

He said, 'Can't we at least be kind to one another?'

'We can try.'

'I think we should. I think we could both use a little kindness.'

Ronan lifted his head and looked up at the cliff, feeling an almost infantile sense of wonder that its precarious weight should so magnanimously forbear to fall and crush him. The overhanging bulk was goblet-shaped, undercut near the foot, rendering this span of sand invisible from the path above. Not unless you were already on your way down could you learn by chance of the cove's existence. Nor was it possible to trace from here the precise route of their own descent. He saw that she had brought him to an utterly secluded place.

Ronan tried to collect his thoughts, but there were things that bothered him. He had expected, for instance, to come out where the stream met the sea, but there was no stream here. More insistently, he was troubled by a nagging sensation of *déjà vu*, as though the looming cliff were part of a dream-landscape revisited. The hues and tinctures of the rock, the livid mauves and greens, the cross-hatched fissures and striations, the whole ponderous giant's dance of the place – it was all familiar to him. Yet he'd never been to Cornwall before – the thought of English tourism, with its odious flim-flam of caravans and gift-shops and pixies had kept him away. But he seemed to know this place. Tentatively he spoke the thought aloud.

'It's the tapestry,' Leah answered without animation. 'The one you almost bought.' And he remembered the large hanging that had been the centre-piece of the exhibition. Its rhythms and textures and colours had compelled attention at first sight by their immediate correspondence with the

119

deep geology of his own imagination. He'd been further intrigued by the catalogue's account of how Alice worked only with wool from sheep that grazed the Cornish cliffs, wool she had spun herself and dyed with pigments made in her own workshop from the plant-life of the locality. Profoundly struck both by the vigour of the piece and by the integrity of its prevailing vision, he had pondered buying the tapestry for days. Finally he told Leah that, much as he loved the wondrous thing, it was out of scale with both his wallet and his walls. And that was almost true, but the nearer truth (and he knew Leah knew it) was that he could not see how to explain such a momentous purchase to his wife.

Thinking again about the old woman under whose eyes he'd woken back at the house, he realized that an imagination adequate to the secrets of this place must have been present also in the gaze that measured him. 'She's a remarkable woman,' he murmured, but the thought left him feeling transparent and insubstantial. 'It seems to run in the family.'

She heard the attempted lightness of his tone. She wanted to respond to it, she wanted to condemn it. She wanted to hit him, very hard.

In the lukewarm pool where she had dipped her feet Leah found a mirror of her own dissolved condition. Cloud and light were there, it was filled with unstable reflections, with delicate forms of life that swayed and flinched at every change. She leaned her shadow across the surface to touch a shiny cluster of mussels clinging above the water-line. It seemed they were listening for the tide which approached with soothing noises some distance away, but they might have been waiting like this for ever. The day hovered over her in warm suspension. She breathed his name twice over, almost soundlessly, in remembrance and regret for so much that had passed between them, for so much lost; though if sadness was there, so too were traces of remembered passion; and when he lifted his gaze she could not withhold a smile as tender and rueful as his. Leah no longer quite trusted herself to speak, for she was fondly recalling how often his expansive nature had brimmed with admiration for other people's skill or beauty or brilliance. From the first she had flourished under such bounty herself, though later it became a cause for amazement how the same man could be driven by a narrow, grasping rage; and now, as he slipped off his jacket and stepped on to a slab of greenstone overlooking the place where she sat, she felt stranded between hope and dread.

This could be so much harder than she had guessed. She saw how her weakness might give him room to recover his talent for saying whatever served the situation best – that seductive gift brought to his nativity by a fairy from his Irish side, one who liked to wreak confusion in the world. She knew how skilfully his tongue enchanted and bewildered her. And there was so much she might try to say herself, but she was afraid he would mistake every word of it, hearing only what he wished to hear, while some figure from his dreams eclipsed her separate existence. Should that happen again as it had happened before, she knew her own mind far too cloudy to bring the mingled elements in his to clear solution.

Ronan sat down where the greenstone slab offered an angle on her face. To his right, in a sunny culvert, lay a clear pool left by the morning tide. A smooth drift of sand shelved into its green depths. He could smell the sea-light caught in there. He wanted to strip and cleanse himself, to bathe his face in that lucid world, then wade naked towards his lover where she would be lying with her hair splayed across hot sand.

In those moments he had no desire for speech, for it seemed they could only wound one another with words; yet, for the moment, words were all he had.

Light burned in the standing pool as, slowly, uncertainly, he began.

Part Two
INWARD

'You are in the Land of Marvels at the Castle of Marvels, about to enter the Bed of Marvels, whereon your end is going to be death.'

'Then,' said Gawain undaunted, 'you had better give me your advice.'

Wolfram von Eschenbach, *Parzival*

6

DREAM

Far above them in the vertical blue day, a flight of choughs wheeled round the cliff and vanished inland. The sea moaned with the noise of an enchanted crowd.

'It's all right,' he whispered, fascinated by the light-stippled flecks of colour in her eyes, 'I'm here. We can come to our senses now. You can let go.'

He had forgotten how beautiful those eyes were. Now they evoked a sensation close to awe. He felt himself trembling with the nervous elation of a man who has come unexpectedly into possession of new powers and is, as yet, uncertain how to master them. But as he hesitated those eyes turned, teasingly, away. She was making for the dark cleft in the promontory of rock from which she'd first emerged. He moved quickly, striding across the slab of rock to leap down, laughing, in her path. She stopped, panting. Against the swish of the surf everything was very still. Then a nimble change of direction took her at a run across the shiny beach towards the sea.

Now there was a gamy feel to the chase, a tantalising catch-as-catch-can across the strand. He was within a stride of grabbing her when, impossibly, she vanished. The air was empty.

But he was still running, unstoppably, into that vacant space, where the ground gave under him. With a sickly lurch his feet sank, and the wet beach was dragging him down inside itself, digesting him in quick-sand, or quick-shingle rather, for the stuff in which he was sinking had the dense, drenched feel of mortar about it. There was nothing to hold, nowhere to stand, already his hips and waist were gripped. Panicking he grabbed and floundered, but his chest was taken, and the stuff was sucking up against his face.

Then his head went under in the coarse, obliterating dark. Only his wrists and hands were left frantic above the surface, reaching for help that would not come. He knew that he was going to die, that nothing could prevent it. When he tried to shout his mouth gagged on darkness. He reared upright, out of the dream, still shouting. His head crashed against rock. The light that had been scattered across sea and sky gathered itself to a viscous black spot inside the sun. The day darkened like a cinema.

For long seconds afterwards he felt sure he was still subsiding into death. He could feel the blood behind his eyes. He thought his ears were bleeding. Then the densely enfolded blackness frayed, the sea shimmered again. Light dazzled at the cutting edge of pain. When he lifted his hand to the place of fiercest hurt it came away bloody.

Gathering his stricken senses, Ronan vaguely remembered how he'd come to lie inside that low cabin-shaped crevice in the cliff. He swung his legs out of the cleft and sat there shaking. After a time he dabbed a handkerchief at the temple's broken skin. When he opened his eyes again the cove was luminous and unstable. There was a dizzy cast to it. It shook like foil.

He'd eaten nothing but a couple of digestive biscuits since the previous night and was famished now. His watch said well after five: he must have slept for hours. Then the weird thought struck him that this might not even be the same day.

His metabolic clock urged otherwise. No more than a few hours could have passed. It had to be the same disastrous day.

His head brayed with pain.

The first clear thought was that this was not the cove to which Leah had brought him. Then a picture surfaced: he was turning to look back at her, and she'd gone from where he'd last seen her. There were only scuff-marks in sand.

Other pictures came: far to the left, he'd caught the slide of green silk among black rocks before it was swallowed by the cleft under the ridge from which she'd first appeared. He remembered thinking, *She's gone to get her shoes and tights, she'll come back and look at you, then it will be over, and you'll have lost, and there's nothing to be done.* Then he'd sat for a long time on the hot scuffed beach, waiting for her, but no figure returned through the narrow cleft.

Worried, he'd crossed to stare between capsized shelves of rock into that slanting rift. Daylight had stopped within a few feet of the entrance. There was cold shadow and a standing water smell. His voice had entered the defile with her name and come back empty. But Leah had gone that way.

So – yes, that was it, he remembered now.

Loathing himself, appalled by what he'd done, and labouring therefore under a crushing weight of dread, he'd gone into the cleft, propping himself on both hands as he shuffled between the sloping walls. The rocks dripped. There was a slime of weed. The passage narrowed ahead. He felt his scalp prickle at the dense volume of stone above him.

At a sharp bend where he had to step, head ducked, from boulder to boulder across a dingy pool, pale light had shafted mistily around him. Beyond its watery chill, the afternoon reprinted itself in soft blues and greys and browns across the rubble of another cove. Seconds later he'd entered that place as one can enter a house and instantly know it empty. Nowhere was there any sign of Leah.

Over the sound of surf he'd heard the noise of water rushing under greater pressure. Mounting a whale-backed rock he saw what he'd already guessed: this was where the stream shallied one last time among smooth stones before entering the sea. You could climb those stones like a stair, up into the gorge he'd seen earlier as they crossed the cliff. Leah would be far down the glen already, and for all the chance he had of meeting her again she might as well have been snatched away into the underworld.

And hours had passed since then. The tide had flooded while he slept, leaving the strand so far submerged that the defile back to the other cove was deeply awash. There would be no way through for a long time yet, not till night had fallen. Ronan considered his situation now. So strangely was the world altered it felt inconceivable that he'd left home only the previous morning. Neither time nor place was familiar. Even the overcast light was odd, as though the day was sickening for something. He stared out to sea, trying to imagine walking that way, but the dream had left a terror of death on him and he shrank from the thought. He lifted his gaze from where the tide pushed a curdled froth of foam into a brackish sump among the stones, then watched the stream careering in twists of white water till it clashed with the swell. For as far as he could see he was stuck on the wrong, sheerer side of the gorge. He would have to find another way back to the car. He would have to find other ways everywhere. Everything was altered now.

Cold, hungry, lacking alternatives, Ronan began the climb. Beyond the high stair, a rampart of rock stood hard against the path over a drop to the stream. It was damp with ground-water draining from the higher bastions of the gorge, and where the track veered upwards round a bluff he saw footprints in the mud that might have been Leah's. Ahead of him the high cliff banked on to more open space, becoming crag. Patches of bracken were already turning bronze and faded campanula blew among the outcrop rock. Somewhere out of sight below he heard the clatter of the stream, then the sound of a waterfall echoing in a hollow place. As he pushed on through the failing light that sound grew louder. Ronan felt its draw.

Eventually he came to a point where the track forked. Of the two available paths, the one climbing upwards through the bracken was the more firmly trodden. The other dropped steeply back into the gorge towards the clamour of the fall. Ronan stood in a haze of mist seeping off the sea, uncertain which way to take. With so little remaining light it made sense to bear upwards where he could more easily see his way. Yet he and Leah had followed the stream from Alice's house, and its course offered the only sure guide back. He decided to go down.

Shadow gathered round him. He was treading an ancient stair carved into the cragside. The sound of falling water came louder though he could see nothing of it, not even when a sharp turn brought him to an incline with a broader view. A length of chain had been fixed into the rock-face to ease the descent. Its links were cold under his hand. As he lowered himself he felt suddenly sure that Leah had not come this way.

His foot slid on the last damp step, and he was out into a flat arena of rock. The stream hurtled away among black stones towards a distant bend of the gorge round which high seas were breaking. He could taste salt on the wind.

Turning, he saw that a high buttress of crag baffled the

sound of the waterfall. A few strides took him round the obstruction, then cold spray was blowing at his face through an arch in the rock. Above him, sluicing down the sixty-foot drop of its mossy culvert, the fall shone in the gloom.

It was as if he'd burst in on a naked living presence. Ronan gasped aloud. He felt dizzied by the white gleam streaming through the dark cleft. He averted his eyes as from a blow. Casting about, he saw there was no way past the waterfall. If one descended that rocky stair it was to come here and nowhere else, for the steps were a pilgrim's track to this pagan baptistery and he no pilgrim. The air was raw and wild. He was breathing too quickly, filled with a dreadful sense of transgression.

There was intelligence here. Ronan felt inundated by its presence, as though he'd stumbled in on a royal audience of which he was unworthy. He stood in the din of the fall as he'd stood in his dream before the hag in the underworld, and his dread was so much the same he thought he might quickly wake to find that the day's defeat had been no more than a further chapter of that dream. The torrent sounded round his head. His head hurt. It was damaged and unreliable. But the place . . .

The place was sentient. There was a glut of intelligence here.

He turned away, back round the buttress of rock. When his eyes shifted across to the far side of the gorge he saw a figure sitting among the stones. She wore a long russet gown. Something was lying across her lap – an empty scabbard with hangings so frayed they could no longer bear the weight of a sword. The woman was examining the tattered cloth, apparently with a view to making repairs; but then she leaned to one side, picked up a clumsy pair of iron scissors such as might be used for shearing sheep, and began to hack at her hair. He was about to shout when he realized he must be seeing things.

Ronan closed his eyes and put a hand to his head. He felt the pain crashing there. When he looked out again the woman had gone. He stood appalled, staring at the place where she had been, and saw only shadows among stones. Then he emitted a brief, punitive laugh that brought no relief, only a harsher sense of his predicament. The landscape he'd adored earlier that day – that he'd wanted to carry off like a bride – had turned against him. He couldn't count on the earth any more. In his dream it had swallowed him; now in the failing light of waking day, it was toying with his mind.

Blocked by the fall, dismayed by the smell of dusk, Ronan turned back to the stair. The hand that gripped the chain was trembling. He wanted to pull himself out of that place quickly, he wanted what was left of the light up there, for the downward draw of the fall was darkening around him. He was groaning as he climbed, and out of breath by the time he got back to the place where the path divided; but he took the upward route without looking back, walking quickly.

He pushed on for another quarter of a mile until the track made a steep descent back in the direction of the stream and he came at last to a place he recognized: the fork in the path where Leah had taken him the other way. The musty green lichen and oxidized stains powdered across the dividing-stone made him think of his wound. Gingerly he dabbed it with his handkerchief, but even that light touch made him gasp. Resting his weight against the stone to catch his breath, he saw how less than a yard away the stream made its first steep plunge into the gorge. Presumably if you scrambled down that ravine you would reach the place where the fall plummeted into the pool. He could still hear it booming over the collisions of the tide and the nearer clatter of the stream. The sound throbbed on the gloom like a deep bass note out of the earth itself, the kind of sound that gravity might make. Again he pulled away.

The track twisted and ahead of him were the trees. Now the going was harder and darker. More than half an hour had passed since he'd climbed out of the cove, and he could no longer see the sky. He could see nothing to prove he was still in the same century even. How had he got himself into this wretched pass? How to get out of it? He was furious with misery by now, and as he stumbled through the glen images travelled towards him. He might have been peeping into the wings of a theatre, for in this dusky place behind the scenes Ronan saw ropes and fly-wheels, drapes, a panel of power-switches and dangling painted flats. Lit by a dim red bulb, an old man was panting as he changed out of his particoloured showman's gear, his skin pallid and flabby, his breathing hoarse. There was something pitiful in the wispy, grizzled hair at his chest and the soft swagging of his belly over wrinkled tights. He might have been an acrobat or a circus strong-man once, but had gone to fat and was little more than a makeshift juggler now. Bottle-shaped clubs lay on the floor beside him. The bulb went out. Immediately another figure stepped from the gloom – a woman caped in green with a golden girdle at her hips. In both hands she carried what Ronan took at first for a silver platter holding a joint of meat, but as she hurried towards him he saw it was a dish of blood she brought, and the object in it was a severed head: a man's head lying on its side with the mouth slackly open. The woman glistened with purpose. Her face, with its plucked eyebrows and carmine lips, was as pale as a clown's. She seemed delighted by the gift she bore.

Ronan flinched in recoil. He was groaning aloud as the

132

track made a turn among the trees and he saw a building ahead on the far bank of the stream. He had passed no such place on the way down the glen with Leah so he must have overshot the stepping-stones while his mind was elsewhere. A flight of dippers bobbed away at his approach. Midges were dense on the air. Obviously he should have crossed the stream earlier – but where? In this deep crag, under the canopy of trees, the light had all but failed. He might trudge the glen all night and not find the right place. So should he go back? Or try to cross here while a glimmer of light still held?

He looked upstream and saw a place where there seemed to be shallows and stones to assist a crossing if he could find a decent stick for support. So he cast about till he uncovered a length of green alder, then took off his shoes and threw them across to the other bank. Pocketing his socks, he rolled his trousers to the calves and tested the bed of the stream with the alder wand. Then he stepped into the flow.

He winced at the cold swirl round his ankles, at the coarse scratch of gravel under the soles of his feet. Four or five cautious strides brought him to a midstream slab of stone where he saw that the waters beyond were deeper and faster than he'd first observed. He was in the middle of an old mill-race, part of which had once been diverted to drive a wheel on the wall of the building opposite; but the leat had been dammed when the mill fell into disuse, and the full volume of water now drove glossily downstream. When he prodded the sleek stretch between the slab and the bank the alder wand sank to such unexpected depth that his balance almost failed. The gap was leapable, but in this dusky, sycamore shade who knew what kind of landing he would find? He could go back, but if he found a better crossing he would then be faced with the ridiculous problem of hunting for his shoes in the dark!

Ronan stood amid the rush of water cursing wilderness. He glanced up and where trees should have been he saw the mast and yard-arm of a square-rigged sailing-vessel running before a gale. The ship was having a hard time making landfall through the heavy swell of a narrow channel. From his place near the prow Ronan saw the old juggler holding a tricorn hat to his head as he cowered against the storm. The woman in the russet gown sat calmly binding the scabbard-hangings with her own shorn hair, and when a lurid spume of phosphorescence crackled among the spars it revealed how a silk canopy rigged over the after-deck had broken loose from one of its ties. The sheet snapped over the reclining figure of a third woman who lay with pale hands crossed at her breast. She might have been sleeping on her crimson bed, impervious to the storm, or dead already. Stars flared among the lesions in the cloud, and when the deck reeled at the next sea Ronan guessed how soon the ship must founder. Now it was each man for himself. High on the cliff above his head he saw two women fishing with rods. His ears filled with the foggy ringing of bells as he made his jump.

There is always a story beneath the story, thought Alice as she came awake, *just as there is always a teller behind the tale. The question seems to be whether we live to tell our own stories, or whether the stories are living themselves out, again and again, through us?* In the moments before she surfaced both possibilities felt entirely feasible.

It was unusual for her to fall asleep in the afternoon, but she had been forced by the press of events to assimilate the experience in the glen more speedily than she would have liked, and her body had decided the task best done through sleep. She had been asleep for less than an hour when the back door was slammed with a force that shook all the glass on the rear wall of the house. Alice's eyes shot open. She was at the desk by the dormer-window in her attic study. On its leather surface lay *The Complete Works of Geoffrey Chaucer* together with a few rarer texts, most of which she had scarcely glanced at since her college days. She heard the sound of feet hurrying up the stairs and the creak of old boards along the landing. Moments later, the door of Leah's room banged shut. Alice heard its small brass bolt click home.

She looked at her watch: ten past three. A soft afternoon glare brightened the open page of her Chaucer where she read:

> 'My lige lady, generally,' quod he,
> 'Wommen desiren to have sovereynetee
> As wel over hir housbond as hir love,
> And for to been in maistrie hym above.'

And of course something must have gone wrong. How could it be otherwise? There was too much bitter animus in Leah and too little repose in Ronan for them to have salved their wounds with a single conversation. Alice had entertained no such hope, though she had thought a start might be made; but with Leah locked in her room, and Ronan nowhere in sight, it seemed that only further damage had been done. Sighing, she crossed the attic to peer out of the front window down into the lane where the green Rover waited.

So things were not quite over yet! Alice stood for a moment pursing her lips in thought. Then she descended the attic stairs and knocked on Leah's door. There was no reply; nor again when she asked if she might come in. She tried once more. 'Leah, I know you're in there. What's happened? Let me come in and talk to you.' She heard

Leah's body turn on the bed, then her low voice. 'Leave me alone, will you?'

'You sound terrible. What's happened between you?'

'I don't want to talk about it.'

'Leah, you can't carry on like this. You need to talk. Let me come in.'

When there was still no response, Alice said more firmly, 'I'm not walking away. You're obviously in trouble and I want to help you if I can.'

Through the pine door Alice heard Leah get up and cross the floor. The bolt clicked back, though when the door opened the woman's slim body blocked the entrance. One hand held her shirt closed at her chest. Leah's eyes were narrowed, though the skin around them looked puffy and raw. She said, 'Don't you think you've done enough as it is?'

'What do you mean?'

'You had no right to let him in.'

'Leah, I had every right – not least because he introduced himself as your friend. Though it's true – I might have acted differently if I'd known more about your past.'

'I told you I was trying to cut free from it. You didn't need to know any more than that.'

'But life can't be sealed off that way,' Alice appealed. 'Believe me, I know, I've tried and it doesn't work. It always catches you out. It has to because you *are* it. It can't just go away.' She strove to catch Leah's shifting eyes. 'And we can't talk like this, not properly; and you badly need to talk to someone so it might just as well be me.'

For an instant Alice thought Leah was about to relent, but as though under pressure from enclosing forces the younger woman shut her eyes and shook her head. 'I want you to stay out of this, Alice. It's *my* life. It has nothing to do with you.'

'Oh yes it does,' Alice answered quietly. 'You saw to that

136

when you sought me out. I didn't ask you to come here, but you came anyway; and you were like a piece of my own rejected past finding its way back, coming home, looking for reconciliation. Whether you like it or not, I care about you, Leah, and I'm not going to stand by watching you hurt yourself like this.'

Leah kept her eyes closed under this fierce and tender impact. 'You can't help,' she murmured eventually in a voice that acknowledged the older woman's care while sadly declining it. 'It's over. There's nothing to be done.'

Alice observed the delicate veins in Leah's eyelids. She said, 'That man's hurt you very badly, hasn't he?'

'It doesn't matter. I just want it to be over now.' Leah opened her eyes in appeal. 'And I really do want to be alone.' As she lifted her hand to push back the auburn quiff of hair, her shirt fell open where its green silk was torn around a button-hole. The eyes of the women met. Alice recalled the image that had come while she was speaking to Ronan – the circulation of the woman's blood from wound to mouth by way of the restoring chalice. And how else, she wondered, was the soul to replenish itself in these broken times? She was filled with the desire to hold Leah close, in kinship and comfort, to affirm the indefeasibility of woman in the world; but when she moved, Leah kept space between them, flinching from touch. She too was trembling.

Alice said, 'You're sure I can't help?'

'Not now . . . Not yet.'

'At least let me bring you some tea. Camomile and valerian? With a touch of balm? It will calm you down and help you sleep. Apart from anything else you look worn out.' Assent was faintly given. Alice hesitated, then made to leave, but a further thought stopped her. 'If Ronan comes back . . .'

'He won't. He can't.'

The older woman nodded as though in acceptance of those uncertain claims, but as she went down to the kitchen Alice was silently remarking that she had made no promises.

Two hours later she was sitting in the dusk of her study, listening to the scuffle of bats beneath the eaves. She had spent most of the afternoon in the Middle Ages, among her books, rediscovering the old romances, and pondering the inventive ways those parables of otherworld addressed a problem that remained as intractable now as it had been in Chaucer's day: how to convert the male talent for aggression into energy available for the cultivation of the feelings?

What did one do, for instance, with a man found guilty of rape? In 'The Wife of Bath's Tale' the king's court of law decided that the felon should be executed. The queen's court of love, however, came to a subtler judgment: the nameless knight's life would be spared, but only on condition that he found out what it was that women truly wanted.

Now there, if ever, was an elegant exercise in erotic justice! During the course of that afternoon Alice had re-read Chaucer's tale three times. At each reading she drew deeper satisfaction from its witty masque of trial and transformation. She saw that it might be the story beneath the story she was living now; and being a woman of pragmatic disposition, once that was seen, she committed herself – as the bats whistled and stirred under her roof – to its imminent enactment.

At the moment when the door opened to his knock, Ronan was certain only of Alice's astonishment – at his appearance probably, for she had switched on the outside light to reveal him squinting against its glare, dishevelled, and surely a little sinister even. Blood was drying in a brownish crust over his left eye, the skin around the cut was jaundiced and blue, his muddy trousers gave off a damp stink as he opened his hands in a gesture of dismayed self-revelation. 'My car won't start,' he said. 'I'm sorry.' His hands, he saw, were grubby and raw.

'Dear God,' she answered, 'look at the state of you!'

He glanced, ashamed, away.

'That's a nasty graze. It needs cleaning.'

'If I could just use the phone . . .'

'No point. Come in. Let me take a look at it.'

She turned and led the way into the kitchen where she took a first-aid box from a wall-cupboard before plugging in an electric kettle. Then she pulled a stick-back chair from under the table and ordered him to sit down in the light where she could see what she was doing.

He stopped at the kitchen door, declining aid. Plainly she did not understand. Some explanation must be made; but by then he lacked the clarity, the heart, the will. 'I think it's best if I just clear off,' he said. 'But I need a phone. I can't get the engine to turn over.'

Alice said, 'I've taken the spark-plugs out. Now come and sit down while I look at your head.'

'You've done what?'

'I didn't want you to leave without seeing me.'

A smell of antiseptic sharpened the air. It might have been an exhalation of the woman's astringent smile. Her tone suggested that no explanation could be more plausible or less exceptionable. She held a cotton swab against a bottle's tipped mouth. 'Come here,' she insisted. 'Let me cause you pain.'

That the old woman might be mad dawned now as an alarming possibility across Ronan's bloodshot mind. But surely this was disproportionate? Not mad, but batty – yes,

139

the fey, autocratic battiness of a lifelong eccentric. In any case, she must be humoured; and then made to hand over his plugs, quickly. With luck they might be undamaged. But he couldn't count on luck these days, so he might still need to use her telephone. What were the chances of getting a new set of plugs on a Saturday night? Not good, he thought, not good at all. And even if a set were available, how far would it have to come across this derelict peninsula? How long would it take? The calculations would not stay in place. His head ached with the wound, with the stress of his predicament. His stomach was faint, making him irascible and rash. It was an effort even to stand. Ronan remembered making his leap from the stone in the stream, but everything since was a blur inside his mind, and he was unsure how much later, or in what strange land, he had come eventually back to earth.

'Be sensible,' Alice distantly recommended. 'If you turned up anywhere else looking like that they wouldn't let you in.' And so, finding in that bewildered moment no reasonable option, he crossed to the proffered chair. He heard her tutting over him as she examined the wound. He caught the warm smell of wool off her cardigan, then the stinging tang of antiseptic. When her crabby hands swabbed the cut he sucked his breath. 'How did this happen?' she chided.

'Does it matter?'

'Was it Leah?'

'No.'

'I see.'

He was reduced to a disagreeable boy by her attentions. 'Why are you doing this?' he demanded. 'What do you want?'

She unpeeled a plaster and applied it with gentle force. 'Justice,' she said.

The word hissed on the air, no more than a whisper, but

she was standing over him and it was close enough to catch. Its abstraction startled and bothered him. It made no sense. When he opened his eyes everything in the kitchen was too sharply outlined. The yellow and tangerine heads of the African marigolds in a green glass vase on the window-sill were fierce and brash. His throat was very dry.

Then the front door rattled open and a woman's voice called, 'It's only me.'

'We're in here, Dora,' Alice answered, and a moment later the woman with white dandelion hair came through into the kitchen, wearing the same disreputable tennis shoes he'd spotted earlier. 'I've been talking to old Reg Sessions,' she was already saying, 'he's in a terrible state after all that questioning.' Then her eyes fell on Ronan and at once the familiar kitchen became entirely unreliable.

'We were just about to have a cup of tea,' said Alice. 'Will you join us?'

The cleaning-lady's eyes briskly skirted the man's continuing existence, though she took in the plaster at his temple and the dishevelled state of his clothes before giving a dubious nod of assent. Her face had lengthened, her eyes were askance. She said, 'Have you warmed the pot or shall I?'

Ronan got up from the chair. The room bristled with unspoken questions, but as Dora took over the tea-making, Alice blandly forestalled him. 'You really should get out of those wet trousers. You'll catch your death.'

Mrs Pascoe turned, wide-eyed at the suggestion.

Ronan's scowl withered under Alice's mild gaze. 'Look, things have . . . They haven't worked out well for me. I was at the end of my tether when the car wouldn't start. If there'd been anywhere else to go . . .' She did not respond. He blundered on, touching the plaster at his temple, loathing this public attention to the most intimate failure of

141

his life. 'Will you tell Leah I didn't mean . . .' But the moment foundered on silence. He tried again. 'Just say I'm sorry. Tell her I'm sorry for everything.' He lifted his hand from the chair-back, declaring his intention to leave. 'I really have to go.'

Alice said, 'But you can't, can you?'

The thought that he might be hallucinating trembled across his mind; but the trousers were moist against his thighs, he could smell their damp heat, and the hands of the kitchen clock stood at a plausible time. He decided that reality checked. If there was craziness here surely it belonged not to him but to this old woman? He saw then that she had designs on his mind. He saw that this place was no more a refuge than the cabin in the rock where he'd dreamed the bad dream and hit his head. He said, 'I think you'd better give me my plugs,' but if Alice heard the unpleasant change in his voice she disregarded it. She turned her smile on him: he saw the danger in it.

She said, 'You didn't come all this way for nothing, did you?'

His gaze backed away to glance at the scarcely saner figure of the cleaning-lady who mopped a spotless surface with a green sponge. Dismay was as evident as curiosity in her frown, and both were subsumed within a general mistrust. There was no help available there, no point in appealing to reason. Again he tried to outstare Alice. 'I've had a hell of a day. I'm very tired, very upset. I just want to get away from here.'

'Taking your defeat with you? What good will that do? You'll only become more of a menace to your kind. I can't countenance that. It's not my way.'

From the spout of the electric kettle, steam hustled the silent air. Then the switch clicked off.

He must have been swaying a little as, with no logical

force but with absolute premonitory conviction, a thought entered his mind. It was simply this: *If I stay here I will die.*

Meanwhile, as if to confirm his growing conviction that time had broken down and everything that should never have happened at all was happening at once, the telephone began to ring. Mrs Pascoe muttered, 'I'll get it,' and hurried out.

He could feel sweat rising at his neck. The subdued menace in his voice sounded hoarse and far as he said, 'Don't you think you'd better hand them over now?'

Amazingly she made no move. He couldn't tell what she was thinking or feeling, except that the foolish woman apparently took a weaver's unhurried view of time and had no idea how desperate the man she was dealing with. Her hooded eyes were weirdly imbricated in shadow. Stupidly he said, 'You really can't do this kind of thing.' But she had done it, the thing was done, and he had no notion what queer fantasy of power had possessed her mind. He understood only that he was trammelled in its consequences. Even his words seemed determined by a pre-existing script as he progressed to the first open threat. 'Do you want me to call the police?'

Alice smiled at that. 'I think you'll find they have more serious things on their mind. They won't appreciate being brought out here over a practical joke. Now let me pour this tea.' She turned her back. Cups chattered to their saucers as she took them down from the dresser. Then Mrs Pascoe shouted from the hall. 'It's Amy. She wants to know if she can come over and spend the night.'

'You'd better tell her that it's not the most convenient time.'

'I already have, but she sounds frightened half to death. Her parents are out, she's on her own at Perangarth and she says a bat's got in. She's all on her own in that big house and she can't stand it fluttering about. She says if she can't come here she's biking down into Porthmallion to find her friends.'

'She shouldn't do that.' Alice looked across at Ronan as if in silent consultation, then she raised her voice. 'In fact, thinking about it . . . Yes, it's all right. Tell her to come.'

'But she might run into . . . you know. On the way, I mean.'

'Tell her to use her bike and not to stop for anybody.' Mrs Pascoe was already speaking into the phone as Alice added, 'And remind her not to forget her toothbrush this time.' She shook her head at Ronan – 'The girl's a complete scatter-brain' – and so conversational was her tone that for a deceptive moment he could imagine things much as they'd been that morning when they sat over coffee in the tranquil parlour discussing the allegory of the heart. He was filled with nostalgia for that vanished age when neither hope nor eager trepidation were yet extinguished. He tried to reclaim a touch of its lost amity now. 'This is crazy,' he said. 'I'm sure you mean well, but there's no point. Leah must have told you what happened.'

Alice glanced up from where she poured his tea. 'I haven't heard your side of the story.'

For an instant, across a generation, across the black gash torn in his life, her voice soothed him with understanding. *Relax*, it said, *drop your guard; there is wisdom here and sympathy.* He had done so once already that day. Why not again? In these desolate extremities, when so little around him was stable or trustworthy, was he not entitled to a morsel of comfort? Then, with a contrary recoil he detected what might also be her prying condescension. Coldly he snapped, 'I don't think it's any of your business.'

'I'm sorry,' she said, unruffled, 'I didn't think to ask whether you take milk.'

144

'Just give me my damned plugs.' Again he heard his own voice, the ugliness in it. Infuriated as much by her composure as by the studied disregard, he briefly saw himself through her deliberate eyes: a man whose behaviour offered no standard of sanity, one in a barely suppressed state of great emotional confusion, a muddy fool. Subverted thus by his own dislocated perspectives, there was only one certainty: he must get out.

He said, 'Or I can take this place apart.'

The whole room should have been shocked to attention, every drawer and crevice rigid at the prospect of being roughly frisked. Alice simply shrugged. 'I wonder if you know how many rooms and sheds there are, not to mention fourteen acres of garden and glen? But do feel free.'

Tense with exasperation, Ronan turned in appeal to the nervous cleaning-lady who averted her eyes, evidently ignorant of the object of his demand – what plugs could he mean?

'This stupid woman', he said, 'has removed the spark-plugs from my car. Don't ask me why. Anyone in their right mind would want me out of here. That's all I ask – to be allowed to go. But I can't get any sense out of her. I think you'd better try, because if not . . .'

Even as he spoke Ronan saw himself ransacking this tidy kitchen, and the picture made no better sense than Alice's behaviour. His hands were white at the back of the chair, his head was clanging like a belfry. He observed the exchange of glances between the two women, and he saw dread gathering in Mrs Pascoe's countenance as Alice said, 'It's all right, Dora. Leave this to me.' Otherwise the situation remained unchanged.

But the night had grown big outside. He thought of the tide crashing through the blow-hole, of the stream plummeting down the fall; he saw himself clinging to a rock-face, struggling not to be swept away – all of this in an instant which barely ruffled the surface of consciousness. Then he remembered that Leah must be somewhere in the house. His heart lurched at the thought; but she, he knew, would want none of this, she would want him out of there, out of her life. If he needed help extricating himself from this mad situation, it was she for whose sake he had come here who would, with a last foreclosing irony, provide it. Every muscle in his face was clenched as he said, 'Leah doesn't know about this, does she?' and caught the first uncertain flicker in Alice's eyes. 'I think I'd better speak to her.'

Nimbly Alice moved to cover the door. She stood with the tip of her chin raised. When he said, 'Would you get out of my way?' her unflinching gaze silently demanded whether, in addition to his other delinquencies, he was prepared to use violence against an elderly woman. And, oh dear God, it was a question to be asked; for if he was the decent man he believed himself to be, then who was this grim bastard threatening her now? He no more wished to harm Alice than he'd wanted to hurt Leah; yet both thwarted him in ways that left him estranged from himself. They allowed no room. 'Why are you doing this?' he demanded. 'Why are you making me act like this?'

'I see,' Alice reflected calmly. 'Isn't it extraordinary how soon it becomes our fault? No doubt something similar was said to the girl they found this morning.'

For the second time that day the face of a raped and murdered woman was conjured into Ronan's mind. He saw its blood and bruises, the damaged, unseeing eyes. Every detail was briefly impressed on his imagination with the precision of a forensic photograph. Instantly he sensed that Alice saw it too. There was a presence – an almost tangible, intolerable presence – between them. For a split second his hand might have been raised either to fend the image off or

146

to hit the wrinkled, undefended face of the old woman across from him. But to Dora Pascoe only one of those possibilities had reality. Ronan heard the shock of her indrawn breath across the kitchen. His hand continued upwards to close across his wound.

And Alice released her own pent breath. 'You look awful,' she said after a moment. 'You really should sit down.' When he opened his eyes she was staring into his face. She must have seen the moral exhaustion there, the physical distress; but something else was happening too, for it was as if, for the first time, she had seen the situation from the outside and been shocked by what she saw. Or perhaps it had occurred to her that she was trying to short-circuit a process which could evolve, if at all, only of its own volition? In any case her face had clouded with questions – had she read things wrong? What would Leah make of this? What authority did she have to interfere in other people's lives this way? She sighed then. Her shoulders sagged.

All three of them jumped as the rap of a door-knocker sounded through the house. 'That can't be Amy already,' Mrs Pascoe muttered.

'Would you go and see?' said Alice, smiling in re-assurance when her friend wondered whether she would be all right on her own with this unpredictable man. As soon as she and Ronan were alone she said, 'I'm filled with pity for your wife,' and left him smarting for a time.

'But you're right', she added before he could speak, '– it was wrong of me to detain you here against your will. Obviously it was pointless too.' She crossed to the dresser, took the spark-plugs from a drawer and rolled them across the table. 'Do you have a spanner,' she said, 'or do you wish to borrow mine?'

Ronan stood baffled and angry under her contempt – struck also by a pang of disappointment at this sudden backing-down. He wasn't ready for it, he felt no triumph, only frustration. It was as if he'd somehow failed to qualify for her further persecution, was deemed unworthy of it. Yet he was left alone in the universe with this difficult old woman; and if he felt an unrequited need to justify himself before her, to compel some vestige of respect, he had left it too late, for Mrs Pascoe was back in the doorway with a fraught mix of alarm and vindication on her face.

'It's the police,' she was saying as she stared directly at Ronan for the first time since her arrival at the house. 'They want to talk to you.'

7
CRIME

His first thought was accident: that this older man wearing an unbuttoned overcoat and thick-rimmed glasses, and the younger, bulkier figure with a quarrelsome moustache, had come bearing terrible news. It would concern one of the children, or his wife; or perhaps, in a disaster consistent with the malign character of this hideous weekend, all three had been taken from him while his back was turned. For what else could have brought the police in search of him across the country? But it occurred to him almost immediately that the duty of bringing such news would fall to the uniformed branch, and these men – both of whom appraised him without sympathy and with no other sign of creaturely feeling – were detectives in plain clothes.

The blood drained from Ronan's face as he remembered the swan. He saw the white apocalyptic wings go down under the wheels of his car. Somehow Alice must have learned of it. She had told the police where he was and detained him there till their arrival. Now he would be charged with slaughtering one of the queen's beasts; already his face was a confession of guilt. In no shape to defend himself, he would be taken away. And, look, the older man was greeting Alice in familiar tones. They knew each other; they were in impossible collusion after all, though briefly the policeman let his eyes drift round the room with the discriminating attention of a prospective buyer before they settled on Ronan. Then he introduced himself, politely, enough, as Detective Inspector George Nankevill of the local CID. 'And you, sir,' he asked, 'would you be the owner of the vehicle in the lane outside?'

Ronan could do no more than nod.

'Then I wonder if we might have a few words?' Moments later Ronan was supplying information with which, at that deranging time, he felt only tenuous connection: his name and address. Both sounded odd on the air. Yes, he had once known a man of that name who did indeed live at that place, but he had lost touch with him some months ago, they were estranged, it felt unfair to be made to answer for him.

'So can I ask,' the Inspector pressed, while his attendant sergeant sucked his teeth in the doorway, 'what brings you to Cornwall?'

A compulsion, Ronan thought, *so powerful that a man of your phlegmatic temperament could scarcely begin to understand it. A kind of madness in the heart, one distinguished by the pathetic and desperate belief that life remained a possibility for him here. He had come like Orpheus to reclaim lost hope, lost love.* But Ronan gave no such truthful account of himself. Weakly he said, 'It's a sort of holiday, I suppose.'

'I see. Do you mind telling me what sort?'

'Actually I came to see a friend.'

'I see. A friend. So am I to understand you're staying here?'

'No.'

'Then where?'

'Last night you mean? I was booked into a hotel.'

'A hotel?'

'In Porthmallion. The Anchor.'

Some minimal change — the slightest flicker of the

150

Inspector's eyelid, a tautening of attention? – brought Ronan up short. Instantly he understood what this must be about. Not the swan after all; nobody cared about the swan any more, for far more terrible slaughter had been recently done. How could he have forgotten? His sigh of relief was audible. 'But why are you questioning *me*?' he asked, as if the real nature of these enquiries, and therefore of his utter innocence, had now been established between them.

'We're interviewing a number of people, sir. If you'll just bear with me.'

'Yes, but . . .'

'Am I to understand you stayed at the Anchor all night? You didn't go out at all?'

'I went out for a walk.'

'Around what time would that be?'

'Seven. Or seven-thirty. I didn't check my watch.'

'And where did you go, sir?'

'Along the cliffs outside Porthmallion, but . . .'

'And you got back about what time?'

'Late,' Ronan equivocated, for a greenish stormy light had just broken across his mind. He caught his first glimpse of hazardous horizons. 'I got something to eat at a pub along the coast and had a drink or two. Then I got a bit lost.'

'So how late would you say?'

'God, I don't know. I didn't expect to be questioned.'

'I understand, sir.' The Inspector looked away, then back. 'Would you say before or after midnight, for instance?'

To be truthful or not, when truth could only darken counsel? It seemed at once impossible that he should find himself on such treacherous ground, and at the same time, given the general decomposition of his universe, utterly inevitable. Ronan's hand went to his head. He was no longer convinced that the time of which he spoke had any verifiable links with reality, for too many complicated

151

things had happened since, and it was in another country, and besides the wench was dead. 'After, I suppose,' he murmured vaguely. 'Yes it must have been after. I was wandering about for a long time.'

'That was when you hurt your head, was it?'

'No, that was today. Not more than an hour ago.'

Nothing in Nankevill's face revealed whether he credited this answer. The question itself might have been no more than a gesture of passing sympathy, for he picked up one of the spark-plugs from the table and casually examined its condition before saying, 'I'm sorry to hear that, sir.'

But if it was obvious why the police might take a lively interest in a lone male roaming the cliffs late the previous night, only now, when he was already compromised by his earlier prevarications, did Ronan guess how they had come to single him out. Images flickered through his mind – the previous day's events which had become the obsolete currency of a discredited regime. 'Unless . . .' He uttered a nervous, dismissive snort, picturing the nervous woman at the bend of the stairs in the hotel. 'Oh God, yes. Of course. You must have spoken to the people there? That's it, isn't it?' If he was pleased by this evidence of resumed mental acuity, the relief it brought was instantly dispelled by Nankevill's quick, sceptical glance across to his colleague. No one but Ronan seemed impressed by his remaining powers. He thought, *They obviously have no idea what it's like in here*. Then he added, 'I suppose it must have looked a bit strange. Especially in the circumstances.'

'What's that, sir?'

'My not being able to get back in till the doors were opened this morning.'

'Is that what happened? You remember that now?'

'I remembered before, but . . .'

When the tardy admission expired, the Inspector said, 'I

suppose you had your reasons for not wanting to tell us, sir?'

Ronan looked up in appeal to the arched, disbelieving brows. 'Anybody would have done the same in my position.'

'I'm still not quite clear what that position is.'

'Come on, Inspector. Innocence is notoriously difficult to prove, right?' He stood there with his palms open: they were bloodless but dirty. 'It just gets confusing, doesn't it?'

'If people don't tell us the truth as they know it?' The policeman judged his pause. 'Yes, you might say that.'

'So now we know where we are,' said the other man, 'I wonder if anything else comes to mind?'

Exhausted, frustrated, doubly cornered and confused, Ronan lost patience then. 'I don't remember killing anybody, if that's what you mean.'

Eventually the Inspector sighed. 'It's been a long day, sir. I'm trying to be polite, as I've already been with a lot of other people today. So if you'd just like to tell us what you do remember about last night.'

What he remembered was the instant when his gaze met hers across the public bar and recognition seared his mind. One could imagine a stroke like that. And she was, he realized, his only alibi; and for only a brief part of the night. The rest was undocumented, without witness. Fog. And if her testimony were invoked what could it show but an obsessed, unstable man?

Ronan heard another little snorting laugh on the air. From the Inspector's beetling frown he saw that he was himself the source of it. Now it was clear: he had been singled out by capricious powers. They were toying with him. One escaped from each of their traps only to fall immediately into another; such was the ingenious design of their machine. He saw hours of interrogation stretch ahead of him as his life unravelled under scrutiny. It might take weeks. It might take for ever, for when he examined his recent behaviour through alien eyes it appeared unaccountable. Already he could hear question after question gruellingly repeated as each honest answer further embroiled him. He could predict every doubt. Only the stones of the cliff could attest to his innocence and they were dumb. Nor would the stars speak up on his behalf.

'Whether you saw anybody, for instance,' the Inspector suggested.

In pent silence Ronan tried to calculate whether the same wretched truth that had brought him under suspicion might serve to clear him of it. There was no choice. 'The friend, the one I came to see,' he said.

'Ah yes, the friend.'

'In fact, I remember explaining to the woman at the hotel. I told her I'd seen a friend.'

George Nankevill adjusted his glasses on the bridge of his nose. 'Does this friend have a name?'

'He means me.'

Ronan looked up in amazement at the sound of Alice's voice.

Again the pace of events accelerated. Reality slipped further on its winch as, with a wrinkled smile under the white shock of hair, Alice said to the policeman, 'I'm afraid you're off on the wrong scent, George, but I think I can clear things up.' She would have added more but, out in the hall, the front door rattled open, and a voice called, 'Can I leave my bike in here? I think it might rain before the night's out.' A jingling of spokes suggested that permission had been anticipated.

Alice widened apologetic eyes. 'Oh dear, more confusion! I'm afraid it's a young friend from across the glen. Her parents are out and she got frightened so I told her to come over here. That was before this business, of course.' At the same time Amy was saying, 'Do you know there's a police-car parked outside? What's going on?' Coming to a surprised halt in the kitchen doorway, she scrutinized the sergeant's moustache with unembarrassed suspicion.

Alice said, 'Amy darling, these gentlemen are police officers. There's been a mix-up which I'm just about to straighten out. I wonder if you'd be an angel and help Dora scrub some potatoes while I have a private word with the Inspector in the other room?'

For a thoughtful moment Amy surveyed this question-able occasion, then she unzipped her stylish parka. 'Sure, whatever,' she said, and smiled across at Ronan. 'You're still here then? What've you done to your head?'

By now he was too bewildered to reply, for Alice had taken the Inspector by the arm and was crooning, 'Do come through.' Dubious, unprepared for the manoeuvre, Nankevill hesitated, then narrowed his eyes at his sub-ordinate before yielding to the pressure at his arm. Ronan, meanwhile, was staring at Amy's hair, for against the dense blue-black of the kitchen-window, its flow of light seemed to illustrate the way his once reliable sense of the real had dissolved around him into an unfamiliar sub-stance with the consistency of honey in a jar. He could no longer remember what he was doing here, or how this delirious day had evolved in such a way that his head hurt, the spark-plugs from his car lay on Alice's kitchen-table, Leah had vanished off the face of the earth, the police had cause to be interested in him, and Alice was now presum-ably – and for what eerie reason? – telling them lies. Ever since he'd woken from the dream the world had been lurching between menace and farce. His head felt scoured by the indignity of existence; beneath the fat plaster his wound shone with its pain.

155

Puzzled by his glazed stare, a little worried by it, Amy turned to Mrs Pascoe. 'What's going on?'

'You heard Alice.'

'She didn't say anything.'

'She said to scrub the spuds.'

'Where's Leah?'

Mrs Pascoe leaned to a low cupboard, took out a bag filled with potatoes, and tipped several into the sink.

'Is she with Stephen?'

'I haven't been informed.'

Amy's frown made dimples. 'Does she know about . . . ?'

'No.'

'Then what's he . . . ?'

'If I knew I'd tell you. As I don't, I can't. Now are you going to help with these spuds, or not?'

'I don't get it. And what are *they* doing here?'

The cleaning-lady answered only with a significant glare. Immediately Amy caught on. 'They don't think . . . ?' And, when Dora Pascoe's expression contrived to be at once lugubrious and non-committal, she exclaimed, 'But that's crazy!' and looked back across her shoulder at Ronan. Their glances collided off each other. In this world who knew where craziness lay?

For a time the two women scrubbed in silence. When they were finished and the potatoes skewered and placed in the Aga, Dora Pascoe stared up at the silent policeman. 'I hope you've stopped bothering that nice Mr Sessions. I can't think he'd harm a fly.'

The sergeant shrugged but said nothing. There was a further exchange between Amy and Mrs Pascoe but Ronan heard nothing of it. His mind, like the significant action, was elsewhere, beyond his control, as everything in this unchancy day had passed from his control. He was aware of the policeman at the door staring at him queerly. He felt the

156

same slippage of identity that had happened in the car after he hit the swan. He was outside all this, in a separate cocoon. Even his own body was a distant relative, not well these days, neglected, rotten with self-pity. There was a gauzy screen between his mind and the curious world out there: two women uneasy in a kitchen, a policeman looking on, all of them unaware that the suspect across the room was losing his grip on what they took for reality.

Then things were happening again. There was a crackling under the sergeant's raincoat. Frowning, he folded back the lapel to reveal a radio strapped at his shoulder, and turned away to listen to the message fizzing across the air-waves. Ronan strained to hear, but at that moment the parlour door opened and Alice was saying, 'Are you quite sure you won't have some tea?' The sergeant forestalled his superior's answer in some excitement – 'Could I have a word, sir?' – and Alice left them in the hall where the policemen conferred in whispers until the sergeant nodded and left the house.

The Inspector studied Ronan for a moment with a kind of wonder in those bleak, bagged eyes. 'I'm sorry to have troubled you, sir, but in cases like this we can't take any chances.' He smiled at Alice. 'I needn't tell you ladies to carry on taking sensible precautions. Good night now.'

Alice said, 'I'll see you out, George,' and Ronan stared, baffled, at the disappearing backs. Amy smirked at Mrs Pascoe, who despaired of comprehension. A waft of sweet dark air entered the house. Then the front door clicked shut again, and Alice came back into the kitchen blowing through puffed cheeks as if the short walk had worn her out. Without speaking she poured herself a cup of tea, then sat down in the rocking chair by the Aga, gathering silence round her like a shawl.

'So is someone going to tell me what's going on?' Amy asked.

Without opening her eyes Alice said quietly, 'Have you got a cigarette, Amy?'

'Yes, but . . .'

'Light one for me, would you?'

Amy did as she was bidden and was about to light another for herself when Alice said, 'We don't smoke in the house,' and drew deeply on her own cigarette.

'But . . .'

'Don't argue with me, Amy. I've had a very difficult day.' As she spoke the old woman studied Ronan with an air of puzzled distaste. 'Well,' she demanded, 'what are you waiting for?'

The plugs on the table glinted at him, anomalous there, spare parts from the infernal contraption in which he'd been trapped, and from which he could not yet believe himself quite free. He felt sure that if he picked them up and tried to leave with them, some fresh and more sinister obstacle would present itself. He heard Alice say, 'You wanted to leave – leave. Nobody's stopping you.' But for the moment not even his lips would move, and in the middle-distance Amy was saying, 'He doesn't look at all well to me.'

At last he said, 'What did you tell the police?'

'Lies, of course. A convenient fiction. One that covered the facts more or less.'

'But why?' he whispered. 'Why should you do that?'

'Not for your sake, I assure you.'

And at that point Dora Pascoe gave a gratified sigh of realization. 'You didn't want him dragging Leah into it!'

'I think he's done her harm enough as it is.'

'What's he done?' Amy demanded.

There was a considered, accusing silence which Ronan smashed with his snarl. 'You wouldn't understand the first thing about it.' For an instant it was as if all the air in the kitchen had been sucked into his rage. He watched the

158

shock on Amy's face. It left him dizzy with shame, with loathing. Everything he touched seemed to shrivel and char. There was no reprieve, not here, not anywhere.

'I doubt that very much,' Alice calmly retorted while he stood swaying there. 'Everybody here understands perfectly well when a crime has been committed against love.'

Each motion in the room was evident to him. Fascinated by the scrawny wobble of her throat, he watched Alice draw on her cigarette. 'And don't think it wasn't a temptation to let those people take you away,' she was saying. 'But it wouldn't have been justice – not my idea of it anyway.' Blue smoke swirled around her face, her hair was wreathed in it. 'They only understand courts of law. I had something different in mind.' He saw regret in the soft curl of her lip, he observed the sadness wrinkling at her eyes as she said, 'I was offering you a little time in a Court of Love. I think you might have found its ordeals kinder than the slow death of the heart.'

Even as she spoke he was reaching out with what remained of his will to gather the spark-plugs from the table, but the bleakness in that last phrase stopped him short. It lodged inside him. It echoed down the empty days to come. Somewhere, inwardly, a voice was protesting that these women knew nothing about him, they didn't know how deeply he'd loved Leah, what she meant to him, that she had been his very life; and though every silent painful word it spoke was true, he could no longer feel the force of it. By now he felt as little identity with that inward defendant as with the outward body looking out into the room, where a pallid woman with drawn cheeks and hair like the seed-head of a dandelion was glowering at him through narrowed eyes, while the strangely melting face of a younger woman gazed in fascination as she waited for the imminent moment of his collapse.

159

'My life,' a distant, failing voice was trying to insist, 'my whole damned life was staked on this.'

'What does he mean?' he heard Amy asking. 'He's right – I *don't* understand. What's he done?' When her questions went unanswered, she looked at Ronan, directly, undaunted. 'It's between you and Leah, isn't it?' she urged. 'What's happened?'

Ronan closed his eyes against the frank demand. His vision swivelled inward to the cove where, under a candid blue sky, a man was standing some distance away from a woman who sat among the rocks with her feet in a shallow pool. The man's hands were held together in a gesture of imprecation. 'I know it won't be easy,' he was saying. 'I know it's going to take time.'

'We had time,' she retorted. 'I can't go through it again.'

'But you won't have to. Everything's different now.'

'For you. But what about my feelings? Where are they in all of this?' Her face seemed bleak with the thought that they spoke only enough of the same language to create delirious occasions for misunderstanding.

'Didn't you say it yourself a moment ago?' he reminded her gently, ' – that vision you spoke of, the certainty you once had that we'd find our way through. It was real – the realest thing in both our lives.'

'Then why did you let it go?'

'Because I was scared. I was running scared. I couldn't handle the complexity – of being truthful with both of you, I mean. Or with myself even. I wanted to have it all, but without hurting anybody. I wanted not to have to choose.'

Her face declared all of this already known. She knew it to be the truth; she also knew it to be less than the whole truth, but what the larger, undisclosed, perhaps for ever inaccessible truth might be – this evidently remained a

160

mystery no less painful to her now than it had been throughout their time together. So she preserved a reclusive silence, hearing the stubborn labour of his breath.

'But I can't be without you,' he avowed at last. 'Not any more. I don't care what else I have to give up.' There, it was said. A whole world was abolished by that declaration. He quivered with the shock of it. 'It feels as though I'm up against something final now,' he said. 'My life depends on it.'

Patiently the day hovered above her continued silence while his future slowly turned on an axis there. He could hear the sea. When he looked up into her face again the skin had a softer bloom, her lips were open. He reached out a hand. 'Your hair,' he whispered as though in final proof of all the errors they had made, 'look what you did to your hair.'

Reflexively her hand moved to her head. But it had been her choice, that drastic cut, her own choice freely made, a sign both of severance and of self-possession. Why could he not accept it? What was there here that she dare believe? Flinching away as he moved towards her, she said, 'I'm not even sure it's really me you're looking for,' and when he replied that there was no one else she shook her head helplessly – 'That's not what I mean' – though she was unclear what other meaning might be evolving there.

'Don't you see?' he insisted. 'We need one another. We *are* one another.'

No cloud had crossed the sun but there seemed, in the woman, an equivalent diminution of the light. Surely *he* must see how such claims eclipsed her? For an instant, they were overwhelmed by the same wave of sadness. She withdrew further inside herself, lifting her feet from the pool and laying her head against the slender arms folded at her knees. Baffled by what he took as her wilful refusal to

161

respond, he demanded, 'This is what you wanted, isn't it? I'm putting everything on the line. Not just my own life.'

She caught her breath, thinking that she would give up this empty freedom without a moment's thought if she could feel his full presence there, calling her into meeting; but there was no such sense of imminent completion, no faith that if she let go she would be wholly met. Something vital was arrested still. It felt prior to all words, almost primitive in its simplicity; and whatever this unnamed, receptive, stupidly persevering aspect of her being was, it remained, for all his vows and claims, unanswered.

She said, 'Does Marion know you're here?'

'In Cornwall? Yes.'

But he had betrayed himself.

'Does she know you're with me?'

This time he did not answer, and she surprised herself by laughing softly – a weary, incredulous little chuckle that shuddered out of her as a tolerable substitute for tears. He was about to justify himself but she prevented it by saying, 'There's nothing for you here. Nothing except what you're finding inside yourself. Go home, Ronan.'

But what was she asking – that he drag his wife and children into disaster without the faintest promise she would be there when the smoke of ruin cleared? His bewilderment came as an accusation of impossibility. 'I don't understand you. I don't understand what more you want.'

'From you?' Even as she spoke she hated the cruelty of it. 'I don't want anything.'

Yet he was offering his life, everything was at stake. He opened his lips to speak, but in the same moment she glanced at her watch. 'From who then?' he veered bitterly. 'The man I saw you with last night?'

For an instant he could have bitten off his tongue; then he

thought, why not? Let the passion show in all its murky heat. Things were always truest at temperature between them. Flame was where they lived. 'I know you slept with him last night,' he hazarded. 'It doesn't alter anything. We're part of one another, you and me. I know you, Leah. I know your very soul.'

'You know nothing about me.' The sentence scalded from her lips, then she leapt up, staring at him, panting defiance, and turned away, making for the dark cleft in the promontory of rock from which she'd first appeared. He moved more quickly, striding across the slab, jumping from one ledge to another, to leap down in her path where she halted a yard or two away. Both were breathing quickly. Against the swish of the surf everything was very still. She said quietly, 'Let me go, Ronan.'

'I can't. I don't believe it's what you want.'

Glancing away across the strand, her eyes started to remember fear. She turned back towards the sea.

Suddenly his arms were at her waist, restraining, pulling her round to face him. From his vantage-point of larger understanding he was smiling down at her. 'It's all right. I know I've hurt you. I know how bad it was. But we'll get it right this time. I love you, Leah. We can come back to our senses now.' He leaned to kiss her shoulder, the sleek silk felt cool against his lips. When he raised his face she stared into the encroaching eyes, then twisted to avoid the search of his mouth as the pressure at her spine increased. He murmured her name, felt the knock of her heart, her breath warm against him. He was sure it must soon be easy again, this flow of sensuality between them. 'There's so much good to remember as well,' he whispered. 'Can't we hold on to that?'

'There are things that still tear me apart when I let myself think about them.' And then, having tried vainly to pull away, she stared straight into his eyes as she said, 'I think something died inside me for ever when I had the abortion,' and for a moment the sea might have frozen in its tracks. Her eyes were gripped against the tears. After this long time she would not let him see them now.

'I know,' he whispered, 'I know.' But it was not enough, and though he knew exactly where her feelings had taken her, his mouth was packed with silence. Time was passing. There was, he felt, no remedy in words. If everything was not to go wrong he must somehow extinguish speech, pass beyond it to the place where he might offer softer comfort, draw her back inside the dream. He pulled her gently towards him, whispering her name.

She said, 'I don't want you touching me.'

But why else should she have brought him to this lonely place where not a soul could see them? He had been sure he sensed her barely suppressed excitement when they set out together down the glen; he was sure he had felt the desire – however tremulous and disguised – for meeting. He was sure he could feel it still, but there was a tiny screech of silk as she tried to pull away. A button had come free in his hand, its hole had ripped. He could see the hollows at her collar-bones, for in the shock of this sudden unintended damage she had slipped his grip, and was lurching away towards the sea.

He reached her in five strides, grasped at a slender arm, slipped, lost his balance and brought them both down on the sand, where they lay for a time, shaken by the impact. Though his full body-weight had fallen across her legs, he knew she was unharmed. He even uttered a little laugh at their ungainliness. He heard it crackle on the air. Then he wrenched himself upright, shifted his weight on to his hands, and was looking down at her. One of her arms was stretched as though reaching for a mottled stone that lay nearby; the other held white knuckles at her mouth. She was rigid on the sand, the skirt rucked at her thighs. With a pang of regret he realized that the torn button was lost. He wondered whether she could feel the heat of him, the confusion; that he had desired this without expecting it; that they were an accident which had seized its chance to happen, she the casualty, he the shocked perpetrator, assessing consequences, who must be overwhelmingly big against the sky.

There was a warm smell of sunlight on sand. He stroked back the quiff of her hair, seemingly less indifferent to her distress than unaware of it. 'It's all right,' he whispered. 'We're together now. You can let go.' His fingertips traced the contour of her cheek, he was fascinated by the colours in her eyes. He saw them wince as she felt the push of his erection.

Only her voice had room to move. 'Don't do this, Ronan.' But his hand moved on. 'I can't breathe. You're hurting me.'

'Don't fight it, Leah. It's what we both want.' The closure of his mouth on hers silenced protest and she gasped for breath against the intrusion of his tongue. Then her head twisted aside. Her hips threw off his hand. There was spittle on her chin. He was nuzzling at torn green silk as, with a driven will of its own, his hand moved back to her thigh.

Leah brought her fist down hard against his ear, she heard him gasp. Ronan pulled back, covering his immediate dismay with another laugh that sounded derisive of her spirit. She hated him for that. From a place beyond volition, her hand lifted again and cracked across his face, hurting him, she wanted to hurt him, to make him feel something real if it was only pain – no, particularly pain. She wanted him to understand pain. But when her angle of vision widened she saw his face all white offended fury. For an instant both of them quailed in the shock-waves of this sudden violence; then he pushed her down against the sand and was kneeling over her.

If there was a mind at work in there its workings made no sense to her. She struggled to throw him off, but he pinned her hands and his body-weight pressed the air from her stomach, so she could only snarl at him to leave her alone. When he failed to move, insults came spitting from her tongue, her voice was ugly with hurt and frustration. He wanted to shut her up, to put a stop to this vileness, was staring down in anger and dismay, uncertain how genuine her fury. When he saw that it was undeniably so – that all her lithe strength was knotted up to rid herself of him – cold things began to happen in his mind. Shocked by his excitement, by a sudden access of power, he looked down where she lay trapped beneath him. This was real as nothing had been real for months. They were back where they belonged, on elemental ground. She was his, had always been his. Need and passion, ferocity and tenderness had left them deeply interfused; and if he couldn't have her, whispered a compelling voice inside him, no one else would have her either. But it hadn't yet come to that; nor need it. Ronan shifted his centre of gravity. With calculated force he thrust himself against her groin.

She gasped at the brutality, wondering what she had done so wrong that a body she had once loved with such care, with such utterly vulnerable devotion, should turn into a weapon that meant her harm. 'Don't,' she whispered, but he lowered his mouth to silence her again. Already the thumb of one hand had wrenched the side of her knickers down across her hip, the fingers were closing over her groin, and still he said nothing. Winded by shock and fear, she was numb, sickened, unable to help herself.

He felt her body go briefly lax beneath him. Look, he was right after all! Time only for the honesty of bodies now, nothing held back, no half-truths, no duplicity, no lies. He felt the sun's heat on his head. There was the pleasing warmth of sunlight here, and the arriving urgency of the sea. He uttered her name, over and over, in reclamation, until he heard the hoarse whisper of her voice above the surf. 'Is this what you want? Is that why you came all this way, to do this to me again, like last time, whether I want it or not? Well do it then. I can't stop you. I can't stop you any more than that poor girl last night could stop what happened to her. So go on, do it if that's what you want' – and when her face twisted towards him the white features were tense with scorn – 'but you'll find I might just as well be as dead as she is.'

Ronan was frowning, hot, confused. Something terrible had been said which he didn't understand. Like the first sag of a detonated building before it toppled, there was a sensation of things collapsing round him. 'What girl?' he was saying. 'I don't know what you mean.'

She opened her eyes and took in his bewilderment. 'On the headland. You must have seen when we crossed the cliff. The police, that crowd?' Staring up at his harassed gaze, she realized his confusion unfeigned. 'You don't know?' Leah forced through her teeth a statement that stunned the air. 'A woman was raped and murdered there last night.'

'And you think I . . . ?'

His mind staggered. Perspectives were unstable now. They gave the illusion of looping through various planes until he was left looking down on himself lying over a frightened, dishevelled woman in a place he did not know. And none of this was as intended. It was all misfortunate, ill-starred. The man, he wanted to plead, had not been himself for months now, was unsettled and confused, perhaps not entirely right in his bewildered mind. Surely allowance must be made for stress, for loss, for terminal despair, for involuntary membership of a savage species?

His eyes gaped open.

Only seconds had passed, and though centuries might elapse before this situation changed he saw no possibility of forgiveness anywhere; for Leah had gone and Amy's gaze was insupportable, and when he looked away, Alice's stare was as imperious and undeceived as that of a judgment angel.

And how was it possible, he found himself wondering, that through the failure of his loving intentions towards women he should stumble into a world governed by their craziness? The thought filled him with grief, which opened on to deeper grief, a grief which must quickly prove arterial, for once released he knew it could not be staunched; it would sweep away what little remained of his strangely evacuated life.

It was needful therefore to regain control; but even as he told himself this, Ronan felt the flags of the kitchen floor shifting under him, a torrent was sounding in his head, and quite suddenly he was swept from his dark cleft, down over white rapids to a primitive, bare place where he was staring up at the featureless head of a stone-age Venus.

There was, he saw, no mercy there. In a final effort of refusal, he turned away. A door came open under his hand. He stepped through the wall of this unsafe house into the smell of night and otherworld. The sky was intensely black. Somewhere a nervous horse was whinnying; there was no other sign of it. Ronan was breathing through a needle's eye; and it was possible, he thought, as he picked his way through a turbulent darkness in which the bright stars radiated pain, that time was winding backwards on its spool.

In the kitchen the three women had watched the changes pass like weather across Ronan's face as he swayed, stammering for words at first, and then in stricken silence. Each of them felt sure he was about to collapse, and that the emotional breakdown must be physical too. Yet the man radiated a hostile power that kept them at bay while his command-centre raged in deep confusion far behind the lines. When Alice got up from her chair, he turned his face away, in shame or revulsion, it was unclear which. Perhaps he had intended only to press his face against the wall, but his forehead came to rest against the outside-door, and the hand carrying his weight found the knob of the mortice-lock, which turned, and he was out in the night, leaving the door ajar and the three women standing uncertainly in the sweetly damp smell off the darkened garden.

'But he hasn't taken his plugs,' said Dora Pascoe.

'He's in no state to put them back.' Alice got up and drummed her fingertips on the pine table, trying to preserve a calm she did not feel.

'Do you think I'd better go after him?' Amy suggested.

'No. This is my responsibility.' Alice unhooked an old coat from the peg by the door and slipped her arms into it. 'He can't get far like that. I'll try and talk to him.' She took off her shoes and stepped into green rubber boots. 'Wait here and don't worry. I'll be all right.'

Dora Pascoe was about to dispute the wisdom of Alice's action when all three women jumped at the sound of the front door opening in the hall.

Standing closest to the noise, and unafraid now that she was in the company of others, Amy looked out into the hall.

'Leah,' she exclaimed, 'what are you doing?'

Alice looked up from where she reached for her stick, but heard no reply. 'Leah?' she called, agitated by her knowledge of the way sound travelled through the lath-and-plaster ceilings of this ancient house, and by the knowledge therefore that, if she had not been asleep – and how could she possibly have slept through all this activity? – Leah must have heard every word that had been said. Amy was asking, 'Where are you going?' as Alice quickly crossed the kitchen, pushed the young woman aside and, calling Leah's name again more urgently, looked out into the hall; but she was in time only to catch the brief, betrayed stare that Leah silently threw her way before pushing Amy's bicycle out through the doorway and riding off into the night.

8

QUESTION

Why then had he come out of the house into this soft wild night where he teetered among shadows, bereft of purpose or direction? But he was looking for something – wasn't that supposed to be the point? Wasn't that why he had come across the country to this shifty, damp peninsula? Yes that was it, he was on some kind of quest, he was knight-errant on a dream-adventure. And now he remembered: they had stolen into his chamber in the night while he lay dreaming, and they had cut the heart out of his chest, so he must go looking for it. He was looking for his defected heart. He was looking, in fact, for Leah, his lost love, and the life they had forfeited; and if he remembered rightly, wasn't she to be found somewhere at the foot of this dark garden, picking at the wrinkled paintwork of a gate?

Ronan stepped deeper into the gloom, the earth spongy at his feet, his balance wavering. The night dilated round him. He could hear the sea; or it might equally have been a roaring in his ears, for there was no telling now where inner world ended and outer world began – only this debatable zone where one darkness floated seamlessly into another like those impulsive thoughts which might also be taken for the flight of bats.

But when he came to the gate there was no sign of Leah. He called out her name, and the silence said, 'Not here,' which brought anxiously to mind an earlier stage of the search – one which had happened a long time ago – when he journeyed beneath the earth to be told by a crone that she whom he sought would only be found in an impossible place on unmeetable conditions.

Ronan swayed among the swaying shadows of the trees. At a loss, he pushed through the wicket-gate down the steep bank, looking for such a place under the sky where there was neither sun nor moon; but it was wholly night there, with no glimmering of day. The stream babbled like a mad lapidary, polishing its stones. He remembered that if he picked his way through the dark he would find that stream and come to a place where a leap could be made. It might take him back to where none of this had happened. He would return through the gorge and find the narrow defile where Leah had been snatched away into the underworld. Once there, he would know what to do; this time he would put things right; he would conjure happiness back into existence were it not so dark down here in the smell of ferns among the trees. But he could feel a path firm beneath his feet, which was leading him onwards and down into a clearing where, against all expectation, a light came on inside his head. Briefly it dazzled everything in brilliance – the leaves were luminously green, the shadows abashed, the ivy refulgent where it clung to the stones of an ancient building.

A woman – not Leah – waited on a bench outside its door, but either she was indifferent to his appearance as an intruder on her world, or she might have been asleep, for she had an air of quiet, impenetrable repose about her, undisturbed by the light. Ronan stopped in his tracks, reluctant, even ashamed to waken her. He turned away, listening to the obsessions of the stream. What was he doing here? At the skin of his face he felt the first cold rain. There was nowhere to turn, nowhere left to go. Out of the night of the glen an obliterating sense of hopelessness swooped down on him. He had failed, he *was* failure; and worse, more bitter, more filled with torment than the pain of failure was the pain of loss. The air he breathed was dark with loss, his lungs were brimming with it. Then – quite suddenly – the soft, demolishing commotion of his tears welled up and overwhelmed him. Their sound flooded round him, hoarse and gasping, gathering force, converging with the sound of night and rain and sweeping him towards the plummeting tumult of the fall.

Someone was calling his name, not loudly or from a distance, more as invocation of his presence, as an invitation to shelter; but that was no longer possible for he was falling through a dark space tautly strung like the inside of an upright piano – except that the strings were fuzzy and soft, and made, he realized, of wool. The air was redolent of fleece and smoke, and tinged with sharper smells. He was falling down the warp of an enormous loom, but so slowly that the sensation of fall was reduced to a dust-mote's leisurely downward drift, until he alighted at last at the feet of a patient giantess.

She was dressing her hair. Its dense volume was looped across her shoulder to a raised hand, from which a further shining length fell to her waist. She stood in a rocky dell with her neck tilted gracefully towards the comb and her head strikingly caught in a nimbus of light. Wearing only a white cloth loosely knotted at her hips, she was so tall, so lovely in her massive poise, that Ronan's heart was instantly ravished by devotion. There was a voice, a soft, anointing voice that spoke to him, at once permitting his dissolution and containing it; and if those were her gentle tones, then he wanted to be taken up in the vast arms, to wander the plain

173

of her belly, to forage the alpine meadows of her breast. He gasped as she let the long hair fall, and when, patiently, the giantess looked down on him he felt he had found favour there. He would do what she wanted, he would go where she asked, unquestioning; he would face whatever ordeals her service required. His spirit lifted as she beckoned him closer. It seemed there was a gift, a token that his vows of service were accepted, a sign of her faith and affection. Reverently he approached. She laughed – a thrilling vault of laughter – and opened her hand to reveal a ball of scarlet wool. With the loose end of its thread pinched between thumb and forefinger, she leaned towards him, tossed the ball lightly down, and set it rolling across the floor.

Ronan watched the scarlet trickle unwind, gathering pace until it reached the edge of the blow-hole which stood suddenly open in the stone flags. Without teetering a second there, the ball dropped over the lip. Only its fine red wake remained, like an incision in the stone.

Now the giantess was leaning towards him as if to confide a secret; she was whispering that certain problems were so intractable the only practical response to them was magic; then she laughed again, and held out her huge left hand to offer him the twine.

Ronan glanced up into her distant face, finding neither dare nor derision there, neither hope nor expectation: only a giantess's grave invitation to his duty. Quailing a little, he took the thread. Perhaps she felt him tremble, for she gave him a contemplative smile and told him that at the beginning of all magical work lay a resolute imagination. So he turned away, following the thread, regathering it, and when, briefly, he looked back, he was uncertain whether she had already receded across far distances, or simply diminished back to human scale.

The wool felt soft against his skin. Making a bobbin of his

fingers, Ronan walked towards the blow-hole's edge where soft flakes of spume floated on dark air. He gazed over the brink and saw the first twist of a spiral stairway roughly cut into the stone. Far below him, indifferent either to exhaustion or dismay, the woollen ball bounced down.

Ronan put his foot to the first step and began the descent. Distantly he heard the grieving sea. This was, he realized, the most perilous thing he had ever attempted, and were he to let himself look beyond the edge of each narrow step he would be overwhelmed by the dizzy drop beyond. He progressed cautiously, therefore, his breath quailing as he concentrated on the action of re-winding the yarn, while his steps wound round the wall of the shaft. The wool's slow growth to a second ball in his hand soon became his only measure of time.

He turned at last in a space where the steps ended and his foot dangled over the mouth of a pit. There was no way round or across, and no way of telling from the lie of the thread how deep the drop. Yet the long climb back was unthinkable.

Ronan sat down on the brim of darkness, trembling, then he let himself fall.

A bell chimed — a single struck note, round and naked as a pearl, as softly luminous. He woke in perfect dark, not knowing who he was or what his life was for.

Out of a fissure in the rock came a young woman carrying a taper. Its glow gave the only light across the universe until she applied its tiny flame, one by one, to lamps in their stone sconces and gradually the light increased. Ronan stared into the growing space around him and saw that the walls were not, as he'd first thought, solid rock, but softly woven out of woollen yarn. Or perhaps they were covered in a vast, abstractly patterned arras which had been wrongly hung so that its reverse was showing rather than its face. He would have found this entirely strange had there not been something familiar about the design of the weaving. Then he realized: he was now *inside* Alice's tapestry of the cliff, the one which he'd admired, and almost bought, in the exhibition long ago – except that here it was hugely much larger; as large, he guessed, as the actual cliff-face that had first inspired it.

As lamp after lamp was lit, its subtle range of earthy colours was disclosed – the greens and bracken browns, the ochre and chrome yellows, the mauves and greys of minerals and stone. He saw where sunlight glanced across the rock. He felt the rock's density and bulk. Even here, viewed from the wrong side, the character of the cliff was so forcefully established that Ronan could imagine how the cove where Leah had taken him must lie just beyond the far side of the tapestry, on the face-side of the cliff. It was as if he'd walked into one of the yawning caves and passed on through. And it would have been as dark in here as only the inside of a dense cliff could be dark, were it not for the lamps that gleamed like ingots in the rock.

Only when the last of them was lit did the young woman turn towards him. Ronan saw the glister of her hair. 'Thank God it's you,' he cried as she offered her disconcerting smile, 'I need your help.'

'It's all right', she whispered, '– really.'

'But you know I'm looking for her?'

'Yes, but . . .'

'Do you know when she'll be back?'

'Not yet, not for a while perhaps.' The young woman studied him in concern. 'Don't worry about it now. I just wanted to let you know I've drawn your bath.'

'Yes,' he said uncertainly, and then, a moment later, 'but would you keep this for me till I'm done.'

In some bewilderment the considerate young woman looked down at the unravelling ball of scarlet wool he pressed between her hands.

He had forgotten how soft the water in these parts. Scrubbing himself with the abrasive green soap, he was soon cocooned in so voluptuous a lather it would take patience to rinse the suds away. Ronan lay in the hot bath by the soft light of blue candles, immersed in pure physical sensation, and refusing for the moment all consideration of his altered circumstances.

When he placed a finger to his injured temple each delicate probe was answered by flashes inside his skull. Then he was taken by the fancy that the pain might be drawn out again, that if he concentrated all his mental forces on the procedure, he could mobilize the pain and direct its energy back towards the exit of the wound where his fingertips waited to syphon it away. He tried the operation, but without success. Yet it should, he felt, be possible. In a world where all the usual rules were abrogated, why should he not be possessed of unusual powers? He might summon, as he seemed to have been summoned here, for instance, so that Leah would come, obedient to his will, and this time there'd be no mistake. In the revised version of events they would forgo all claims and assumptions, there would be no attempts to explain or justify, no rebukes, no argument; only the mutual desire to glide together as smoothly as a water-bird and its reflection on a still lake. He would find words to moisten her.

But the bath where he lay was surrounded by nine tall figures in white tunics who looked down on him from a vaporous height, and if their gaze was sympathetic it was also stern. They reminded him that a grievous wrong had been done, that he could not stay here for ever, that he would be expected soon in court for sentencing.

Embarrassed and daunted, Ronan covered himself with his hands; there was a curious feeling that he was not in a bath after all, but in a huge silver cauldron; then he laughed with the realization that if one chose to bathe at the bottom of a blow-hole then one must expect to see illusions in the spray. Yet he felt himself observed still, though invisibly now, as he lurched out of the bath to dry himself.

When he came to look for his clothes he found nothing to wear but an old bathrobe of white towelling with a belt of the same stuff that knotted at the waist. He put it on and stood for a time staring into a full-length mirror at his reflection. The hair was spiky and wild, his eyes mistrustful under the bruise, the mouth recalcitrant. His legs shone white as wax beneath the hem of the robe, and the naked feet had a stubborn, remote existence of their own. He felt ashamed to represent himself. But there was no alternative; so he drew in his breath, summoning a derelict's pride, and stepped through to where the girl and a nervous woman stood up to meet him. They took his arms, ready to lead him down, but at the top of the stairs he began to struggle. Worried by his agitation, they saw eventually that he only wanted to retrieve the ball of wool left on a window-sill.

He was brought into a court where the atmosphere was tense with nervous excitement: the king was already doing justice there that day, but the mood of the crowd seemed rancorous and unpredictable. Ronan saw a shackled prisoner step down from the dock under guard, having just been found guilty. A sudden sweet stink of well-hung game tainted the air as the evidence which had condemned the man was lifted up and tied about his neck. Arrayed thus in the odium of his guilt, the felon hobbled off through the mockery of the crowd. Ronan was left staring at the way the bloodied white carcass hung from the man's shoulders like a mutilated angel, with its huge wings dangling to the floor.

Trumpets sounded across the hall. When their brilliance faded the next case was called. The mood turned uglier. Fists were lifted, there were shouts and jeers, a sudden emotional surge. Near the front of the court, not far from the throne, a woman howled, and was caught up in the unruly scuffling among her neighbours when pikemen pushed her roughly back. Ronan could smell the danger in the air, but not until he was ushered through the crowd and stood alone in the dock did he realize that he was himself the object of this execration.

Wearily the king signalled to his chief counsellor, who banged his staff till silence fell.

For an instant in the ensuing stillness Ronan caught the king's eye. He saw the resignation there, and the regret of a once powerful but now ailing man who had tried, and failed, to save a valued friend. It was the sight of mercy aborted in that brief glance that made Ronan, for the first time, truly afraid. Distantly he heard the king's voice as judgment was given. All the testimony had been considered and the evidence weighed; no grounds had been found for extenuation. Only one verdict was possible – the Nameless Knight was guilty. And for so grave an offence against the vows of his service, there was only one appropriate sentence – death.

Ronan heard the gasp of the crowd, and the surge of its murmur to a gratified roar as the king pushed himself to his feet and beckoned to the tall headsman wearing a black hood who stood behind the throne. The man stepped forward, unwrapping his axe. Ronan saw the woman who had been howling put a hand to her whitened face: she understood now that she would have to watch the execution, she would see his head roll, the arteries spurt. It would be done there, in the hall, right under her eyes, and nothing in her life had prepared her for this. Was she sure she wanted this? There was no longer a choice. Guards were at Ronan's back. His wrists and arms were gripped, he was pushed forward. He could smell sweat, the air was depleted of oxygen, his eyes widened, reaching everywhere. He glimpsed the bluish sheen of the blade. Had it been possible he would have fainted then; and at the same time, to his own amazement, in a secret, scarcely acknowledged place he was thinking, *Let the bastard die.*

The queen and her ladies entered. There was no fanfare of trumpets, no announcement of their arrival, but their grave appearance instantly commanded silence. There were nine of them. No longer in white, they wore brocaded gowns of satin and velour, with lace collars and ermined sleeves that dangled to the floor. Veils hung from gorgeous hats over high-piled hair.

Stately and proud, the queen stepped forward. She had come, she declared, to assert an ancient right. The crime in question was a crime against woman, therefore it should be tried by women. It was, moreover, a crime against love, and only a Court of Love was competent to reach a proper ruling in such matters. It was the ladies' right to summon such a court. They did so now. The knight must be handed over to their jurisdiction.

The crowd was confused by this development, its mood shifted. Among the counsellors on the king's bench there was a hasty whispered conference, but the queen spoke over it, addressing the king directly. 'The right is ancient and inalienable. You can neither grant nor deny it. It is ours.'

As the blood drained from the face of the haggard king, Ronan realized how infirm he was, how little authority was left to him. Swaying, the king reached to the nearest of his counsellors for support, but too late, for the front of his robe had flushed with a sudden dim stain where an old wound was opening. He uttered a little gasp, and then, abstractedly, as if lacking the strength to be more than mildly curious about his condition, he put his hand down there. When it came away the palm was bloody. His eyes glanced up in bewilderment; his gaunt body sagged where he stood groping for the throne at his back. 'Let them have the man,' he panted. 'Take me away.'

A pattern of words repeated itself in Ronan's head:

> Do not fall on a bed of sloth,
> Let not intoxication overcome you,
> Begin a voyage across the clear sea,
> If perchance you may reach the Land of Women.

He had heard those injunctions before, a long time ago; but where had they come from? And there was a smell associated with them, a mingled smell of camphor and peppermints. Surely they were words from a story, but not one of the stories he'd heard recently; they came from much further back than that, and there was, he thought, a ring of Irishry about them. He remembered then: the smell was his grandmother's smell, and the story one she had told him as a child. It was about the voyage made by Bran, son of Febal, to magical islands across the wide sea. The words came from the song Bran had heard after being lulled to sleep by the music of a silver branch. And Ronan remembered how the tale had both frightened and enchanted him, and how once it was over he had wanted to hear it again immediately, even though, at the time of the telling, he had wanted it to end.

Who would have thought those words could have lodged for so long in his brain? Yet he seemed to have arrived at last in the place they promised, for this, if anywhere, must be the Land of Women, and though his life had apparently been saved by these women he had no clear idea what their purposes were. Nor was he in any state to speculate – except for the feeling that someone must have been telling stories about him; or recounting experiences; or even some fusion of the two that the teller seemed to understand little better than he did himself.

No matter, for he was in the queen's care now, and more than a little in awe of the mature repose of a beauty which relied on nothing theatrical or cosmetic – simply the clear, discriminating presence of an adult female face at peace with the years. He had marked also a certain impervious strength in her grey eyes which would respond neither to argument nor charm. Intellect would not impress, nor eloquence sway her; yet she seemed unaware that a serious mistake was being made, and was unmoved by his efforts to explain that he was not the Nameless Knight, that he did indeed have a name, and was not the man the authorities had been looking for. Nor was he in any way responsible for the terrible thing that had been done.

There seemed to be other confusions too: about the precise nature of the offence in question, and even about the time when it had happened, for these women seemed convinced he was implicated in an atrocity that had been committed, as far as he could gather, many centuries before.

Did he not remember, they asked, the time when the land had been ruled by the Rich Fisher, the magician king of the Grail, who could change shape at will, and whose reign had brought abundance everywhere, so that the whole island shone with gold and silver, with furs and costly fabrics, and there were food and animals and birds of every kind? When he denied any such knowledge they sought to remind him of how, in that time of plenty, the springs and wells of the land had been watched over by maidens living in the woods, whose duty and delight it was to refresh tired travellers with food and drink. A wayfarer needed only to approach their sacred groves and state his wishes, and one of the maidens would instantly appear, bearing a golden bowl which held all kinds of food, while another presently followed, bringing a white towel and a dish containing whatever else the traveller might need or desire. In that time, he was told, all wanderers were received in this gracious way until a king named Amangons ravished one of the damsels of the woods and stole her golden bowl. His men were let loose to follow his example, and after this savage violation of their rites, the well-guardians withdrew into the hollow hills, never again coming forth to welcome travellers. Thereafter the springs dried up, the waters receded, the trees shed their leaves, crops withered, the land fell waste, and the Rich Fisher's Court of Joy could be found no more.

Listening to their account of the destruction of the land, Ronan was taken back to the days when his imagination had first come alive to tales of Arthur and his knights, to the flash and gleam, the misty stirrings and vanishings of a magic world through which he'd caught his first glimpse of a possible magnificence in life. He recalled the summer garden of his childhood home, and the buttery light over the sloping field beyond. He thought of cloud-shadow drifting across the distant English hill, and remembered the particular smell to the pages of the book the boy was reading. He felt a piercing sense of loss for the dreams sullied in the time between then and now, for all the hopes defeated or relinquished on the way.

The story evoked deeper, nearer losses too. He was ready to admit as much, but otherwise he couldn't understand why the women thought those remote events had anything to do with him.

That was surprising, they said, for they were sure they had recognized his face, and they made him look at a picture he would have preferred not to see. It was a photograph of himself at the moment when Leah had lain beneath him in the cove, of his face as she must have seen it from where she lay trapped under his weight. He was appalled by the queerly fanatical smile across his features. All colour had been washed out of the picture to yield the grainy, monochrome texture which artfully renders atrocity indelible on the imagination. It left the eyes devoid of light. They seemed fixated on things invisible to everyone but himself. It felt as though any thoughts behind those eyes could bear no persuasive relation to the smile twisting the corners of the mouth; yet he recognized the peculiar icy heat of the places it came from.

The sight sharpened the pain in Ronan's head. He turned away, squeezing the thumb and forefinger of his left hand across his eyelids, and when the patterns of trapped light expired the image in front of him had changed. He was staring into the shadows of a candle-lit chapel where the body of a man lay stretched on a purple cloak across a bier. Ronan recognized the wounded king – he lay there barely alive, his breath rasping like a saw across green wood. Under his tunic the bare legs were stained with blood. It oozed from his covered thighs, splaying in a scarlet delta at the knee. A weak, beseeching hand was lifted. Hope glimmered briefly in the narrowed eyes.

Ronan stood above the bleeding man aghast, his first thought was *murder* – someone had tried to kill the king, and there was so much blood. He stood, sickened, a hand at his mouth, making small moans. Then he gagged when he saw where the blood was welling from: it was as if an adult circumcision ritual had been horribly botched. He stood there helpless and appalled. The man needed help. He should help. How should he help? What should he do? He wasn't qualified. He was afraid to tamper with that dreadful wound. He was faint with urgency. What was expected of him? How was he supposed to cope with this? He looked away and saw a lance leaning against the wall. It too leaked blood. Rivulets and pools of blood were leaking across the cracked stone floor. And he had to act – the air of the place was pent with expectation. He felt that at any moment the walls might roll open like a blind to reveal an urgent host of presences. He stood in an anguish of inaction, obscurely convinced that the right form of words might heal the wound, yet unable to remember what those healing words might be. He felt sick with the failure of it.

Now the floor was a deck heaving under him, he was at sea, and if it was up to him, the wounded man was certainly a goner. With a shudder of recoil, Ronan imagined him suddenly lurching up like the dying Nelson to clutch at his neck and whisper, 'Kiss me, Hardy.' So he backed quickly away, out of the chapel into another, brighter room where the consultant surgeon and his team were still in conference. Again Ronan listened in dismay to their prognosis. Scalpels were laid out in accessible array. Their enthusiastic sheen appalled him. But what use had he been himself when the man's blood was flooding at his feet? Better to leave the case to them; they were professionals, they were reliable, they had been doing it for years. But the chapel door opened behind him and a woman came out cleaning her spectacles on a man-size handkerchief. Where had she come from? Only a moment ago there had been no one in there but the wounded king. 'It's a nasty graze,' she was saying, 'though I don't think we need worry about it. As you say, his real trouble's emotional. I'm afraid you've got your hands full there.'

Ronan dimly heard the words, but they were so far out of

scale with what he had seen of the terrible haemorrhage that he could not take them seriously. The wound still bloomed across his vision like an evil flower. He would have raised his voice in protest but already his eyes were gluing with honeycombs of sleep. Someone placed a soothing palm across his head. Inside his mind there was only darkness then.

Some time later he surfaced again in a room which had the smell of night about it. The curtains were undrawn, the light of a standard-lamp reflected in black window-glass. By now it must have been far into the night. He had no idea how much time had passed. His watch had gone from his wrist, forgotten somewhere – left in the bathroom perhaps, at the time when his dirty clothes were removed and he found nothing to wear but this white bathrobe. Ronan heard the wind blowing through the trees in the glen, he imagined the stream and the fall's steep plunge, and the sea beyond, crashing through the blow-hole. He thought of the stars gathered there like spectators at an accident. This landscape had crowded round him all weekend, nudging and distracting, waylaying and bewildering him. Sometimes he wondered whether it was Alice's voice or the earth's voice that he heard; or whether the sounds of the night were in fact distinguishable from the exhalations of his grief. He didn't know, except the sounds were all around him, though he was sitting alone in the night with Alice, who was stitching something quietly as they talked. He watched her put down a pair of scissors. Vaguely he remembered being alone with her before, he remembered the soft, consoling flow of her voice.

It felt utterly vital now that she again be kind, for somehow she had coaxed him to talk. She was saying he must try to talk more feelingly, and though he wanted to try, it seemed he had lost the way of it. He had lost it a long time ago, and despite the gentle, vellum lamp-light and the embers of the fire, it remained so dark in here. He said it aloud. He said, 'It feels utterly dark inside me now.'

'Then have faith in that darkness,' Alice advised. 'You're not lost, others have been there before. It has been named.' But the silence prolonged itself, and his hands were trembling, so after a moment she put down the stitching and took one of his hands in hers, offering the confidence of her smile. 'I think you're beginning to discover your aptitude for vulnerability,' she said. 'Try to go on.'

Ronan pulled his hand away, his glance shifted uneasily from Alice's encouraging gaze, and travelled the room until it came at last to rest on the book that lay on the table beside him. He opened it at random and was looking at a picture of an armoured knight accompanied by his squire who wore a floppy hat and a smart quilted doublet, white, with flames embroidered round its skirts. They had emerged on horseback from a deep wood, and had come to a chapel where they were talking to a deformed hag with mad hair. Her scowling head had jug ears; a single breast dangled unpleasantly from the skins roughly slung across her body. She had feet shaped like a swan's.

Ronan moved his eyes to the opposite page where they latched on words. He read how the hag was supposed to guide the knight to the castle of *Bon Repos*, but out of pure malice she was misdirecting him to the Forest of the Long Wait instead. The hag's name, it seemed, was Jealousy.

Ronan snorted. Who in their right mind would trust such a loathsome creature? He looked up at his companion and was about to speak, but his mouth opened on silence, for something was happening to the queen's lovely face, and what he had taken at first for shadows round her eyes had crumpled into bags and wrinkles, the eyelids were hooded now, the skin of her cheeks sear as a leaf, her neck withered. It might have been his mother's face he was looking at, except he found more cunning here, more penetration, more scope for ruthlessness.

Then he was surrounded by several such women, of uncertain outline, blurring softly into one another. Their patience, it seemed, was limitless, and therefore somehow sinister. He was entirely in their hands, and could see nothing to be done about it. He was trying to explain himself, to apologize, but there was, they said, no need. Of course they understood how hard this was for him; but he should try not to struggle – he would only make things harder on himself; if he just let it happen he would find he really wanted it after all.

And then he could only watch as the oldest of the women reached a mottled hand into the basket at her side, took out a pair of sewing-shears and severed the line of scarlet thread.

Thus cut off, he was left alone for hours to face the facts of who he was and what he had done and what he had become. During that bleak time there were moments when he came to see himself as these women evidently saw him: a violent fool who had tried to take by force what could only be freely given; one of Amangons' men, caught in the atrocious act, and brought at last to justice. But he could see no justice, for of all the possible versions of his life, they had settled on the one where he had been least typically himself, where what had happened could only be understood as aberration, as an almost daemonic seizure.

In a moment of weakness, an emotional moment when all finer distinctions of feeling had blurred into a hot mix of rage, frustration and despair, he had briefly lost control; now, in consequence, he was being held answerable for all

188

the harm ever done to women by men. So you could forget all the high talk of courts of love and erotic justice. Their tender interest in him was a sham, a sick charade arranged for his humiliation. He had been thinking it over. He had been trying to work out what these women wanted, and it was obvious now: what they wanted was revenge. This was no court of love but a war-crimes tribunal, and its logic was simple: he was male and therefore guilty; no further evidence required. What's more, their designs on his mind had left him so confused that he half-believed it himself. He saw how even a vigorous defence could only further condemn him. So he would have to be careful now, and cunning, because who knew what they were planning to do?

He was frightened by the memory of what he had seen in the chapel where the king lay bleeding. That was what they could do if they chose. The laws of this court were crazy enough. He had seen the scalpels. And if it was revenge they wanted, why not? Why shouldn't they do that to him? He remembered the woman in the green cape who had come dashing towards him with a dish of blood. He found himself thinking, these people keep their promises.

Ronan was trembling when the nine women eventually returned. Their heads were wimpled in white like an order of nuns. Each of them held a treasure that shone with a cool lustre in the gloom, and because the movement of their feet was concealed beneath long skirts they seemed to float across the floor. Not one of them looked his way as the grave procession neared the dock where he stood transfixed by the momentous beauty of the sight.

The women assembled in a white crescent across from him. Ronan lifted his head, invoking stubborn pride. Whatever their sentence, he would outstare it. And at least, he thought, this must be over soon.

But he was wrong.

It was the queen who delivered judgment. This case, she said, had not proved easy. The defendant would understand that a due process of erotic justice must consider matters that might appear inconsequential to a court of law. Everything must be taken carefully into account – the feel of things as much as the facts – for, as he had surely gathered by now, a court of love was less concerned with punishment and retribution than with transformation. But how to bring about the needful change?

She let the problem hang for a moment on the silent air. When he made no response, she smiled briefly at her companions.

Having reviewed all the options open to them, she resumed, they had decided to strike a prudent balance between summary judgment and merciful remission. The court was to be adjourned for a year and a day. At the end of that time the defendant would be asked for the answer to a question which they would shortly put to him. If he gave the correct answer he would be free to go. If he had no answer, or if his answer was wrong, they would hand him back to the court of law where the headsman would be waiting. Did he understand these terms?

Nervously Ronan considered the new situation. Distrusting it, he saw no choice. Yes, he said at last, their terms were understood.

And accepted?

Irritable with tension now, he told them to put their question.

The women moved in closer, they linked their hands, and surrounded him with the measured steps of a circle-dance, which gathered speed until a dazzle of white light was swirling round him, and words came chanting out of it in a single voice. Ronan had to strain to make out the question, for it was pitched in the quaint, lilting dialect of some remote country parish:

> 'I grant thee lyf, if thou kanst tellen me
> What thyng is it that wommen moost desiren.
> Be war, and keep thy nekke-boon from iren.'

Then he was out of there, waking up in the difficult world, thinking it over.

At first, tasting the freshness of the air, he couldn't believe his luck; then the sheen of the headsman's axe squinting through the last line quickly clarified his mind.

Shaking awake, he applied himself, and at first sight he thought this shouldn't be so hard. Women were not scarce, there were plenty around to ask, he was in the Land of Women, after all; and, despite recent events, he had always got on well with them. He respected their intelligence, their pragmatism, their rights. He had given a lot of thought to women in his time, and already he had some ideas which might be confirmed and refined by a little research. But as he got up, resolved to approach the first woman he saw, it occurred to him that there were questions lying behind the question. He thought of the women he knew most intimately – Leah, and Marion his wife – and how very different they were; as different as passion and order, as different as risk and playing safe. He thought of the confusing demands his mother made, and of the women closer to hand – Alice and Dora Pascoe and Amy – and how little they seemed to have in common for all the obvious affection between them. When women were so various, how could there possibly be a single thing wanted by them all? So which of them were most representative? Who to ask? Would any woman do, or were particular qualities required? The question might have as many possible answers as there were women to ask, and if you didn't already know the correct one how would you recognize it when it came? Might it even be necessary to learn the curious language in which the question had been put? He began to see that things were not so simple after all.

In increasing agitation he travelled far and wide, putting the question again and again. He accosted women of many kinds – working women and shoppers, women chatting as they waited for their children outside schools, brisk professional women, bank-clerks, traffic-wardens, doctors, politicians, whores. He spent time with head-hunters and hairdressers, with lollipop-ladies and social-workers, with the driven, the dedicated, the deprived. Some told him plainly to mind his own business, others rambled on and got confused. There were fearful women who suspected his motives, troubled women who could barely speak at all, and hostile women who treated him with scorn. Some seemed clear about what they personally wanted – love, babies, security, to lose weight, a larger house, a quick fix, good health, wealth, success, world-peace, or peace of mind; but even the more confident were uneasy making claims for women as a whole; and even happiness as an object did not entirely answer, for there were some he met who nursed their spite and misery like sickly children, feeding them with grief.

As the weeks went by he tended to disbelieve all answers. There were times when he grew sick and tired of women with their demands and incoherencies; and others when he was filled with admiration for the way so many of them coped against the odds. Increasingly he came to share what he felt to be their inwardly consuming difficulties of self-belief.

He saw the weeks accelerate. Months blurred; he

watched the seasons swishing by. Then he caught the smell of woodsmoke off an autumn bonfire, and the year was over. Just the one day left. The irrational extra day. The leap-day, the one that lay beyond the rim of ordinary time.

By noon, exhausted, heavy-hearted, he was back at the glen. He was approaching from the sea when he saw a group of women dancing near the sunlit culvert of a waterfall. Enchanted by their grace, he approached, wondering whether to pose the question one last time, but as soon as he stepped into the glade their circle vanished, leaving a single figure behind.

Derelict, in battered trainers, among a tawdry squalor of rubbish and plastic bags, she was feeding a crow with bits of pie. The bird took flight at his step. Tutting, the woman glanced up and was so hideous he could scarcely bear to look at her. Everything about her was foul with neglect. Her breath was rank, the stink of fish clung to her skin. There were bristles at her chin, her yellow teeth protruded tuskily, the rheumy eyes were cunning as a sow's. Ronan visibly recoiled, and though she could not have missed the reflex of disgust, she didn't seem to mind. She was used to it, she'd learned that people had a hard time seeing through appearances; yet she was partial to a little company, and always ready for a chat. So she beckoned him over to the dump, and was soon taking a sympathetic interest in his plight. She asked what ailed him, she coaxed out all the facts. She smiled.

Ah yes, he had come to the right place – she knew the answer to his question. She would certainly divulge it. But there must, of course, be some exchange. She would tell him exactly what he wanted to know, but first he must promise to do whatever she might ask in return.

No more than he'd been able to hide his revulsion could Ronan now conceal immediate mistrust. It came as an ugly thought: wasn't this always the way with women – withholding the desirable thing till the latest moment possible, then proffering it only as they wet their lips to swallow you whole? But his mistrust merely amused her. She tossed a last morsel of crust to where the crow squinted up with its sleek head tilted, then she grinned slyly back at him. Perhaps, she suggested, he was also having trouble knowing what he wanted himself?

Her smile had a take-it-or-leave-it glint which was almost whimsical. Yet both of them knew he would be mortgaging his life to her, and that the price of rescue might be everything. But he was out of time now, his life was already on the line, there was nowhere else to turn.

Ronan drew in his breath – a long juddering, hypertensive snatching at the air. He had seen so much of life throughout this year – its glory and its awfulness, its valour and its pain – that he was unready to part with it now. At almost every turn of his travels he had been exampled in endurance; in a stubborn willingness to persevere; in the capacity to make a life, and try to love it, however great the odds. He knew now that he wanted to live. He felt how good it was to breathe!

For a moment he tried to reassure himself that there was something familiar about this repulsive creature, that she might be on his side, that she might mean well for him; then he shrugged such palliative thoughts aside and faced stark fact. He sniffed, rubbed a nervous hand across his mouth. He asked what he must do.

'Marry me,' she said.

There was unconcealed relief in his incredulous laugh. 'But I'm married already.'

The hag nodded her foul head, unsurprised, pointing out that he had defected from his marriage some time ago, that his lover had gone, and there appeared to be a lot of empty space in his life right now – or in what little there would be left of it if the two of them did not come to some arrangement.

Alarmed to discover himself so completely known, Ronan changed tack: what guarantee did he have, before committing himself, that she knew what he needed to know?

The hag nodded at that too, craftily. She invited him to take a look at her. Wasn't it obvious that she'd been through everything? She knew it all, forwards and backwards, inside and outside, upstairs and downstairs and in my lady's chamber. She'd seen it all, it'd all been done to her one way or another, she'd been destruction-tested. And now there was nothing got past her. Oh yes, she could tell him what he needed to know all right. She could tell him in a single word.

'Tell me then,' he said.

A thin cackle hissed between her teeth. It wasn't that she didn't trust him, of course, but temptation was a terrible thing; and in any case, hadn't she already been very nice to him when there was no need for it, and wouldn't it be more loving on his part if he was to give his promise first?

When he still dithered, she added, 'Either way, *I'll* survive, my love. It's more your future I was thinking of than mine.' And so, bewildered, exhausted, afraid either way, Ronan at last nodded his assent.

'Why don't you say it properly?' she wheedled. 'It's just that I'd like to hear you say the words. Say it for me. Say that when the time comes we'll get married, you and me.'

'Yes,' he answered, 'when I'm free.'

She smiled, accepting the equivocation, and craned her neck, offering the loathsome mouth. He remembered her then – where he had seen her before – the hag in the cave from his dream on the cliff, she of the impossible place and unmeetable conditions – grown older, uglier, more foul with neglect; but in this desperate moment of his possible salvation, Ronan was more thankful for her fidelity than oppressed by it. He felt almost affectionately towards her now. Yet still he withheld the expected kiss. 'Tell me,' he demanded, 'what do women want?'

Smiling, converting the intimate approach of her lips into a whisper, the hag answered in a single puzzling word.

9
ANSWER

'But I don't understand what you want from me,' protested Stephen, who was angry about many things, not least his present inability to eliminate the note of petulance from his voice. 'I mean, you finally agree to come out with me last night, only to leave me feeling you wished you'd stayed at home. When I try to talk straight all I get is evasion. You drag me out of the hotel without a word of explanation, tell me that you want to come back here; you agree to share the damn bed with me, we even start to make love . . . and then it turns out I'm not a lover after all – I'm a bloody bolt-hole! Just a convenient back to hide behind! How am I *supposed* to feel about that?'

Leah stood at the foot of the stairs in Stephen's flat with her head lowered. Her hair was drenched, there were dark patches along the thighs of her jeans where the rain had soaked them. She said nothing.

'Especially next morning,' he persisted with diminishing vehemence, 'when you start bossing me about, getting me to drive you back, barely speaking except to say that you don't want me hanging about the place while you set yourself up to get burned again, and it's suddenly *Goodbye, Stephen, thanks a lot. See you again next time I have a use for you!*'

Pausing for breath, he looked disconsolately down at the bright cornelian rain-drops in the fuzz of her hair, and felt things softly shift inside. If it was difficult, in this silent humiliated presence, to sustain a grievance which, in any case, merely betrayed the pain of disappointment, the moment she looked up it would be impossible. But the grievance was real enough, though its grounds were other than those he'd listed, and more injurious to his self-esteem. Stephen had not minded being used; the truth was, he'd been glad of a practical chance to demonstrate his care. Nor, in those emotional circumstances, had he been greatly discomfited by the wretched failure of their effort to make love. What really bothered him was the knowledge that, for everything she might say to the contrary, Leah had been disastrously ready to make herself vulnerable again to a man who – as far as Stephen could see – was a despicable bastard. Increasingly, throughout this difficult day, the hurt to his feelings had been aggravated by a nagging sense of injustice. And now here she was again, throwing him into new confusions.

Still without looking up, she said simply, 'But you said you were my friend.'

'I am, dammit. Or I've tried my best to be. But you're impossible, Leah. You give me so many different signals, I don't know what you want any more. I had you naked in my arms last night, for God's sake; and then today . . .'

He could, for an exasperated moment, have beaten his head against the wall.

'I know,' she said, 'I know.'

'And look at the state you're in! Where've you been? What the hell's gone wrong for you now? How did you even get here?'

'I took Amy's bike.'

'You cycled all the way from Alice's? In this rain? Without a coat? Oh Christ, you must be wet through.' Out of frustration and his despair with her, Stephen might have been accusing Leah of an infectious condition.

'Do you want me to go?' she said.

'No I damn well don't. You shouldn't have been out on your own in the first place. There's a murderer out there, you know; or have you been so caught up in yourself you've forgotten? He could be anyone, anywhere. I've even had the police questioning *me*, would you believe? They came out to the nursery late this afternoon.'

'But why? Why you?'

'Someone spotted the car when we parked on the cliff last night. It gave me a hell of a shock I can tell you. I hadn't thought about it before – not with everything else that's been going on – but it might have been happening right then, while we were talking to one another in the car. It makes me sick to think about it . . . still, right now.' Stephen saw the distraught white shock on Leah's raised face. 'Luckily I had the receipt from the hotel in my wallet,' he went on, caught up by the survivor's need to convert a bad experience into narrative, 'and I knew my neighbour had seen you and me coming out of the house together this morning; so the police seemed to believe me – as much as they believe anybody these days.' Stephen glanced back at his nervous listener again. 'But for God's sake, Leah, it's just bloody stupid, biking about on your own in the dark like this. Anything could happen. And whatever you don't feel for me, I care about you. I care about you so much it hurts.'

Leah stood in her damp clothes shivering. She had pedalled for miles through the rainy darkness without switching on the lights of Amy's bicycle; she heard the tyres sizzling along the road, she felt the wind's resistance off the sea, the bike buckled and shied beneath her on the hills. After the first flush of escape, and with the night freewheeling past her down the gradient through Treligo, she had tried to imagine herself singular again, truly single, as she had been in the days before Ronan, careering through the manageable world on her Silver Dream Machine; but Ronan had given her bicycle that name, and the memory conjured him back to her harassed brain. He was alive inside her. He encircled her days, there was no part of her life left untouched by him. He knew her memories, her dreams; he was intimate with each trick of her thought, with every fold of her flesh. And when—with the damp wind whistling at her ears – he returned to her thoughts, it was not as the desperate, fumbling creature in the cove, but as the man who had commanded the entire attention of her soul in the days when their adulterous life frightened and exhilarated her.

Had she been crazy to believe herself utterly alive in that time – to have been delivered into her own womanliness? She had known what was real, she could prove reality on the pulses of her skin; every flicker of hope, each returning tremor of despair – they were all testable against the immediate temperature of her feelings the minute he was in her company again. The knowledge was heart-knowledge, body-knowledge, it was honest and sane. So far had it preceded questioning that sometimes she'd been afraid to question him because his answers, however careful and scrupulous – and they were not always so – were bound to tell less than she already knew. And it had gone impossibly wrong, and her confidence in the delivered heart was destroyed by it. So perhaps she had been crazy after all, crazy to risk herself then as she had been crazy to put herself at risk again today; for she had wanted the man; she had wanted him to come in strength of heart, to make a considered space in which he would allay her doubts by gentleness, in which words would be found to heal the intolerable wound. Yet she had been driven so far from her senses that it was hard even to admit this to herself; and there were other, more exacting needs. She had wanted to rage round him like a lean sow, to make him feel her hatred and her hurt, her spite and pride. If he had come for her, let him confront her whole – not just the adoring lover of his dreams, but the dark moon too, the unappeasable queen of savagery and sacrifice, the flayer of skins. But she had lacked the strength, and she could not forgive him for that, any more than she could forgive herself for the pity she also felt, or for this terrible aptitude for laying waste her life. And so, as she'd lowered her head over the handlebars against the rain, listening to the turmoil of the sea, Leah was so dazed she hardly knew whether she was cycling away from the man or towards him. She knew only that she was alone under the big Cornish night, that she did not want to be alone, that her howling in the cove had been, above all, a wail of loneliness, and there must, please God, soon be an end to it.

So she had come to Stephen's house, for there was nowhere else to go. Both Amy and Dora were at Alice's, and Alice had betrayed her; and so sheltered had Leah's life been since her arrival in Cornwall, she knew no one else well enough to knock on their door on a calamitous night and beg to be taken in.

But Stephen would look after her. Stephen would go to Roseleye the next day and pick up her things. Then she would take a train out of Cornwall on Monday, she would go somewhere else, she would find a way to replace herself.

Except that Stephen was no longer quite so tractable. He had injured feelings of his own, he had grievances against her, and those grievances were just. And still he stood above her on the stairs, in cardigan and brown corduroys, his shirt loose at the neck, his hair adrift, his unshaven, affronted face confessing with each silent second the continuing problem of his love.

'But you mustn't,' she whispered.

'Not care for you? Then why are you here?'

'Not like that, I mean,' she answered weakly.

'I wish I didn't,' he retorted. 'I'm sorry it's a bore.'

'Oh God, it's not that. It's never for a moment that. It's just that . . .'

When she faltered, he said, 'What is it, Leah? What is it just? That there's no damn point because you're still more than half in love with a man who's turning you into a nervous wreck? Is that what you're trying to say? That you don't want care and consideration; that you'd rather be roughed over by someone who's already hurt you so badly you had to cross the country to get away from him? Is that what you want?'

'I don't know,' she said, 'I don't know what I want.'

'Except that it's not me.'

Leah put a hand to her drenched hair. 'I never meant to hurt you like this. Truly I didn't.' She turned away, whispering, 'I think I'd better go.'

'Wait a minute. You're not going anywhere, not on your own.' He came quickly down the stairs and caught her by the shoulders. She flinched at his touch. When he turned her round, he was appalled to see the light go dead in her eyes. He thought of the girl who had been found under the cliff. Hastily, but too late, he withdrew his hands.

Was there no hope for friendship anywhere between men and women then? Did the brutal aspect of their sexual destiny always take over, even in the tenderest of lives – love and death, sex and death, the eventual death of love itself? Leah's eyes were crowded now. There was no fight left in her; she had never wanted to fight; she had never wanted to form this icy shell, which was, in any case, strangely melting round her; and the feel of it was soft and menstrual, though also cold, like ice-floes calving from a glacier before the warmer currents swept them melting out to sea. And

Stephen was talking through the sounds of dissolution. He was saying that if he'd got hurt it was only because he'd set himself up to be hurt, it wasn't her fault, she wasn't to take it upon herself. But she couldn't respond, could barely receive his words for the tears flowing through her. He spoke on anyway, a patient gathering of sound, holding the space between them, and when he came closer, offering an embrace that wanted nothing in that moment but what she wanted for herself, she felt no urgent need to pull away.

'But what on earth do you think we want?' asked Alice, perhaps too sharply, for she was very tired by now, and worrying about Leah, and all but in despair to feel him slip back into black hostility again after the far journey she and this man had made together through the strenuous night.

And having put the question in one world, Alice could not know that it was heard in quite another. He was back in court and ready for the question, readier than she knew, for he had slipped behind the women's lines and found an informant there. He smiled now at the despondency in the questioner's voice. He knew the answer, it was guaranteed correct, and the longer he'd thought about it the more it made a wicked kind of sense.

'Sovereignty,' he replied. 'What you want is sovereignty.'

His answer met only a moment's surprise before Alice utterly discountenanced him by shaking her head in a complicated little laugh expressive of her incredulity, her amazement, her weariness. What delicious irony that a man half out of his mind should suddenly out-trump her in her own suit like this!

'*Wommen desiren to have sovereynetee*,' she quoted. 'Is that what you're telling me? Well it's true enough, but I wonder what you imagine it means?'

Alice was unable to keep from her voice a note of

203

amusement which he took for scornful condescension, and to him it seemed they were no longer alone. He was standing offended and exposed – a ridiculous figure in an ill-fitting bathrobe, holding a ball of red wool, vulnerably male among a vast parliament of women. The higher he lifted his gaze the more women he saw. There were hundreds of them looking down on him from serried benches. Some of the faces were famous and had arrived there from all periods of history; others were vaguely familiar from his travels; a few, in the best seats on the front row, he recognized instantly – his heart almost stopping with shock to see them gathered together there. The hall, which a moment ago had been shrill with murmuration, was now perfectly still.

'Power,' he said into that stillness. 'That's what I imagine it means. What you want is power. Power over men.'

He heard Alice's weary sigh.

She said, 'Is that really what you think we want?'

'What else am I to think?' he snapped back at her. 'Look what you've been doing to me.'

'Look what you're doing to me,' howled a voice behind him, and when he turned the woven walls of the hall had drawn open. He was looking through the cliff into the cove. Perspectives looped and zoomed into close-up. He was staring down at a dishevelled woman who lay helplessly under him. He heard her voice. 'Is that why you came all this way, to do this to me? Well, do it then. I can't stop you – you know that don't you? Go on, do it if that's what you want.'

The words echoed in his head. He heard the defiance in them, the injury and bitter grief. But the face that stared up at him was no longer Leah's.

It was young, not yet twenty, and must have been pretty once, though there was a pinched intensity to the features that gave them a famished air of concentration – the lips full, slightly prognathous, the unplucked eyebrows meeting over black gem-stone eyes, one of which had been pulped in its socket by a blow to the head. Already dead for many hours, the skin was bluish and cold, with a rancid cast to the places where it wasn't clotted and torn. In the gape of the mouth two teeth were broken, and a trickle of blood had crusted under the nose, which was embellished with a small ornamental stone set into the flesh above the right nostril. The pathos of that last detail lacerated Ronan's heart. He could have wept for the pity of it, but the undamaged eye was flickering round to look at him, holding him in focus, with a miniature of his own appalled gaze reflected there. It was this living-dead face that had spoken. Now the rigid lips were loosening again. She said, 'Is it time to tell my story now?'

So his trial wasn't over yet. There was more evidence to hear. Hardly any time had passed since he'd left the kitchen and his breakdown began. He saw what had happened, how he'd been beguiled. He had been nowhere; he had been here all night. The ordeal would go on. There was, it seemed, no end to it.

He watched the girl step through into the court, he heard the gasp that rose from the assembled women at the sight of her injuries. Her voice was thin, little more than a whisper. 'It begins', she said, 'a long time ago, with the story of the causeless blows.' She hesitated, frowning as if in difficult recollection. 'In those days a man won me for his water-bride. Three hard puzzles I put to him: he solved them all. So I came out of the lake at his bidding, bringing my dowry of fairy-kine. I saw he loved me dearly. I vowed to stay with him all my days unless that time should come when he had given me three causeless blows.'

Sadly the girl shook her disfigured head. 'He swore he would never lift a hand to me. I was sure he meant it too, I wanted to believe him. Don't we always want to believe?

205

But the first blow fell when I refused to attend the christening of a child. He struck me again when he was publicly shamed by the noisy way I wept with sorrow at a wedding. And the third blow came when he heard me at a funeral laughing out loud for joy.'

There was a responsive murmur from the court. 'Each time', she went on, 'he told me my behaviour was shameful and strange. He wouldn't believe I had my own sufficient reasons. But I did, of course, and when the third blow fell I told him all.'

The voice grew louder, more confident. 'His eyes were opened then. He saw there were more ways than one of making sense of things, and other ways of feeling than his. Oh yes, he was sorry, he wanted to make amends. But it came too late. Does consciousness always come too late?' For a moment she left the question hanging on the air. 'In any case, I kept my word. I left him there to grieve his hasty ways. I vanished back into the lake. That was my first time in the world of men.' Sighing, the girl paused there as if to savour the profundity of the women's silence, drawing strength from it. 'The second was much later, in King Amangons' days. I was one among the damsels of the woods. I was in the glen that day. I lay against bare rock watching a buzzard circle while they held me down. I heard my sisters screaming and the whinny of the horse. I smelled the blood. We knew the end of sovereignty had come. The stars and waters spoke of it. Already our lady of the fall had seen our passing in the glass. Only the men imagined that the day's events were their invention. We'd waited for hours beside the fall in full knowledge of what was to come, preparing in silence for the end. I held the drinking-horn. My hands were trembling all that time. Do you think that knowing a fearful thing must happen makes it easier to bear?' The girl held her battered head high. 'I tell you it does not. And when it came the pain was terrible, though, yes, the fear was worse. Always the fear is the worst of it.'

Again silence settled over the hall. The girl stood among a daze of memories, recollecting herself. 'Then there was the pretty time with Gawain,' she said, 'he who would one day bring the daughters of the damsels of the woods to Arthur's court, who later sought the vanished grail, and achieved the mystery of the bleeding lance, yet first stood trial as the Nameless Knight because he forced my maidenhead and broke my heart. And then again, last night . . .' She faltered a moment, then tilted her brutally damaged head to catch the light. 'You see how young I was once more. It began like this: I'd had a fight with my lover, it was late, we were on our way back from a concert, at a road-house off the Bodmin road. We'd been fighting on and off for weeks, it was getting worse and worse, but this time it was very bad. This time he said we were finished now, and when I said I was glad he just got up and left me there. He said he was going back to London. I saw him start the bike and ride off in the night. At first I couldn't believe it. I thought he was bound to come back for me soon. I couldn't believe he'd leave me there like that. So I waited for ages but he didn't come. It started raining then. I hitched a lift, I got into the first car that stopped – an older man – he looked respectable enough – but you can guess the rest.

'Strange I should wash up on this shore. I left home years ago. None of my family knows I'm dead. No one will have missed me yet. I hear they're looking for him all around these parts, that everybody's answerable. Perhaps they've caught the man, perhaps they never will. For me it doesn't matter now. His name is legion. I am everywhere. There is no end to this.'

Again, in the silence of the solemn hall, the girl shook her head. After a time Alice looked up at Ronan and quietly

207

asked if he would like to explain to the girl his understanding of what she meant by sovereignty. The offer defied acceptance. In any case Ronan could not speak. Overtaken by enormous grief, he could see no reason why it should not be Leah telling some version of this story, or his wife, or his own daughter. Given ill-luck, mischance, a moment of poor judgment or of misplaced trust, what mercy could they hope to find in a world where he – lover, husband, father, fool – had driven so close to atrocity himself? And this nameless corpse had once enshrined a life as irreplaceable as theirs, as rich in its own sufficient reasons.

In a moment beyond all argument, Ronan had looked into the girl's dead eyes and found an image of his own degraded soul. Too late he began to see what sovereignty might mean. He had tried for too long to live solely on his own male terms, but he had encountered the power of a countervailing principle now – one he had failed to honour both in women and inside himself. And once its sovereignty was recognized he understood why he stood among the accused – one of Amangons' men, personally arraigned for a crime against love, immediately answerable. If he was not to indulge himself in lies, or denial, or empty breast-beating, the time had come to accept his share in the general guilt for the suffering and death of this particular girl. For whom there was nothing left to do but mourn; and nothing to bring to that mourning but the fierce current of compassion that was quickening through his body now like pain.

Poor swan, he was thinking, *poor smashed and desecrated swan, I had not meant such harm.*

Nor could it stop there. Alice was still speaking to him. 'And what of Leah?' she asked. 'What of your wife?' Had he ever truly seen either of them? Had he ever freely recognized their sovereign existence, ever accepted the claims of relationship such recognition made? Had he ever dared to meet either of them on their own irrecusable terms, beyond the constraints of his own powerful control? Had he ever dared the truly erotic life?

Ronan endured the painful questions, and for the first time in many months – in many years, perhaps – he was seeing beyond the confines of his need. Then all the structures that he'd built around his life began to fold as, one by one, the shoring-posts were kicked away. Out of the dusty ruins he watched two women emerge, emancipated into actuality.

His wife, Marion, returned his anguished gaze, not in hurt or rage, but in lightly sardonic appraisal. Under the bobbed, greying hair, the lines around her eyes were as finely drawn as the veins of a leaf. Her skin was clear, softly downed, and when she tilted her chin there was a refined, accomplished pride, a newly achieved singularity in her expression. Ronan had been married to this woman for almost twenty years, and he could not remember when he had last seen her look so beautiful.

From the clarifying perspective of his loss, he reviewed their years of marriage. For the first time he acknowledged the full scale of his defection. Time misspent in mutual recrimination fell away. Like a scrupulous loss-adjuster he assessed at their true worth her daily, ordinary acts of unconsidered love – the kind of love which makes and mends – makes children, makes homes, makes do, makes mistakes, makes up; the tragic, married love which is as close as we may come in our fallible lives to a living symbol for the reconciliation of opposing powers, and yet, like a tethered angel, must perform this hallowed function in a domestic mess of chores and bills, of ceaseless demands and impossible expectations. This was the order of love Marion had availed him of for years, nourishing it, nagging it, keeping it on hold long after he'd put the receiver down, long after it served her self-interest and self-respect to do so. Now he knew it gone. He had forfeited his lien on its valuable freehold. The truth was out. There was no going back to what had once been home.

Nor was the new world that he'd hoped to find with Leah any longer open to him. There too he had forfeited more than he had so far dared to see. For more than two years, in all the ways she knew, Leah had sought to draw him deeper into truthful meeting. Time and again she had shown him how a love wholeheartedly aware of its transgression, and willing to pay the price of it, might enter a world no longer confined in secrecy but vastly enlarged. In their hours of passion he had glimpsed the luminous spaces waiting there; these were the promise of the vision she had sought to share with him, holding that vision open for as long as she could; but the final act of deliverance had been withheld. He had withheld it, he had withheld himself; there was nowhere else to lay the blame.

Only now, as feeling began to flow again, as his heart opened to admit the inadmissible, did he perceive the earlier catastrophic errors of his heart, the true scale of his loss.

And, quite suddenly, like candles blowing out, both faces were gone. For Ronan it was as if the sky itself had been cancelled. He was alone as never in his life before. He was engulfed by loneliness, transfixed by it, by the fear of being left to die alone. He saw himself lying unattended, like the king in the chapel. His body was electric with the pain of severance. But here, on the swiftly diminishing margins of his existence, there was more shadow than illumination – a dusky, blue-black gleaming shadow, like the sheen across a raven's wing. He saw that the earth was closing round him. There was no air, no space, no help; a dense black vacuum sucked against his face, it squeezed the breath from his lungs, snuffed it at his mouth. He knew it would stop at

210

nothing less than shut-down. But this couldn't be right. He'd been promised life if this ordeal was undergone, and justice was miscarrying here as the earth took him down inside herself. Ronan opened his mouth to shout and no sound came. When he tried to move his hands he found them uninhabited.

A stream of images went syringing through his brain, and the story each one had to tell was loss. The dreams of recent weeks re-ran themselves fast-forward. He saw the man in the chapel losing blood, the patient in the operating theatre, Leah vanishing on the strand, the hag in the cave, the swan go down. He heard the blow-hole's mindless din, and every loss he'd ever endured was recapitulated in its surge and howl. Leah was gone, Marion gone, his home and family gone, hope gone, his mind gone, and now even the familiar weight of his body was shrugging itself away. He couldn't speak, couldn't scream, couldn't swallow, couldn't breathe. There was nothing left, what was left to him was nothing, there was nothing now.

'So you are free at last,' came the voice of that nothing like a dark, engorging kiss. 'We have an agreement, you and I.'

The night — it must still be night — protracts itself. Something has gone wrong with the machinery of time, his circadian rhythms are unreliable, and the clocks of hell say only *meanwhile*. But even pain and fear cannot sustain themselves indefinitely. Even shock at one's own death must pass.

For it seems that something quite as absolute as that has happened, and if not death then he doesn't know what other name to call it by, for there is no doubting that a hitherto characteristic function of his being — the person he was, the usual public representative, his constant and familiar *me* — has passed away. It feels as if he has given up the ghost, and

211

the ghost has taken over. He senses it watching, waiting, haunting the discarnate imagination as it pursues a fast-evolving posthumous career.

His body, meanwhile, is laid out on a narrow bed in a darkened room, and there is an old woman close to him whose face he cannot see. She is his night-companion, who rocks him in withered arms. Desolate otherwise, he is filled with gratitude for her company. Her words cradle him among dark gales. He finds her voice medicinal. She is telling him stories.

And who is she now, he wonders, this hag of all the world who has become the midwife to his dreams?

She is, she tells him, who she has always been – the dark lady of his soul, his neglected queen of the night, all the lovers he has used and lost, his ever-available whore, his crib, his marriage-bed, his grave. Hideous as she is, it was always she whom he was looking for, and she will shortly become his faithful wife.

He remembers then the bargain he made, the price of life, the cost of understanding. He remembers her face.

Gratitude is immediately swept aside by panic. The thought is not to be borne. To be for ever humiliated by this grotesque presence at his side, to have his body nightly wrapped in that disgusting embrace. The price is too high. He prefers obliteration.

He begs her to let him go, seeking to renege. She will hear none of it. The deal has been struck – he gave her his promise, she has given him life. Neither can be revoked. Forsaking all others, he will enter with her into the honourable estate of matrimony. And they will marry at the appointed time in the appointed place, where all the contraries improbably converge – where sun balances the moon as day the night, where dark and light have equal measure, and fresh water and salt-tides consort to prove that impossible places can exist, that unmeetable conditions can be met. His life has always been in her keeping: he will find it waiting there.

Then she is gone. He is left restless on the narrow bed, his mind ferrying back and forth across the misty water-margin between sleep and consciousness where it traffics with a flow of images. There is a residual awareness of his actual location – a blue room, somewhere in Alice's house, in Cornwall, near the sea; but his active ghost acknowledges no such limitations. It is elsewhere and everywhere. Space and time are negotiable, as are all other boundaries. The sound of water cascading through his senses drowns out all other sound, and such sleep as comes is no more than a shallow, amphibious dozing through which are accomplished strange, hypnogogic transformations.

Thus there is a time when he experiences himself as a kind of sea-horse, a creature with a sensitive equine head of princely intelligence and great dignity that evolves nevertheless from the curlicued fluke of a reptile's tail. Or, later, he is a shaggy famished animal stalking a winter wood, alarming wildfowl as he forages for nuts and berries, beech-mast, chanterelles, anything to appease his savage hunger. Licking an icicle with a rough tongue, he glimpses a white stag sniffing at the frozen air. He sees its antlers lifted skywards where pink snow-light glistens on the bare crowns of the trees; but as he edges closer, the great beast shivers, turns its flank, and vanishes against white wilderness.

From change to startling change the quest goes on. The seasons pass. His normal mode of apprehension now is wonder. He soars and burrows, flickers, prances, crawls. At times loud cries announce his presence in the night; at others he dips his head in silence to the river's reflection of the moon.

213

He finds in his wanderings the dung of many animals – the droppings of the fox, the otter's spraint, the twice-passed pellets of the hare. He contemplates the humble stuff as a portion of the continuity of things, one of the diligent ways in which existence is passed along the food-chain, from life to life, until he has seen how it is to be both vole and hawk, both owl and shrew, and knows how far beyond the merely human range his flexible intelligence can reach.

How far beyond the animalic too, for there are other kingdoms occulted inside his cells: the crab and cuttle-fish are closer cousins than he knew, as are the minnow and the newt, and the giant saurian drowning in a tar-pit squinting at the stars. Later there are the prodigal fantasies of the insects to explore, and a myriad sheerer creatures too, before he passes beyond what he had once taken for the limits of the animate, and feels his way into the vegetable realm of fern and leaf, of root and fungus; and on at last, downwards and deeper, into the dense glimmering under-world of water and the rocks.

It is here, like a naked miner at the planet's heart, that he knows himself deeply inside the hag. She has opened herself to receive him, and he has become one with her substance. He begins to believe that this was the wedding waiting for him – this intimate embedding of his nature deep within the earth – but even as the thought occurs, he reaches a parting of the ways. It is the exact underground equivalent of a place he once knew in the otherworld: a fork in the track marked by a vertical dividing-stone. This stone too is stippled and powdered in green must, in oxidized stains and sunburst efflorescences of lichen. Again he must decide which way to go.

One path will take him down into still deeper fusion with the earth. He sees its shadows descend through dense green murk until the last distinctions blur in clay and mud and torpid pools as black as bitumen. To go that way would be to cancel out the final spark of consciousness. He would suffer neither heart-ache nor hunger there, but he would find no meaning either, for in that place, beyond the last figure of the dance, he would have passed outside significant existence.

Another way stands open. Its tall stair winds ahead of him, and the effort of the climb will take him up and out. That way he can pass back through the veil of matter. He can pick up the human task again. He can resume the dance.

Instantly his body flashes with pain at the prospect. It scalds across the newly tender, naked skin he wears. He howls with the anguish of it, a prolonged, refusing, animalic howl; but then the anguish too becomes a flourish of a sound he hears inside the howl – a cry, a call, an animating clarion raised against the silence and the dark. The sound extends itself, refining its inflexions of pain and passion into song. It passes through him, he is what passes through, and what it passes into. There is neither division nor blurring of identity; only this quickening, harmonic confluence of song which reaches everywhere. Insistently it tells him how this fund of images is none of his invention, but the stirrings of the earth inside the matter of his mind.

Only then, at the vivid moment of its return, does he understand what he has been looking for, what has been lost. He comes alive to it now; its sense surrounds and embraces him. He feels the song of the earth rising through the soles of his feet. He inhabits it. He knows it for the song of his returning soul. His whole being burgeons. The choice is already made.

He takes the first step upwards. Imagination gathers speed, accelerating back through all the kindoms of the beasts, and he remembers himself capable of more than howls. Hoarsely the breath in his throat takes the shape of words. As he climbs, he staggers back into the limitless possibilities of language, astounded and delighted by the trickery of names, those loops of light that ring and dazzle everything. Through the caverns of the earth words radiate towards him. He wonders at their countless spells to conjure, shrivel, bless, at their capacity for making play, at all the tongue's infatuating weaponry.

Soon there comes a time of images within the images, for he is in touch with a prolific and far-ranging intelligence which contemplates other pictures, other scenes, even as it follows his progress up the winding stair. At each complete turn of the spiral it finds no difficulty in conceiving how his existence has been wound on a generation, from the earliest, most primitive of men, through long millennia, until he is in the time and experience of a maze-dancing people far removed from what had recently been his own monolithic mode of consciousness. He is astonished how spacious their world, how widely its bounds of meaning reach to embrace the planets and the stars. And still the stairs twist upwards, drawing him on through the pattern of his ancestry till he is in his great-grandfather's time, then his grandfather's, and his father's – where he approaches the passionate moment when his present life will be conceived.

At that point he reaches the last skin of rock that stands between this inner and the outer world. The sounds around him merge into the clamour of the waterfall. He sees that he has arrived at a place inside the wall of rock that forms the fall's wild cell. He smiles with recognition, remembering how – not long ago, and from the other side – that very place had filled his mind with dread. Now he can delight in its no longer alien intelligence. He draws strength from it.

This is the place, it seems, but not yet the time. He senses presences around him, and events preparing to unfold. Somewhere a buzzard's piercing call commands the hidden sky. It warns that out there, in the world of light, a familiar figure must soon come scrambling down among the rocks to meet him.

Hearing how the clamour of the fall elides with the urgent arrival of the sea, Ronan savours the moment in thoughtful silence, steadying himself, waiting.

Part Three
MANDORLA

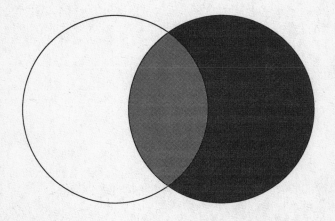

'A child of earth and the starry heavens.'

(Orphic Inscription)

10
SOVEREIGNTY

Dawn over Porthmallion Quay, the tide turning back towards the dark Atlantic, while inland a cloudy, marbled light illuminates the ground-mist clinging to the eastward hills. A bleak mewing of gulls slants down across the harbour-bar. Boats stir. There are lights in wheel-houses, the clank of tackle shifting, the smell of kelp and engine-oil, and of unfolding day.

In one of the row of white houses on the cliff above the bar, Leah lies in a darkened room, somewhere between sleep and waking – dreaming still, but knowing that she dreams, and mingling memories, apprehensions, notions, with images that rise unbidden to her thought. She lies on the bed much as the landscape lies under receding night, still continuous with it, slow to differentiate herself. Not wholly personed yet, she is waiting for something without knowing what she is waiting for, holding herself afloat in this crib of dreams.

Figures come and go across her mind. A version of Alice sits spinning there, lips sealed, all-wise and enigmatic; under her foot the treadle rises and falls. The wheel turns, inside its mother-of-all the spindle whirrs; and the picture widens: Amy lies naked on the rocks, still virginal, feeling her way, wondering in what form the great event will come; while Dora Pascoe wrings her hands, daily assenting to life, but only through remembered grief. Calmly Leah walks among her friends, affectionate and separate, lonely, but open in her loneliness. She is in search of a particular destiny, which can come, she imagines, only from that seamless place on the horizon where the night-sky merges into land and sea without distinction.

Her gaze is fixed on that dark aspect now. She feels the earth under her bare feet. There is a beating on the air, the creak of wings. Through the gap prised open between day and night a great horse flies. The sky is shuddering. White flanks and haunches gleam as the beast wheels against dark wind and touches down. For a moment it stands across from her, snorting, stamping its hooves among the lilies of the dawn, all animal. And then the winged horse rears. Hooves flash. The skin folds open under the neck, along the chest, and a man steps easily out from the cage of bone. Naked, glistening, he treads the earth lightly. Leah stands her ground, knowing that this time she will not run; and in the same instant – to the famished, wild cry of an alighting gull – she emerges into day.

Like wind and tide, men were – Dora Pascoe decided as she eavesdropped, later that morning, on Alice's side of a telephone conversation with Leah – a mixed blessing. Not that she had much use for them herself these days, though it had been odd to come across Reg Sessions weeping by the hedge the other day and feel her old heart flood with more than sympathy.

Out in the hall Alice was saying, 'I'd ask you to come home at once, but . . . Yes, he is.' And, after a further brief interruption down the line, 'My dear, I couldn't blame you if you'd rather walk across hot coals. But he hasn't even woken yet, and I don't want to disturb him.'

What could one do with them, thought Dora Pascoe,

meaning men; and what could one do without them? Take Reg, for example; though she knew it was her weakness to be too easily overwhelmed by other people's grief, for it always brought back sorrows of her own. But, if she was honest, other feelings — unfamiliar to her for a long time, and possibly disgraceful — had also stirred inside her as the unhappy man poured out his heart. She had seen in those watery eyes a mirror of her own disconsolate condition — except that she was long inured to loneliness while this man still fumbled it as from a recent disability.

'You don't think there's a ghost to be laid at least?' she heard Alice ask; and, a moment later: 'I can see perfectly well it might go either way. Feeling free enough to see him again, I mean, or so free of him there's no need any more.'

All of which seemed unnecessarily complicated to Dora Pascoe, who had managed, by contrast, to cheer up Reg Sessions quite simply. In fact, they had surprised one another, those two, and were a little breathless with it. She would be seeing him again, for tea, today, and sooner or later she would have to talk to Alice about what was going on between herself and the hapless widower. It really was most unexpected.

'That would be good if you felt you could,' Alice was saying with warm relief, 'but let me talk to him first. Let me see how he is. And if you could leave it till after half-past seven say? There's a thing I've promised myself I'll do this evening.' A few moments later she rang off affectionately.

When she came back through into the kitchen, Mrs Pascoe said, 'Didn't I tell you she'd be at Stephen's?' For a moment she admired her own percipience, then extended it. 'Are those two getting together after all?'

'I really don't know,' Alice answered. 'Stephen's lent her his place while she sorts herself out, but he seems to be sleeping at the nursery. Which is rather more effective than laying a naked sword between them, I suppose.'

The reference eluded Dora Pascoe whose thoughts were already elsewhere. Various complicated reflections about Alice and Leah, and Ronan and Stephen and Reg Sessions, had been displaced by a sudden joyous remembrance of her husband who was drowned at sea. She was recalling how they used to go biking over to Sankence woods at twilight of a summer evening, and how he'd take his old fiddle out of its case and lay a tune on the air. In those days the wood was filled with nightingales and the lilt of his music would catch at the birds' throats and make them start up singing. He called it fishing for a song. He said it was like laying bait. He had always been able to catch her heart that way, and Dora was stirred by the memory now.

All music as the dark came down, she thought. Sighing, she said, 'They seem to make such heavy weather of it now. In my day once you made your bed you had to lie on it.' Then she remembered that her day had been Alice's too, and that Alice had done no such acquiescent thing; so she relaxed in the reflection that it took all sorts to make a world, and some were more peculiar than others, that's all.

'Anyway, I'd best be on my way.' The cleaning-lady nodded significantly towards the upper floor. 'You'll be all right on your own now?'

Alice said she was sure she would. But she was sure too that she wasn't about to waste the rest of the day waiting for the man to wake, so as soon as Dora had left, she scribbled a postscript to the note she had left for him earlier on the kitchen table. Even then she had to answer the phone twice more before she could get back down to her studio.

The first call came from Amy, who was eager for more news of the evolving drama at Roseleye. It had provided, she declared, one of the most exciting nights of her rather boring life, and was well worth the trouble she'd run into at home for staying at Alice's without permission. Eager to

224

know how Ronan was, the young woman sounded disgruntled to hear that the man was still asleep in bed after all this time.

'You know Leah's at Stephen's?' she said.

'Yes, I've just been talking to her.'

'How is she?'

'She thinks she's replacing herself at last.'

'What does that mean?'

'I'm not at all sure. We'll just have to wait and see.' Wondering whether she had put too sharp a note of closure in her voice, Alice added, 'Though from the sound of her I'm quite looking forward to meeting the replacement.'

But Amy was kicking her heels among the postcards and knick-knacks of the gift-shop in Porthmallion where she worked part-time, and business was drearily slow, so it still took a while for Alice to disengage herself.

When she did so, the telephone rang again almost immediately, and this time she found herself listening to a stranger's voice.

Briefly he came awake to a ringing sound which his excited imagination heard as the jingling of a silver branch, but his eyes did not open. Some time later he surfaced again, amazed by the face he saw advancing towards him through his dream, though it faded almost immediately in the pale light gusting through the curtains. The room was blue. It had an unfamilar smell. He caught lavender and creosote mingled with a musty hint of damp. Then the curtains billowed bringing in a larger taste of day, of lenient morning, rinsed and gusty out there. He sat up in a space that had the patient feel of a room rarely occupied, trying to locate himself. There was just light enough to read the words embroidered on the needlepoint sampler above his bed:

*'The Slumber of the Body
seems to bee but a Waking
of the Soul.'*

Sir Thos. Browne

And he remembered how the night had been.

But his senses were alert to the day, impatiently so. It must have rained in the night. He could smell it on the air. He imagined the garden glistening in damp mist, the day unveiling. He was, he discovered, naked beneath the sheets. A white bathrobe lay tossed across a wicker chair. A ball of scarlet wool had unravelled in the bed beside him.

Then he heard the buzzard out across the sky.

He found a note on the kitchen table telling him that Alice was in her study and that he should help himself to food and drink before joining her there. It had been written at 9.30, but a postscript added nearly four hours later informed him that she was now in her workshop. Now it was after two, and he was dismayed to find how much of the day had vanished. When he'd found his watch in the bathroom he'd thought it must be wrong. Nor could he work out how there had been time to wash and dry his clothes, especially in the dampish weather. But, yes, he was starving. He plugged in the electric kettle, took a loaf from the crock, and cut himself a fat slice. Looking for butter he found bacon also, and decided to make a bacon sandwich. There were tomatoes and lettuce, the coffee was to hand. The smells quickened his appetite.

Standing by the Aga in the silence of the house, he heard the cry of the buzzard thrilling across the sky. He crossed to the window and watched the great bird make an effortless banking turn against the pearly glare above the glen.

Instantly his spirit lifted with a sense of kinship. He knew how it would be to soar on such expansive wings, to feather the wind, to see the green land mapped below. The cry came again, a piercing talon of sound. It penetrated all his senses, its voltage jolted the heart. Ronan came fully awake. His skin prickled with the knowledge that he had come through.

When he found his way down to the mill, Alice was sitting in a patch of sunlight outside the studio where a garden-bench overlooked a bend in the stream. Her chin was tucked into the neck of her smock, the hands lightly clasped, her eyes closed. The scene stirred memories which he could not place.

Reluctant to disturb her, Ronan stopped some yards away. She must, he knew, be exhausted from the long night's effort. She had laboured with him for hour after hour, taking the full impact of his turbulent feelings. She had heard his confession and conducted his exequies. She had midwifed him through into this new, unanticipated place. He felt known to her with a terrifying nudity now.

And everything inside him was raw and tremulous still. So he turned quietly aside and walked down to the steep bank where he stood for a time watching the water as it sluiced between black stones. Presumably it was somewhere near here that he'd tried to cross the stream on his way back from the cove? He remembered seeing the building in the gloom. He remembered how truculent his mood had been, how wretchedly his jump had ended in a muddy grasping slide.

Now blue daylight scattered among trees, he could smell salt on the air, and the damp, glaucous smell of the dells. His senses were cleansed, his nerves scoured. He felt alive inside his skin, he felt renewed.

And these, precisely, were such feelings as he'd wanted to

share with Leah; but she was gone from his life, and this spacious clarity he felt could be no more therefore than the mark of a vast inward emptiness.

'So you're awake at last!'

Ronan turned, startled by the voice. Alice was smiling at him where she stretched. 'I was supposed to be meditating,' she said, 'but it seems to have unravelled into a catnap.'

Almost shyly he said, 'I didn't want to disturb you. You can't have had much sleep.'

'Oh I don't need much these days.'

'But God knows what time you got to bed last night.'

He saw she was looking at him slightly askance. He was conscious how banal his responses, but there was a wry twist at the corner of her mouth, a sense of crossed purposes.

Alice said, 'You do realize this is Monday?' And he stood bewildered, calculating. He'd left home on Friday, spent that night on the cliffs, come to Roseleye the next day, on Saturday afternoon. This must surely be Sunday afternoon? But time had stolen a march on him. 'Monday the twenty-third of September to be exact,' Alice supplied. 'You've slept through a day and a night and rather more than half another day.' He gaped at her smile. 'Where *have* you been?' she said.

'I'm just wondering . . .' But this was so strange, the actuality of the day, the place, the stream – the continuity of things in contrast with the sweet, deranging sense of having tripped out of time completely. A day and a night and most of another day! Yet those lost hours might equally have been the year and a day of the old story. The world might have grown ancient round him as he slept. There could have been mighty increments of history.

A breeze ruffled the glen, bringing cloud off the sea, and

Alice shivered. 'We should talk,' she said, crossing mottled hands at her chest. 'Let's go inside. I'm a bit chilly here.'

It felt as though the large attentive stillness had been gathered inside those walls of random stone for a long time. A shaft of sunlight through the high window was stippled with dust, and there was colour everywhere: the stacks of cubby-holed shelves were packed with balls and bobbins and hanks of yarn – undyed wools of smoky black, cloud-grey and white, then on through a subtle botanical spectrum of colour variations – umber and orange, citrus yellows, soft pastel pinks and blues, magenta, scarlet, indigo, a vernal range of vegetable greens – like a huge, resourceful palette splashed against white walls. Under the northern light of a lower window stood a drawing-desk with a chest of drawers and a metal filing-cabinet to either side. They formed a studious cubicle within the wider space where spinning-wheels and looms were ranged. One vertical loom was dressed with a plain warp but otherwise bare; a large horizontal machine stood empty, and a dust-sheet concealed whatever work might be in progress on the tall frame by the iron gearing system that must once have driven the millstones.

But it was the smells of that lofty space which most impressed him: the oily whiff of lanolin from a pile of fleece, the smell of timber off the looms, and the tarry heat exuded by the pot-bellied stove, all of these mingled with the sharper reek of dyes and mordants, and the smell of wool to give this air a rich, familiar redolence.

Within seconds of stepping into it, Ronan turned to Alice and said, 'It feels as though I've been here before.'

Alice was pulling a stool up to a spinning-wheel. She stared at him, wondering for a moment, then sat down and reached for a rolag on the bench beside her. 'You don't mind if I work as we talk? I hate to let time go.'

'Of course not. I'd like to watch. But . . . the thing is, I don't remember when.'

Alice looked up from where her fingers offered the wool to the spindle. 'You were in here on Saturday evening. You'd walked out of the kitchen. I found you standing in the rain like a lost soul in the glare of the courtesy-light. I brought you in here. It seemed the only thing to do.'

Frowning, Ronan closed his eyes so that only the smells of the studio and the sounds of Alice's wheel impinged on his senses. Memories returned, and he was back there again, on that terrible night, his cracked head a pot of pain, his clothes sodden, his face a wreck of snot and tears as he bellowed out his grief and rage on the studio floor. Then this old woman had crossed the flags to join him there. She had sat down with him, folding her arms round his quaking body, rocking with him, back and forth – for how long? Hours perhaps. He remembered the smell of wool from her cardigan, its warmth at his face, her body-heat holding him, comforting him, keeping him there, contained, as he howled and raged, reviling himself and the world that bore him.

The sound of her voice came back to him – it had been like ointment on the grazes of his brain. She was telling him ancient, heraldic stories, one after another in a continuum of sound – all the stories she loved best out of the old days, and out of the events that were pressing closely on her mind – the legend of the damsels of the woods and of the Rich Fisher's wound, the story of Gawain and the mystery of the Bleeding Lance, the tale of the Loathly lady and the Nameless Knight that Chaucer had given to the Wife of Bath to tell, the story of the Causeless Blows.

She had been at a loss what else to do for him, Alice admitted now, for he had been far beyond intelligible speech, and his body had been so heavy against her that she couldn't move. They were stuck together there; so she had soothed him as best she could by rocking him in the cradle of her stories, spinning her yarns until Dora and Amy came looking for them, and somehow, between them, they had got him back up to the house.

Alice pushed the rim of the wheel into motion again and pressed the treadle. She leaned into the rhythm of her work while Ronan sought to reconstruct the night's events, trying to discriminate between reality and dream. Surely there had been a point, he asked, when there were policemen in the house?

There had indeed, Alice confirmed. George Nankevill and his sergeant had called in to see her on their way back to Porthmallion.

'To see *you*?'

'I was able to help out once when he was getting nowhere with his usual methods.' Alice left Ronan to make what he could of this as she went on. 'He was wondering whether I might be able to help him with the case of the girl they'd found, but he got terribly worked up when he saw your car outside. I had to tell some fibs, I'm afraid, but as it happened they were called away on a stronger lead.' She took in the pallor of Ronan's face. 'Do sit down. I'm sure you need to.'

But Ronan was too restless to settle. 'The trouble is,' he frowned, 'I don't know what's real now and what's. . .'

Alice nodded sympathetically. 'Hardly surprising – you *were* mildly concussed. But I got Charlie Hardy to take a look at your head – she's a doctor who lives in the village – and she wasn't too worried about it.' Alice smiled at the memory. 'You must have caught her name because you kept lurching up at her and saying, "Kiss me, Hardy!" – which rather confirmed her diagnosis that you were in a state of total emotional collapse. Perhaps it's time we talked about that?'

*

Throughout the afternoon their conversation unfolded to the whirr of the wheel as Ronan shared his version of the weekend. The light gradually shifted round them while Alice listened intently, helping him make sense of the way events in the world around him had elided with the otherworld of dream. As his comprehension deepened, the man appeared to change with the light. Even his face had a different cast to it – more open and animated than that of the self-conscious, defended figure who had sat across from her in the parlour two days before.

When all her carded fleece was spun, Alice made Ronan hold out his wrists, and draped a skein of yarn between them. She began to wind it into a ball and the motion reminded him of how he had rewound the scarlet ball of wool that had unrolled across the floor of his dreams. He was frowning into space, remembering. His heart lifted. 'There was a giantess,' he said suddenly. 'I know it sounds crazy, but she was so real . . .'

'A giantess?'

His eyes wandered the workshop, looking both outwards and inwards, seeing the place around him, reliving the enchanted encounter with the giantess of his dreams. His gaze came to rest on the pile of fleeces where he and Alice had lain together while she told him stories. From there he looked up and saw the great cogged mill-wheel against the wall with the covered loom standing in front of it. Alice must have followed his gaze, for she too remembered something.

'I wonder,' she pondered, smiling. 'When you were stumbling about in here the other night you pulled that dust-sheet off. It's draped quite loosely.' She freed his hands of the yarn. 'Why not take it off again?'

Ronan crossed the room and a moment later he was gazing up at the tall, uncovered tapestry. Out of the textured hues of woven wool the figure of his giantess emerged again – dressing her hair, her body softly delineated against the background of the land – and he saw at once why the figure had instantly compelled devotion. He stood in silence, filled with awe and loss, yearning for the impossible in the calm afternoon light.

Quietly Alice came across the room to stand beside him.

'It's so beautiful,' he whispered. 'Even the eyes . . . I don't know how . . .'

Alice nodded. 'They were terribly difficult,' she said, 'but they seem to work.'

'Has she seen it yet?'

'I only finished it the other day, and she doesn't even know about it yet. She would never let me draw her, you know. She thought I was sketching Amy at the time I made the studies. I'm not at all sure what she'll make of it.'

'Surely she could only love it?' Ronan exclaimed. 'It's so truthful. To the deep feel of her, I mean. You can't know how many times I've watched her hold out her hair that way . . . that tilt of her neck towards the comb . . .'

And then, as he looked back at the image, Ronan saw it alter before his eyes – there was an instant reversal of figure and ground, and what had previously been the lithe outline of the standing woman's body had become, startlingly, on the other side, the profile of a hag.

That was how he immediately perceived the newly emerged figure; but then he recognized also how the shift of accent had not been from fair to foul, but from one complex mode of beauty to another, each of them precisely defined by the other's form. It was impossible to hold both images in focus at once, yet each seemed intimately enfolded inside the other, as youth and age, or innocence and experience, are always immanent within the features of the human face. Nor did it stop there, for as he was drawn more deeply into

233

the design, he saw how what he had first interpreted only as part of the landscaped background of the piece had resolved itself into the bodily substance of the crone. He gasped aloud at the marvel of the thing. It was as if the world inside the loom had revolved on its axis. It was as if he had felt the actual earth turn under his feet.

When he glanced in astonishment at Alice he found her smiling at him. 'That's good,' she said. 'I wanted it to take a little time.'

'But how did you do that?'

Alice looked back critically at her work. 'I used only the dyes I could mix from three plants: madder for the reds, woad for the blues, and the yellows I got from weld. Raw wool gave me the neutral tones. They used to work that way in fifteenth-century Flanders, in the ateliers of Bruges and Ghent. There's no comparison, of course – they leave me standing breathless. But I needed that simple armature to hold the thing together, to interlace it all with light.'

'I knew it was more than a portrait, but . . .'

'It's not really a portrait at all. In fact, you gave me the title for the piece the other night.'

'I did?'

'I should have seen it for myself much earlier, of course, but sometimes you get so involved in the work you can't see through it. It took you to remind me.'

'Are you going to tell?'

'It's *Sovereignty*,' – Alice smiled at the sudden widening of Ronan's eyes – 'which is the name this Lady was once known by. Sovereignty or Royal Rule. She's the impersonal, timeless figure who is both the hag of the old stories and the beautiful woman she becomes. She's the living soul of the land. The ground of our being. Everything finally depends on how we relate to her, which is why in the Celtic realms the king was ritually given to her in marriage. She was revered as the true source of power. The whole pattern of natural increase depended on the sanctity of their union.'

'But you've shown her alone here?'

'Isn't that her condition today – a lady in waiting?'

Ronan caught the wry, interrogative glint in Alice's eye. Was she still speaking of the impersonal soul of the earth, he wondered, or did her remark reflect on the unrequited lot of women in a time when few men regarded their relationships as sacramental matters? Was she thinking, more directly, of Leah perhaps? Or even, it suddenly occurred to him, of some aspect of his own evolving soul?

Alice might have been thinking, allusively, of all these things, but even as he allowed their implications to pass through him, she added, 'Though she's still active too, of course – whether we respond to her or not. And we're in terrible trouble when we don't. After all, she *gives* us everything, so if we ignore her when she says it's time to change, why should she *forgive* us anything?'

Ronan stood in silence. She felt his mood darken again as he reflected how little room he had allowed in his life for such considerations. She observed the self-recrimination in his frown, the possibility of resumed despair. 'But look,' she gestured, 'there's a mandorla up there too.' She pointed to the almond-shaped space on the tapestry where the radiant circles of sun and moon intersected each other in the sky above the figure's head. 'It insisted on being there. As a sort of promise, I suppose.'

'A mandorla?'

'The area where two circles overlap,' Alice explained. 'It's an ancient emblem for the coupling of earth and heaven. Of the female principle and the male, if you like, though it has lots of other applications. I see it as the house of the imagination – the place where our inner world merges with the outer world to shape our experience.' She smiled across at Ronan. 'Isn't that where we all live all the time – between earth and heaven? And not just in the public world outside, or in our private world of dreams, but in the mandorla where they meet and deal with one another? It's our gateway to meaning. The problem is to keep it open so that the claims of both worlds are honoured. Which is what my lady here is trying to do.'

Alice sighed, then glanced from the tapestry to the watch dangling from the ribbon at her fob. 'And speaking of inner and outer worlds,' she added, 'something rather special is about to happen out there, and I promised myself I'd take part. Would you like to come?'

Ronan hesitated, bemused by the quick shift of attention; but, yes, he would be glad of the open air, of a chance to gather his agitated thoughts.

When they stepped outside, Alice gasped at what had happened to the day. Already it was after six, the cloud had thickened from the west, and all around the glen a mist was trawling across the hillside paddocks – a soft, darkling blur, like the bloom on the sloe-berry that Alice would pick later from its thorns as they followed the stream towards the sea. She knew instantly that they would see nothing of the heavens that evening. Ronan sensed her disappointment though he had no clear notion of its cause. Midges scribbled on damp air about his head. He heard the sound of water among the rocks like distant rain.

'I think we should go anyway,' Alice muttered, and, grasping her old ashplant for support, she set out in rubber boots across the stream.

They were silent for most of their walk through the glen, though here and there Alice drew his attention to a dipper's flight, or the worrying way that knotweed had begun to choke the stream. Out beyond the trees, as the gorge steepened, there were the last, battered moon-daisies to admire, and the frail pink balsam petals where the bracken fronds turned bronze.

'I've been thinking about the mandorla – in the light of what's happened to me,' he said eventually. 'About the boundary between the inner and outer worlds.'

'I would imagine the distinctions are illusory,' Alice answered, 'even though we experience them as real.'

'That's what I've begun to see. But I'd let my mandorla get very thin. I was allowing too little room for negotiation between the world out there and the world in here. In fact, I was wearing myself out trying to keep them apart.'

'And it can't be done, not for ever. Not unless you stay asleep,' Alice conceded. 'I suppose there are some who do.'

'Too many!' said Ronan. 'But I was thinking – what if you expanded the mandorla until the circles completely overlapped?'

'Wouldn't that be God's imagination? – a circle with its centre everywhere and its circumference nowhere, which was how the ancients used to describe it. It would contain everything.'

'And you think that's how things really are?'

'I don't even know what it might mean.' Alice smiled. 'All I'm sure of is that the wider you hold the mandorla open, in the full sympathetic reach of the imagination – and no matter how fierce the strain can get sometimes – then the richer life feels in meaning.'

'Yes,' Ronan said, remembering how he had felt when he heard the buzzard's cry across the glen.

When they arrived at the dividing-stone Alice paused to catch her breath. She saw the man glance at his watch, then up at the declining light. 'What is it?' she asked.

'I shouldn't be too long,' he said. 'It's getting late and I have to find a place to stay tonight.'

Alice raised her brows at him. 'I shall be most offended if

you don't stay with me! We are intimates, after all. Besides, there's still unfinished business. I had a number of phone calls today, and one of them was from Leah. She may come by tonight. Or if not tonight, then almost certainly tomorrow.'

Ronan stood by the dividing-stone, unbreathing. Resigned to irretrievable loss, he had not anticipated this. He found himself in a further commotion of uncertain feeling now.

Alice said, 'The world goes on you know.'

'But I thought . . .'

'And women are not entirely predictable.'

'Has she said she wants to see me?'

'Not in quite those words. But I think she should be given the chance, don't you? I don't want your shadow haunting her.'

Some moments later, having left Ronan a space to collect himself, Alice proceeded to discompose him further. 'There's something else you ought to think about. I also had a call from your wife.'

'What!'

'A rather intelligent woman, I thought, who sounded very worried. I took the liberty of telling her you'd call back tonight.'

'But how did she . . . ?'

'Through the police. They must have traced your address from your licence plate as part of their investigations. Your local force told her where the car had been seen, and George Nankevill let her know you were here.'

'Did you tell her what I . . . ?'

His question gravelled on silence before Alice's stare.

'Only that you were recovering from a minor concussion,' she replied, 'and that I expected you to be up and about quite soon. I said you would explain everything when you called.'

Ronan looked up and found himself under an inquisitor's gaze. The first reflexive pang of panic faded. Unexpectedly it was followed by a quick sense of release, like the shooting of a rusted bolt. It seemed that an incriminating truth could bring remission too, and he had been caught out by all kinds of difficult truth this weekend. Reflecting now on the cunning quantum-machinery of fate which seemed to be working him over where he stood by the dividing-stone in the failing light, he gave a little snorting laugh of acceptance. 'It seems', he said, 'that the real court of love is only just about to convene.'

Alice allowed a smile, and turned away, taking the path to the left – the same way Leah had taken two days before – up the steep slope towards the cliff.

Long before they were high enough to see it, Ronan heard the agitation of the sea. The dusk was loud with the running tide. Further along the coast the blow-hole's foamy shrapnel would be skimming the air. He felt the wildness everywhere, he savoured its bracing indifference to the cavillings of the human mind. He relished the liberty it brought.

When they came to the place of Alice's choosing he stood a little apart from her, taking the wind at his mouth, watching the blurred sky condense into a sea the colour of wrought iron. Nearer he saw one of the rocky islets flash in a sudden nimbus of exploding surf. Closer still, at the foot of the headland where the body of the girl had been found, the waves were buckling and rising in a mint-green surge of swell.

Ronan turned his gaze inland, looking across the gorge to where the stream plummeted steeply down a crag of rock before twisting away to the sea. Already the trees in the glen were scarcely more than deeper smudges on the buff-grey dusk, and there was so little guarantee of continuity to the hills beyond that he could have believed himself on an island there. It might have been the way-station island from Alice's book, he thought, where *Compaignie* and *Amittié* waited, fishing from the cliff, as his pinnace put ashore after the storm.

Again Alice consulted her watch. 'Our timing's excellent,' she said. 'Unfortunately, for our purpose visibility is nil.'

'What had you hoped to see?'

'What's about to happen, out there,' she answered. 'It's the autumnal equinox today – one of the two points of the year when day and night are of equal duration. But this one is special because there's a full moon tonight. She'll be rising over there in just a few minutes, at the zero point of Aries in the east. And at exactly the same moment' – Alice swung round to point in the opposite direction – 'the sun will be setting at zero degrees of Libra in the west. So for just an instant they'll balance one another across the sky, at twilight, at a time when the dark is perfectly balanced with the light.' Alice lifted her eyes to the occluding blur of cloud. 'And that's no more than a fraction of what's going on. But I'm afraid we shan't get to see any of it.'

In Ronan's eyes a flare of excitement answered to the suppressed elation in Alice's voice. 'We have our imaginations,' he cried above the gusting wind. 'It's happening anyway, right, – whether we can see it or not? And, if we're in the mandorla, isn't it taking place inside us as well as out there?'

'That's exactly right.' Alice lifted her voice. 'The ancients also used to say that there's a sun and a moon inside us, and also the stars. So we can at least consider what we can't observe. Did you know, by the way, that the very word *consider* means to be together with the stars, to put yourself in touch with their intelligence?'

240

Other words than Alice's were ringing through Ronan's imagination now. He watched her gazing upwards where her thoughts were on the unseen halls of space, but an inward voice was drawing his own vision downwards to the earth. He looked back into the little gorge where the stream clashed with the incoming sea. Then his gaze swung outwards through the twin bastions of rock that marked its seaward exit.

The tide stood almost full. It was crashing high among the coastal rocks, sliding across broken stairs and pavements, refunding itself in shattered white cascades. Soon, for all its temper, it would have to turn. Yet before that happened there would be a second or so when the tide would neither ebb nor flow; and in that moment there must be a place where the sea-going stream met the furthest reaches of the turning swell.

Suddenly, without a word, he was running back the way they had come, down the steep damp track towards the upright stone at the division of the path.

In the minutes before the sun declined below the horizon and the moon rose, Alice was reflecting on how their hidden lights would stand as far opposed as they could get across the opaque sky. From that point they could only move closer. And this at the equinox when the sun was setting and the moon was full!

She recalled her vision at the fall. Neptune had been on the moon in her chart that day: it was a time for revelations! She had been shown the violent beginning of the era that was at last coming to an end. Now behind the clouds the exhausted king lay bleeding, and without a new relationship to everything that had been suppressed and denied he would not recover.

Silently Alice stood in remembrance of the murdered girl,

whose name she might never know, who remained bereft of all identity save that of victim, and who was therefore, until the time when her story could be told, entirely representative. Neither the cause of the weekend's events, nor reducible to their occasion, she was intimately a part of them, a sentient ghost, active in the glen, looking for a response from the feelings to her otherwise unanswerable questions.

Alice remembered the girl's body as she had seen it in those moments when she talked with Ronan in the parlour at Roseleye. She remembered how the women in white had bathed it in the pool. She remembered the stone man and the lady of the fall. She remembered the crude wooden chalice and how that mortal wound had been healed – as if the wound itself secreted its own remedy!

Her thoughts were moving quickly now. She reflected on the powerful gains that had been made for consciousness in the era that was ending. With growing ingenuity and vigour men had taken charge of nature, and the increase this brought was not to be demeaned. But nothing came without cost, and in tearing free from the bonds of the natural order, wounds had been torn in consciousness itself. Across the planet now those wounds were crying out for healing. It might already be too late. Yet here, near the end of her days, in the gathering crisis of the times, as the female principle felt its way towards a new balance with the male, Alice sensed that she might be watching the difficult rehearsals for a promising third act in the long passion-play of the human soul.

Turning to share these thoughts with Ronan, she found him gone. Already he was almost half way down the path into the gorge, and hurrying. She watched him go until he dipped below her sight-line and vanished in the gloom. Then he was gone also from her thoughts, for Alice felt her own heart quickening as suddenly she reconceived the new work that had been taking shape for weeks in her imagination. It would, she saw, be huge, more complex than she had first thought, much more difficult; but somehow it must be done. And there would, she knew, be time for it before her own great transformation came.

Once more Alice checked her watch. Smiling, she lifted her head, saluting eastwards where the full moon rose invisibly above the turning earth.

The thoughts passing through Ronan on that swift descent were strange. They were less thoughts than sensory impulses drawn from the touch of wind at his face, from the commotion of the tide, and the stream falling towards it through the gorge. Recalling the moment on the walk to the cove with Leah when he had wanted to take possession of this landscape like a bride, he laughed to realize how close one might come to an insight yet still skid past it till one ended half a world away. Now he felt the constancy of grass under his feet, and the patient stones. He felt himself sustained.

Again he came to the dividing-stone. Clambering from ledge to ledge of the rocks below it, he found and took the roughly hidden third-way staircase down into the gorge. And it was like climbing down into his dreams, except that this time he was wide-awake – more vividly so than at any time since he'd been a child, though with the conscience of a chastened adult heart, and a man's renewed imagination now.

In his eagerness he missed a dark turn of the track and took a sheerer way that brought him down beside the waterfall. There were umbels growing in the grass, and the sky above the gorge had darkened to bluish slate. He could see the waters churning in the trough below. Ahead,

243

through the narrow throat of the channel between the cliffs, he saw the dense weight of the Atlantic heaving in.

Now he was faced with a difficult, risky slither if he was to reach the slab of rock that overlooked the pool. For a second he hesitated, then kicked off his shoes and lowered his bare feet. Ronan slid down the steep crag-side until he was contained inside a broken hollow socket which the stream had carved out of the solid rock-face long ago. He waited there briefly, catching his breath, feeling the round hold of earth.

Then he let himself go.

A moment later he was gasping against the spray, and looking up where white water plunged through its hollow culvert into the turbulent shadows of the cauldron-pool. From there the curved buttress leaning against the crag concealed the sea. He was standing where only the loud torrent of the fall filled his ears. It echoed on the final music of his dream.

Ronan knew he was far into the mandorla now: that he had entered from the outside the same place of transformation that his dreaming body had already penetrated from within. Like two blurred images moving into single focus, he knew himself to be both the dreamer who had been here on the verge of waking, and the figure he had sensed approaching through his dream. He could feel the two men coming to meet each other. Their worlds were converging now.

When he stepped from the shelter of the culvert his ears were assailed by the clamour of the sea. Fifty yards away, a wave exploded against the cliff. Its unexpended force came hurdling round the bend of the gorge to hurl itself with a wide, sliding swish across the stairs of rock. He watched the waters drain in brief flashing cataracts from the ledges in the stone, deepening the blackness there. Then the sea pulled back, leaving a brackish foam to be pushed higher up the stream when the next insurgence came.

Nearer to where he stood, Ronan observed how the overflow from the pool was swiftly decanted through a narrow gully into a sleek dam formed by the random blockage of an amber stone. Water sluiced on either side where the stream hastened towards collision with the swell.

Vertical at sea-level, Ronan studied the progress of the tide. He stepped into the shallow dam. Cold fresh water sucked about his shins. The gravel held firm beneath his feet. When he looked up, not thirty yards away the white breakers crowded higher than his head. They crested at drowning height, hovering there, but collapsing with a great sigh as they came. Their furthest reach subsided just before the amber stone, yet that must surely be the dream-appointed place.

Ronan stepped on to its surface. He waited in the narrow shadows of the gorge, remembering how it had been when he first came there. Though only two days and nights had passed it might have been a lifetime, for the feel of everything was changed.

Now, by contrast, he was entirely in place here, utterly inside his skin. Somewhere above him Alice kept her appointment with the rising moon. Further along the coast, Leah would soon be leaving Porthmallion, making her way towards what might be his last encounter with her; while inland, many miles away across the other side of the country, Marion and the children were waiting for his call. Ronan stood quietly at zero-point, watching the breakers cresting on this quantum wave.

Nothing was decided yet – nothing except the need for all the truth he could bring to the difficult meetings ahead. Yet if he could keep faith there with the open stillness he was discovering then anything might happen – though yes, it felt likeliest he would come out of this alone. Ronan drew deeply on the air, savouring the taste of solitude. He saw how the three women would always be alive inside him now, each of them a vital aspect of his soul, informed by, but no longer to be confused with, their separate sovereign presences out there.

Patiently he waited for the furthest reach of the tide to cross the stone and flood the small dam at his heels. In that instant no one could tell whether the waters there were fresh or salt, and every once-unmeetable condition would be met.

Five more breakers spent themselves against the cliff before he felt the shocked air gasping at a fresh incursion of the sea. Invisibly, over the horizon in the east, the full moon rose. The tide came on. Ronan watched its wild velocity unfold, taking the shape of figures in his mind. He saw the dancing rapture of white women there and the bright descending candour of a swan. Then the wave expired across the amber stone.

He heard the fall resume its clamour at his back. The stream was swallowed at his ankles by the mingling waters of the sea. There was a hush as if a throat was stopped. For a moment all sense of separate identity was gone. Then, knowing that as the tide turned all the instruments of time were turning too, Ronan gave his breath back to the dusky air, and quietly stepped through.